BAD KITTY
Takes the Test

NICK BRUEL

A NEAL PORTER BOOK
ROARING BROOK PRESS
NEW YORK

To Aurora

Copyright © 2017 by Nick Bruel
A Neal Porter Book
Published by Roaring Brook Press
Roaring Brook Press is a division of Holtzbrinck Publishing Holdings Limited Partnership
175 Fifth Avenue, New York, New York 10010
mackids.com

Library of Congress Cataloging-in-Publication Data

Names: Bruel, Nick, author, illustrator.
Title: Bad Kitty takes the test / Nick Bruel.
Description: First edition. | New York : Roaring Brook Press, 2017. | Series:
  Bad Kitty | "A Neal Porter Book" | Summary: Because of a recent string of
  embarrassing behavior, Kitty's cat license has been revoked and she must
  take a test to get it back so she can still be a cat.
Identifiers: LCCN 2016027113 | ISBN 9781626725898 (hardback)
Subjects: | CYAC: Cats–Fiction. | Behavior–Fiction. | Test
  anxiety–Fiction. | Humorous stories. | BISAC: JUVENILE FICTION / Animals
  / Cats. | JUVENILE FICTION / Humorous Stories.
Classification: LCC PZ7.B82832 Book 2017 | DDC [E]–dc23
LC record available at https://lccn.loc.gov/2016027113

Our books may be purchased in bulk for promotional, educational, or business use. Pleas
contact your local bookseller or the Macmillan Corporate and Premium Sales Department
at (800) 221-7945 ext. 5442 or by e-mail at MacmillanSpecialMarkets@macmillan.com

First edition 2017
Printed in the United States of America by LSC Communications US, LLC
(Lakeside Classic), Harrrisonburg, Virginia
1   3   5   7   9   10   8   6   4   2

• CONTENTS •

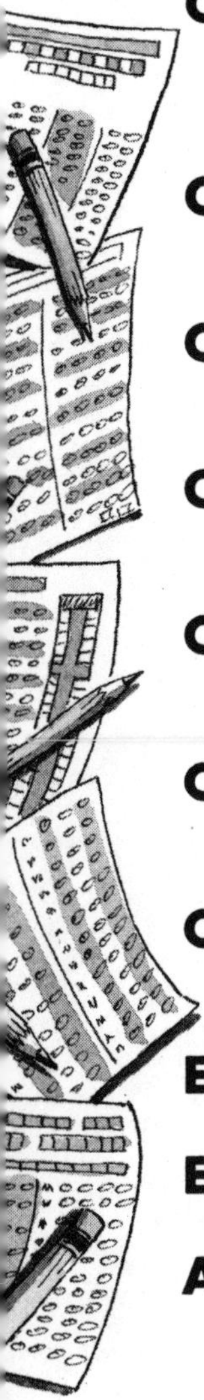

•CHAPTER ONE•

BAD KITTY DOES NOT LIKE BIRDS

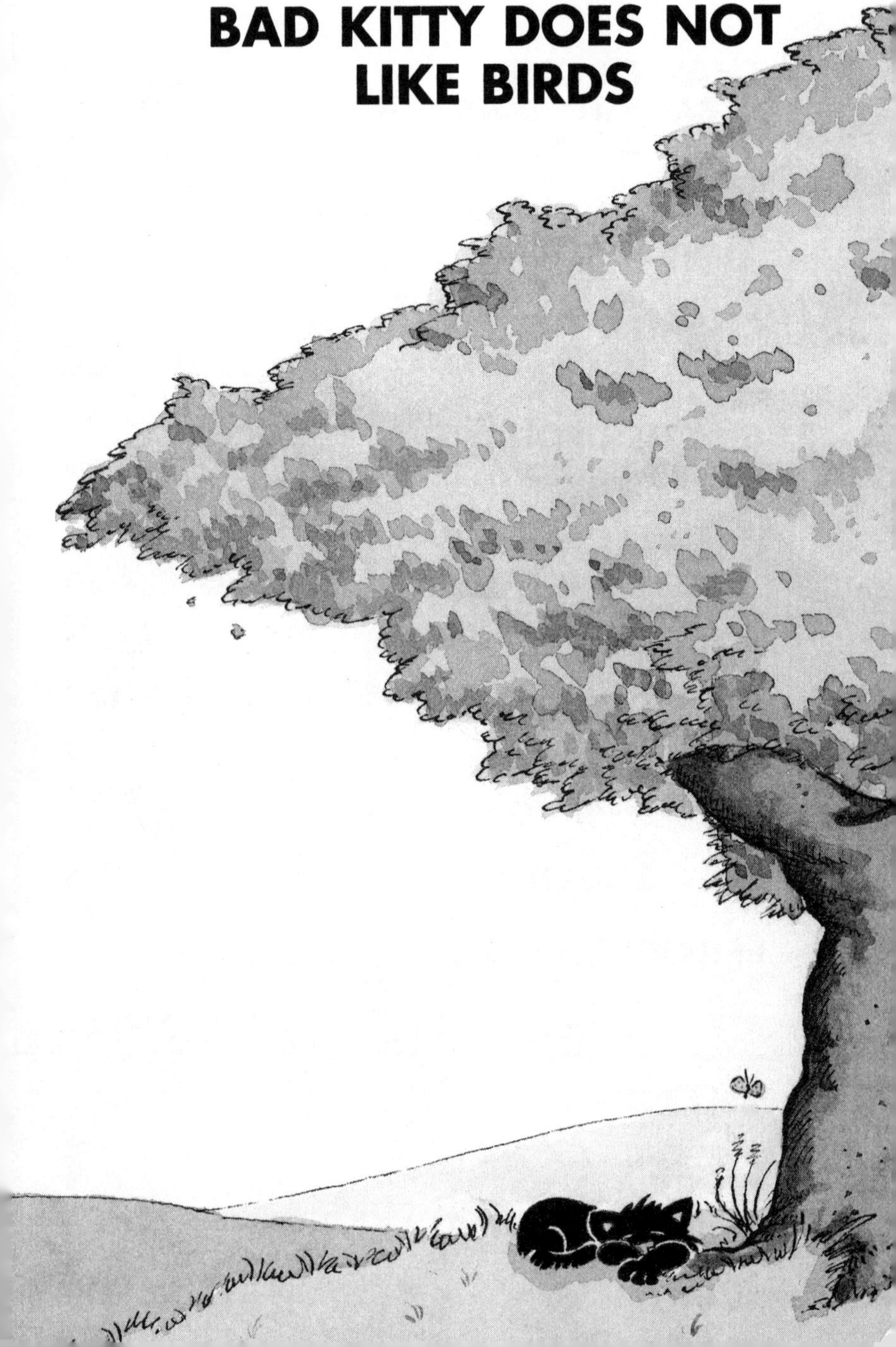

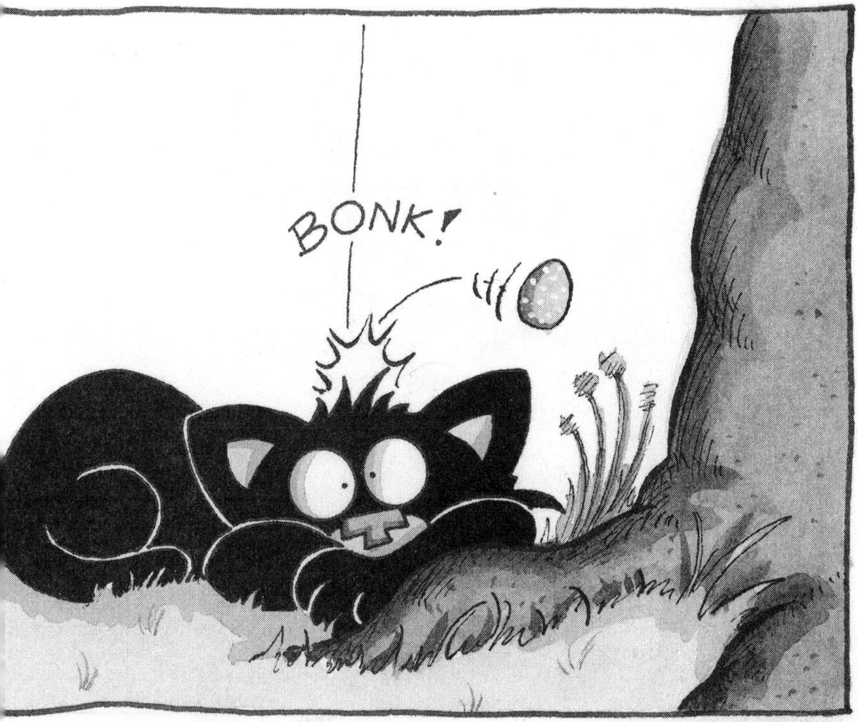
BONK!

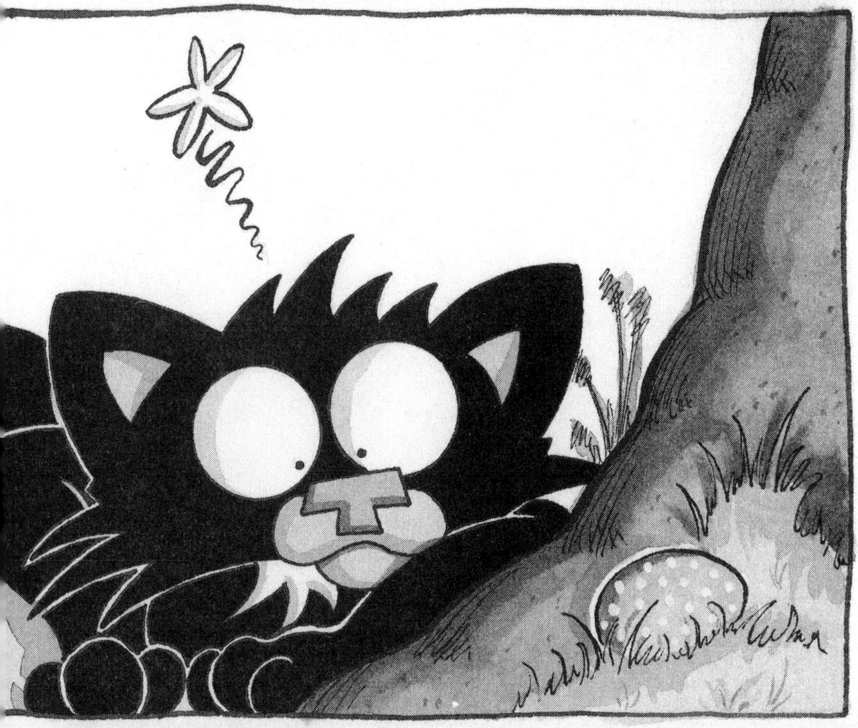

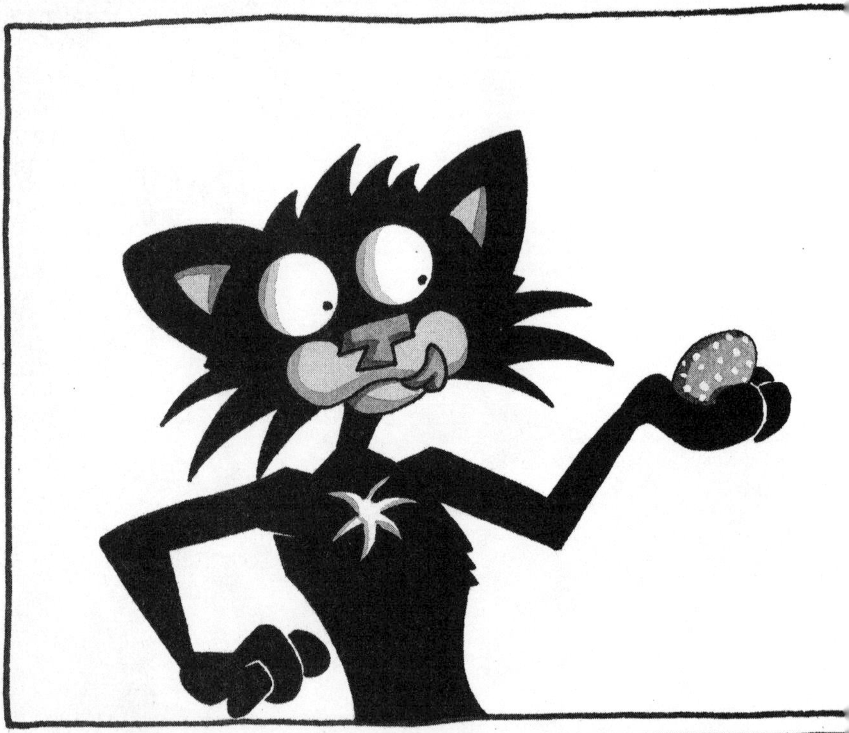

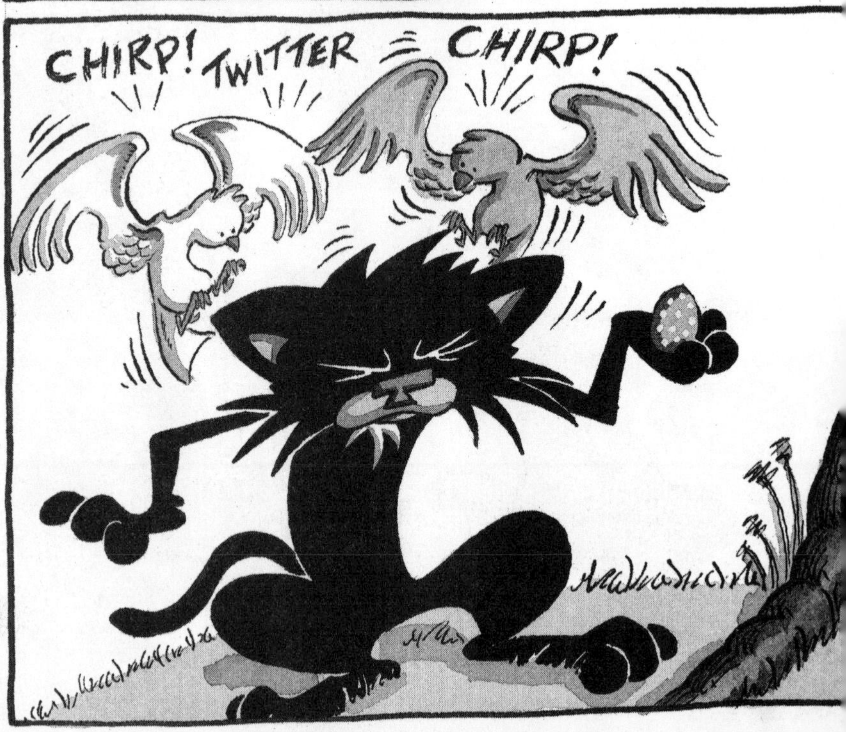
CHIRP!
TWITTER
CHIRP!

Kitty loves birds.

She loves how they flit.
She loves how they flap.
She loves how they flutter.

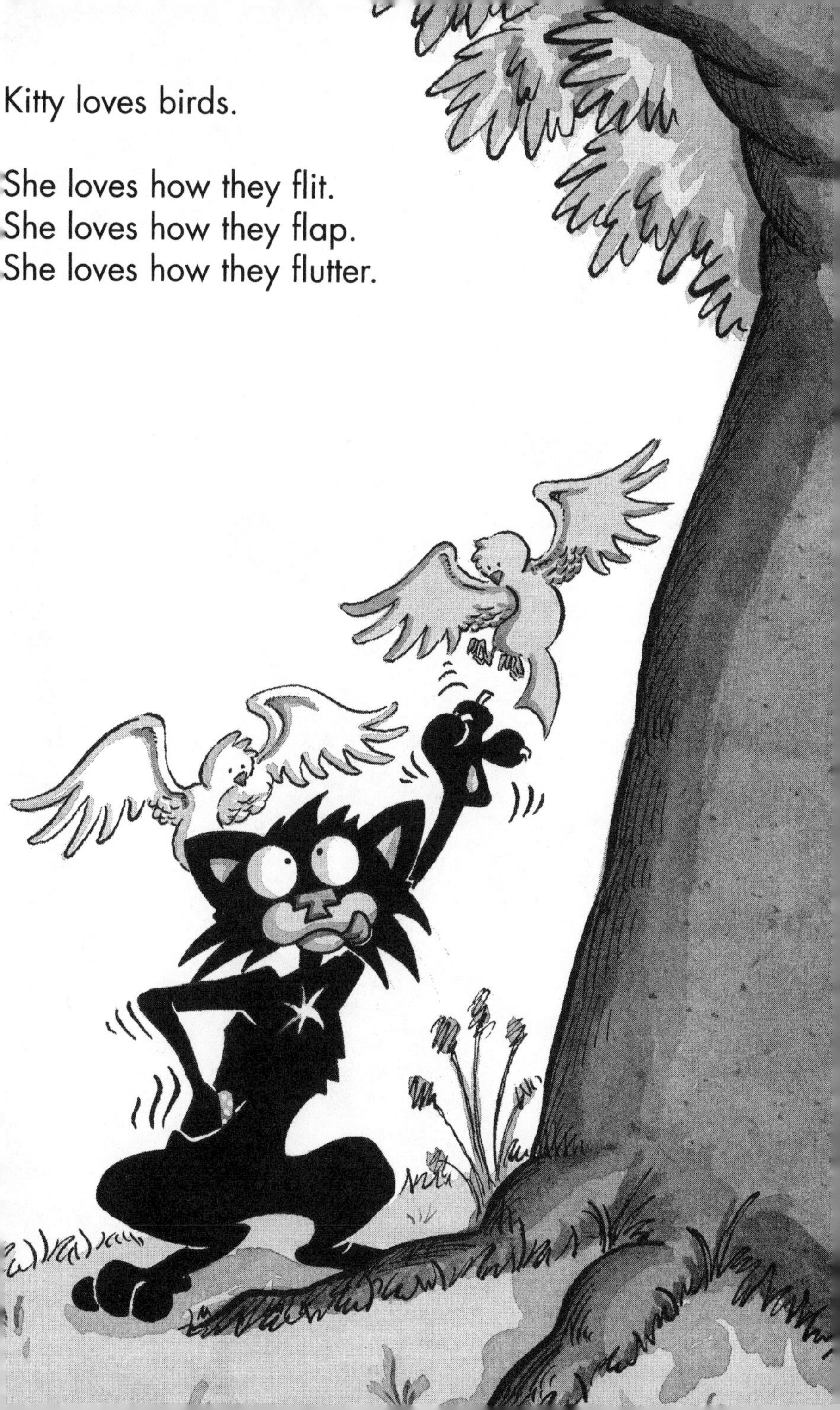

When Kitty sees birds,
she wants to play with them.

She really, really, REALLY
wants to play with them.

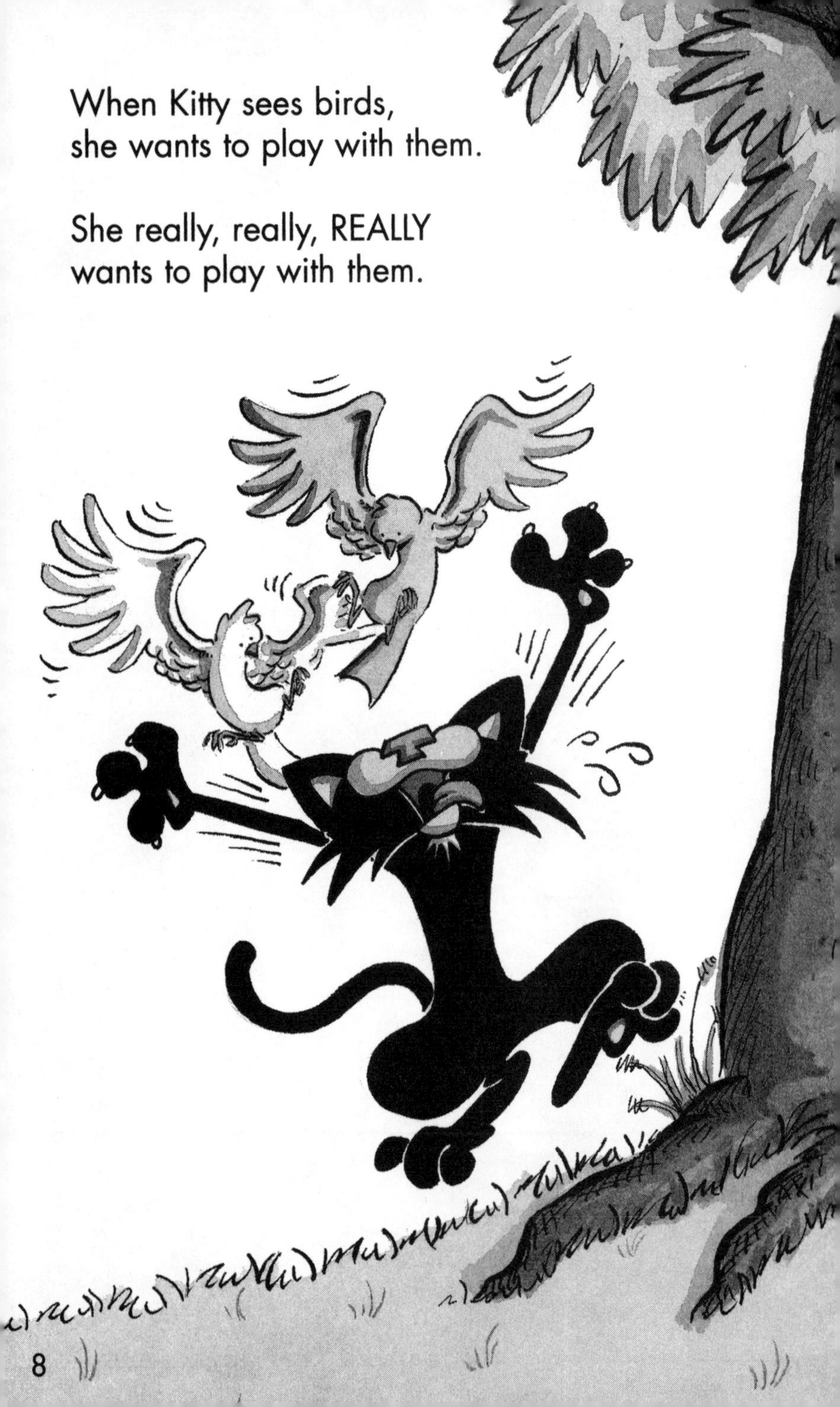

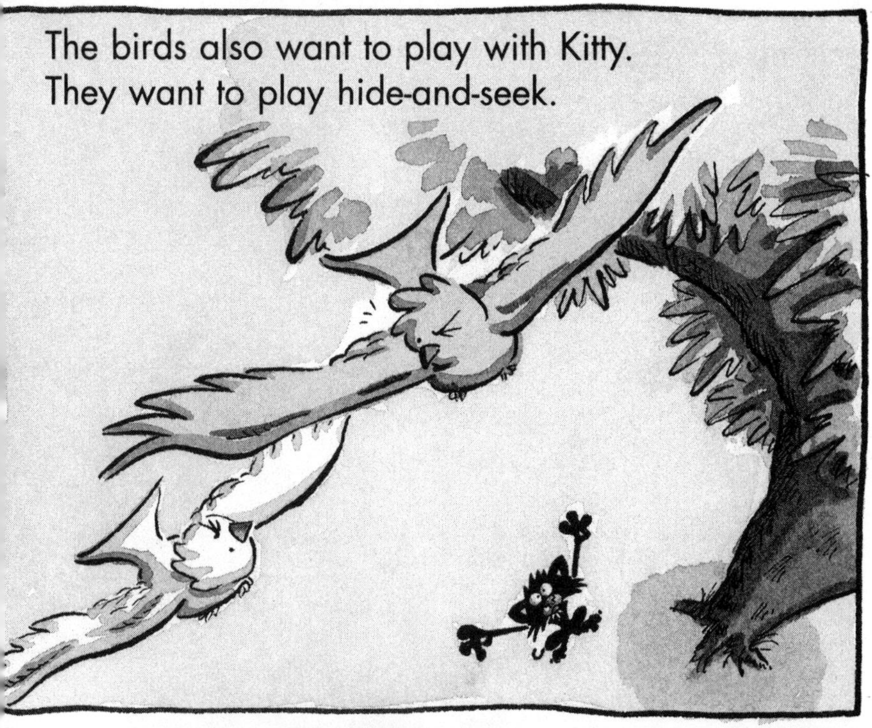
The birds also want to play with Kitty. They want to play hide-and-seek.

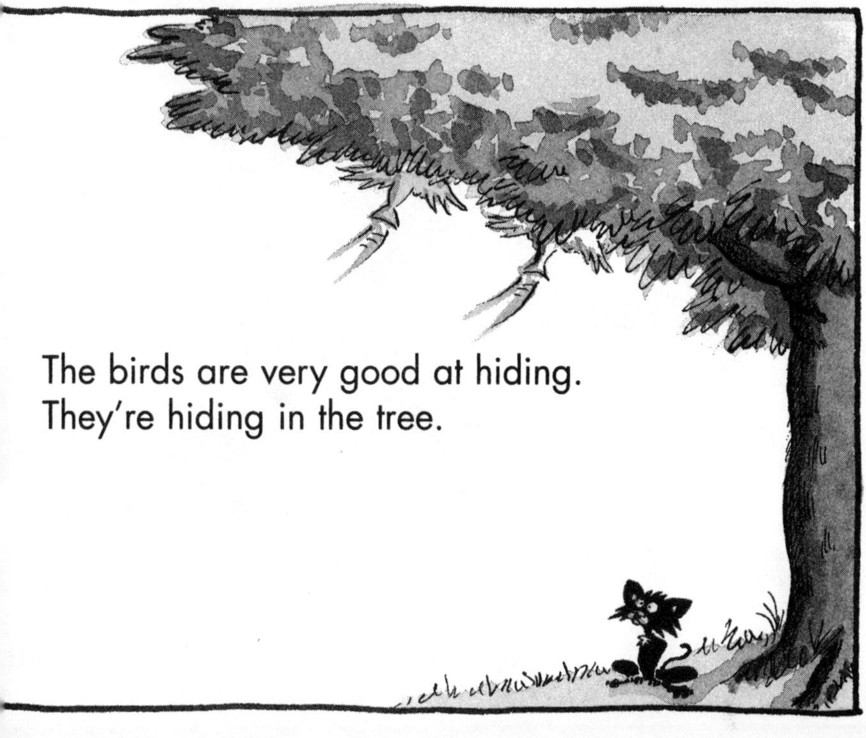
The birds are very good at hiding. They're hiding in the tree.

But Kitty sees them!

Kitty is very good at seeking.
And she's very good at climbing.

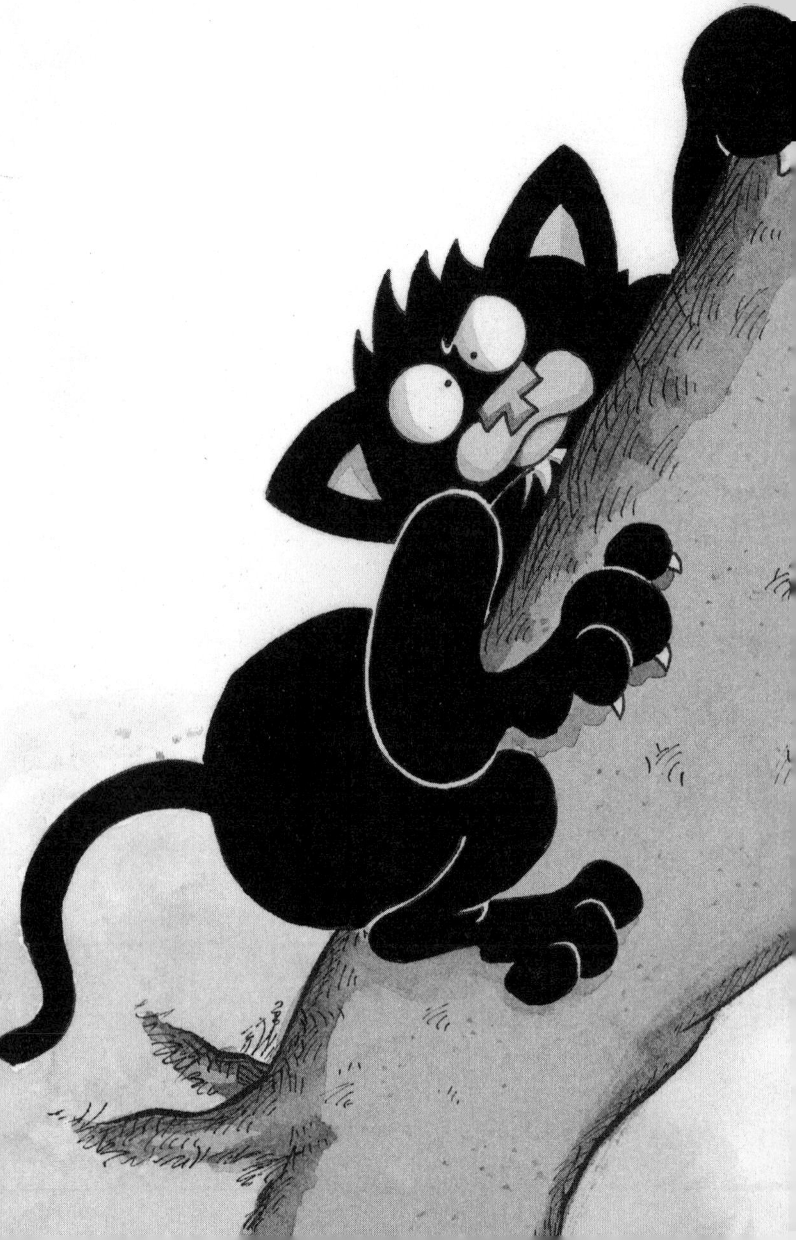

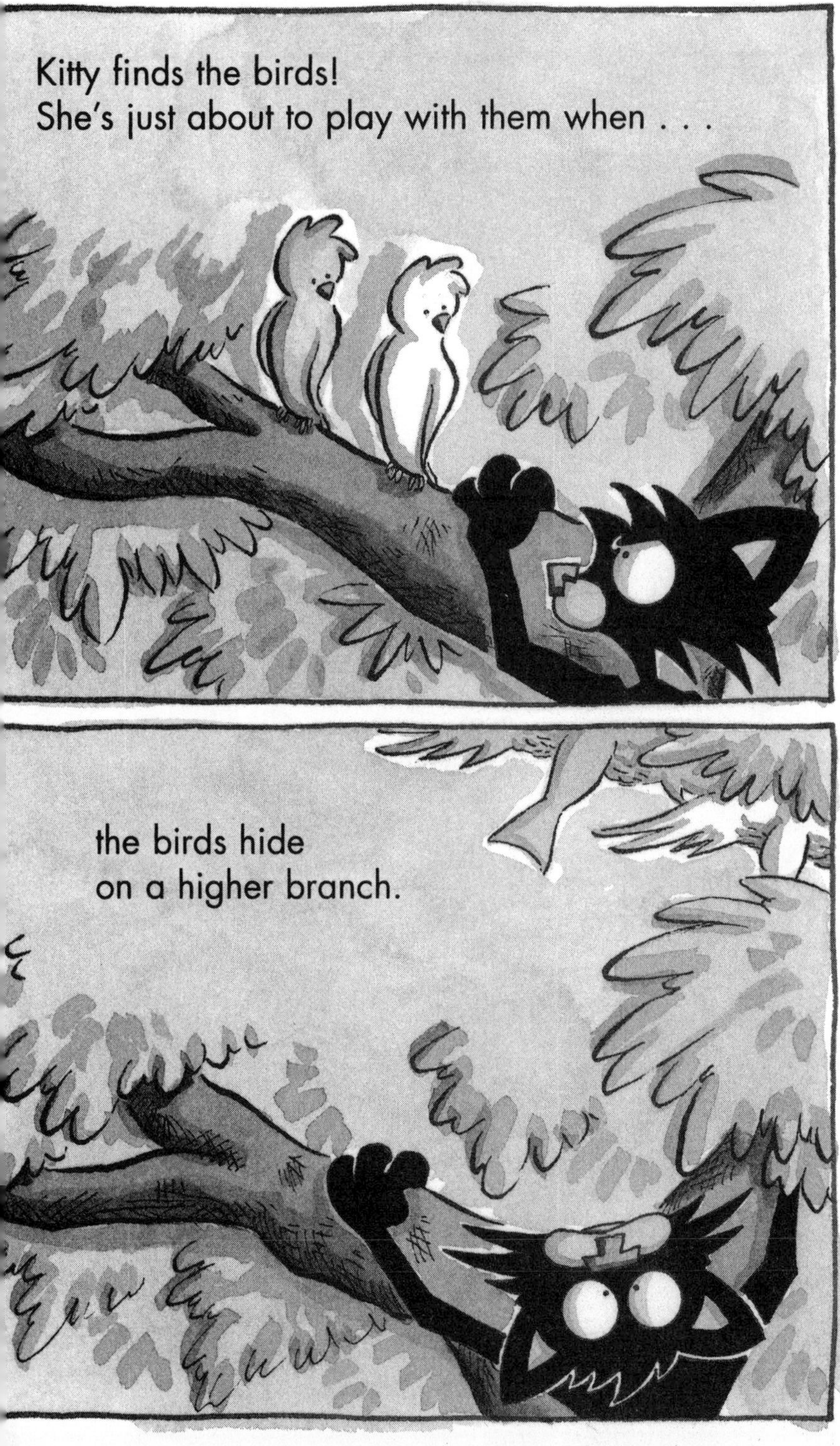
Kitty finds the birds!
She's just about to play with them when . . .
the birds hide
on a higher branch.

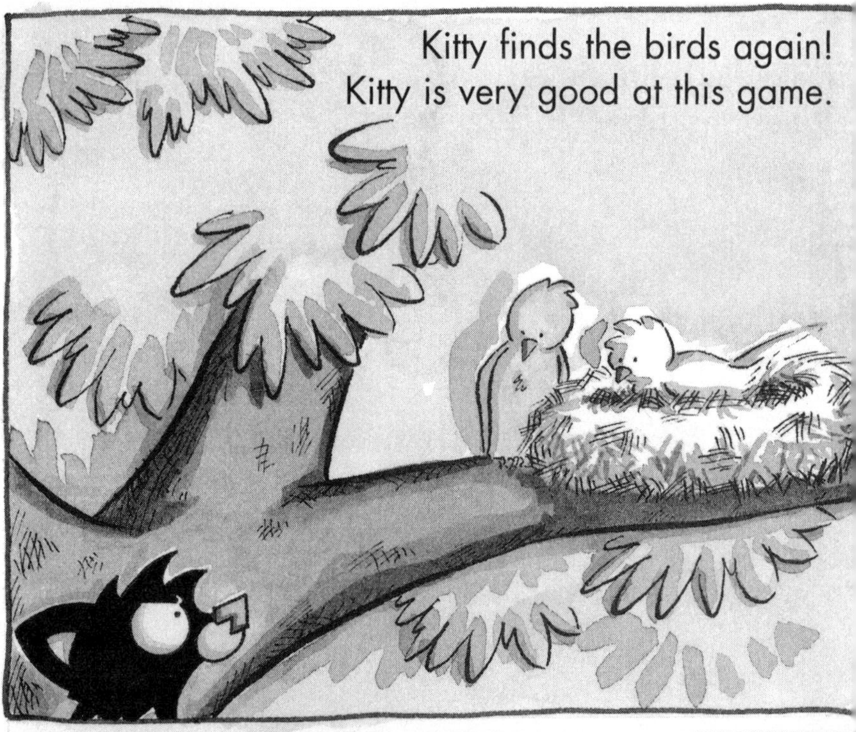
Kitty finds the birds again!
Kitty is very good at this game.

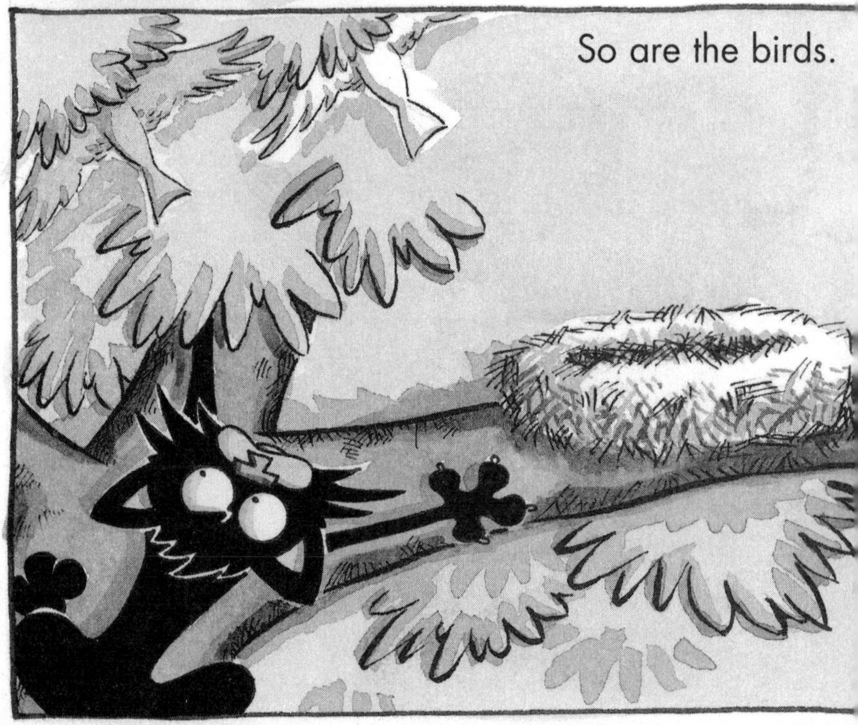
So are the birds.

The birds keep hiding
higher and higher.

Kitty keeps climbing
higher and higher.

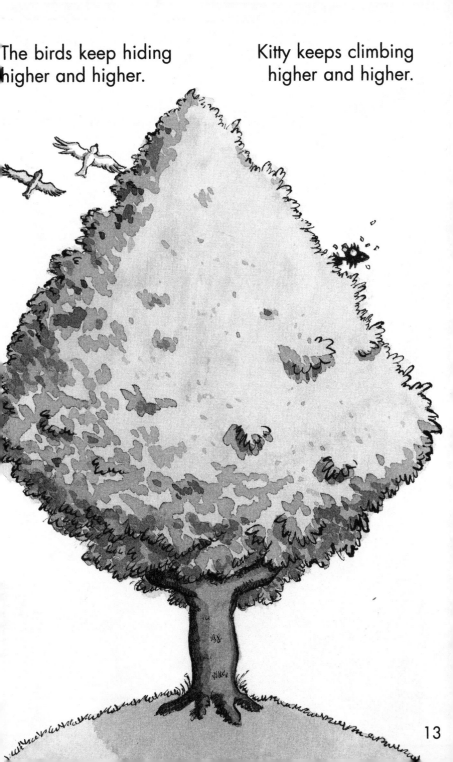

Soon, the birds are at the top of the tree. There is no tree left.

Now Kitty wants to play another game with her new friends: TAG!

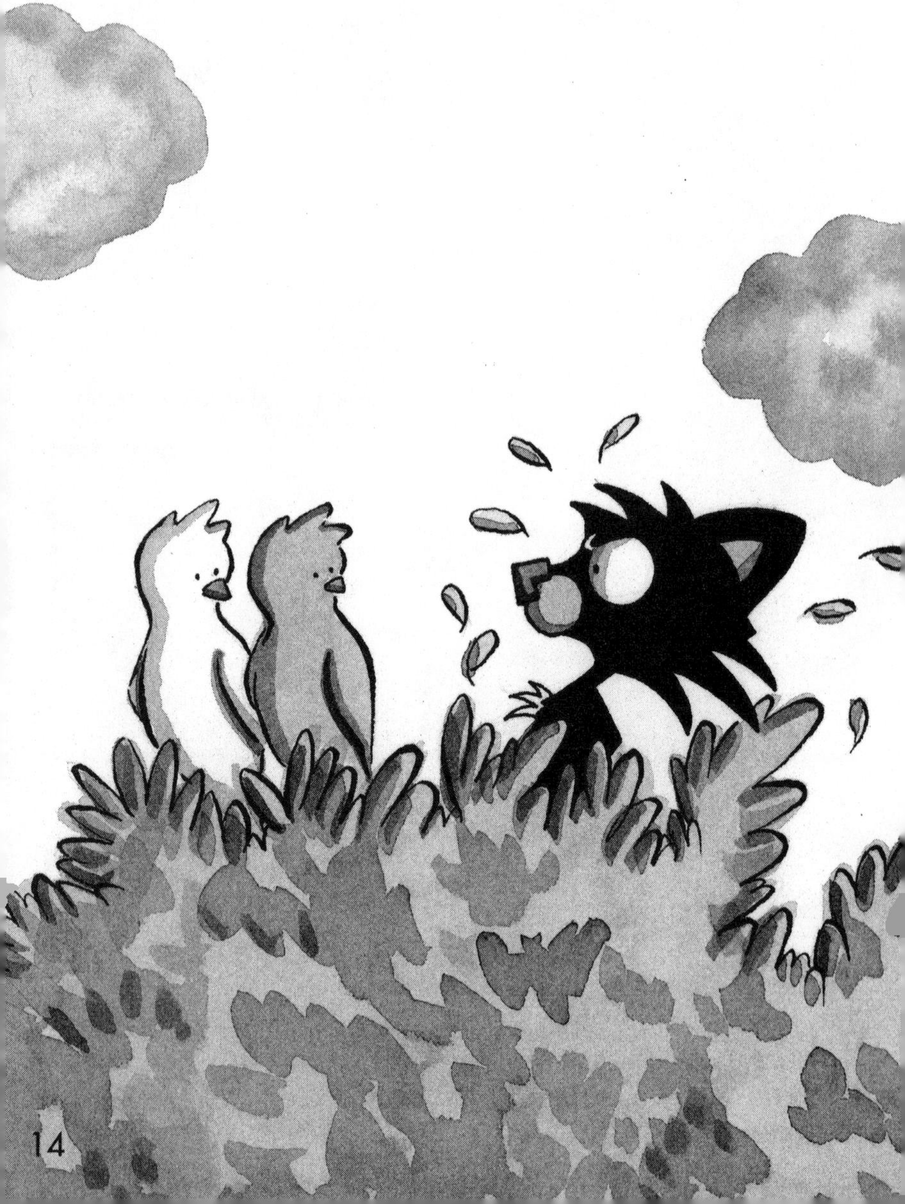

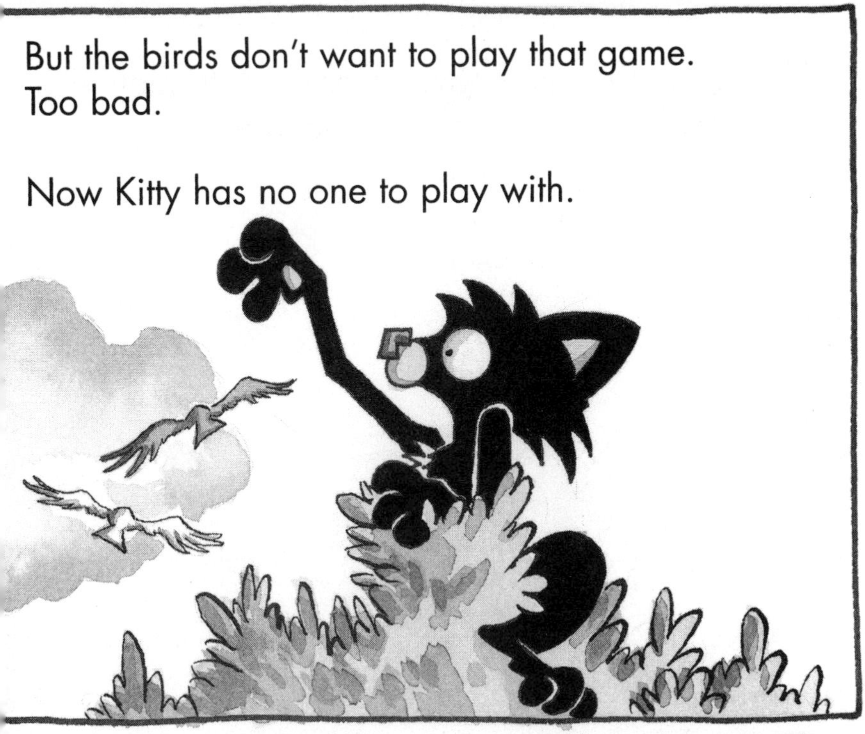
But the birds don't want to play that game.
Too bad.
Now Kitty has no one to play with.

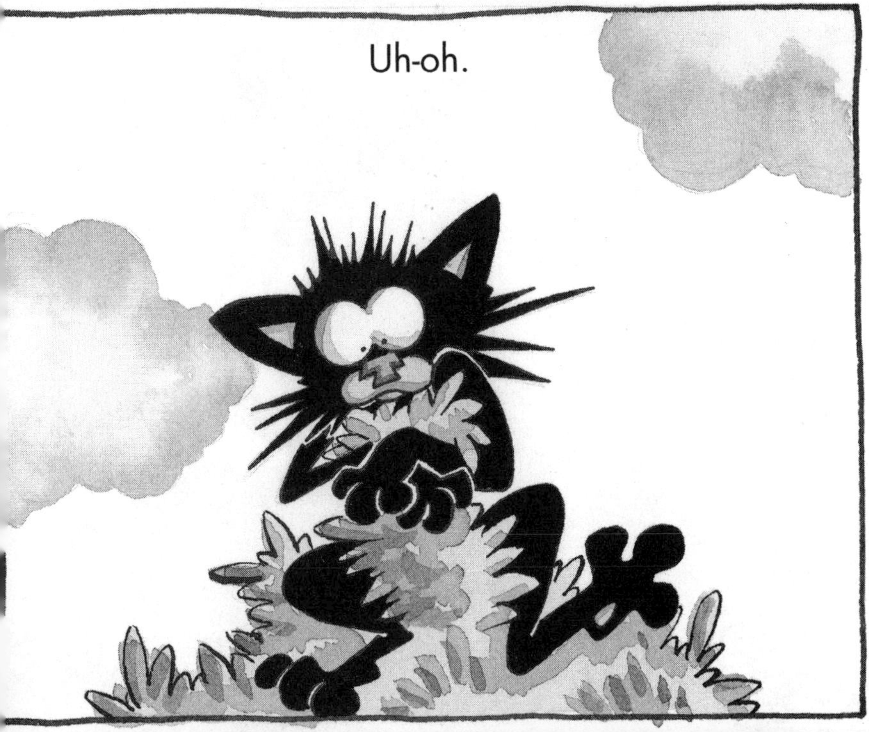
Uh-oh.

Oh, good! The birds have come back to play with Kitty and help her down from the tree.

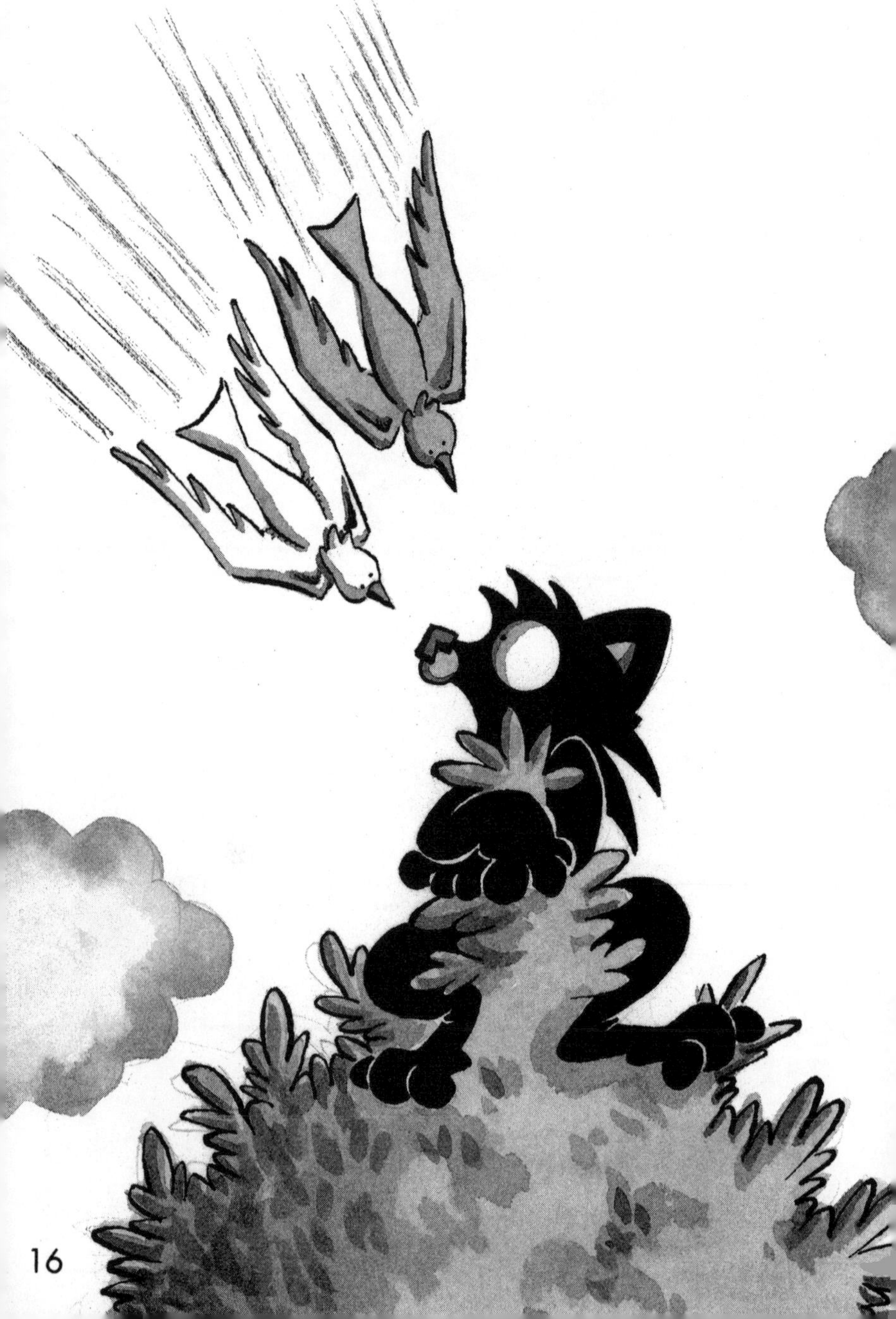

But Kitty does not want their help. She just wants to go home.

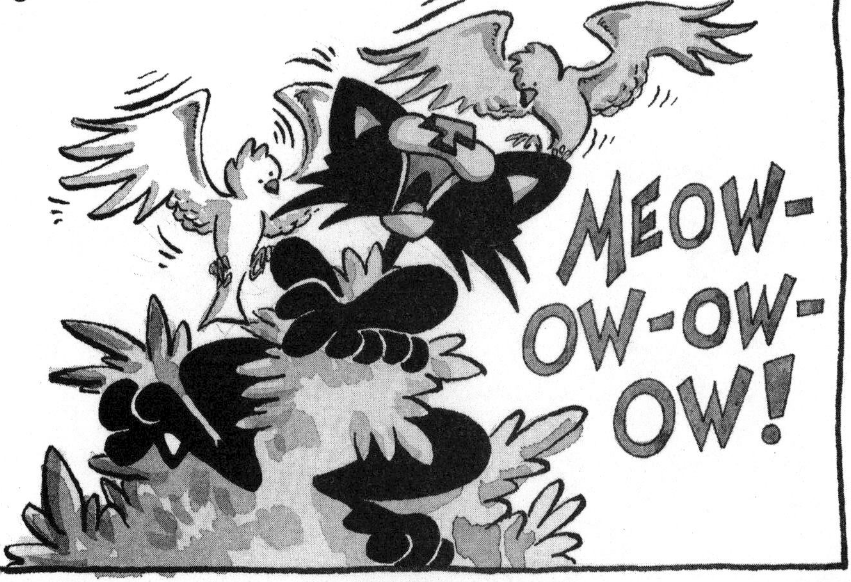
MEOW-
OW-OW-
OW!

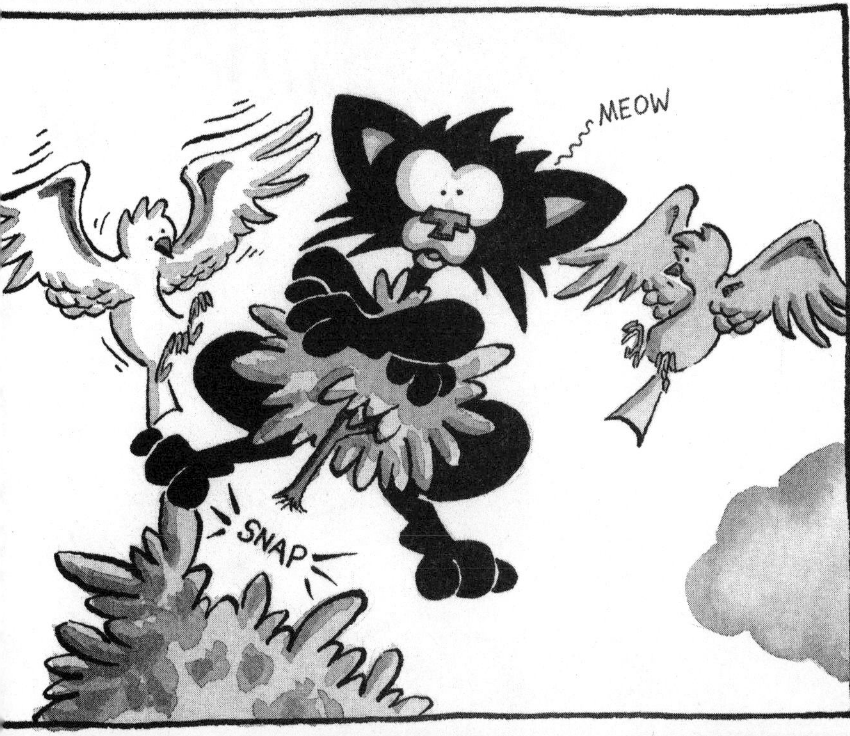
MEOW
SNAP

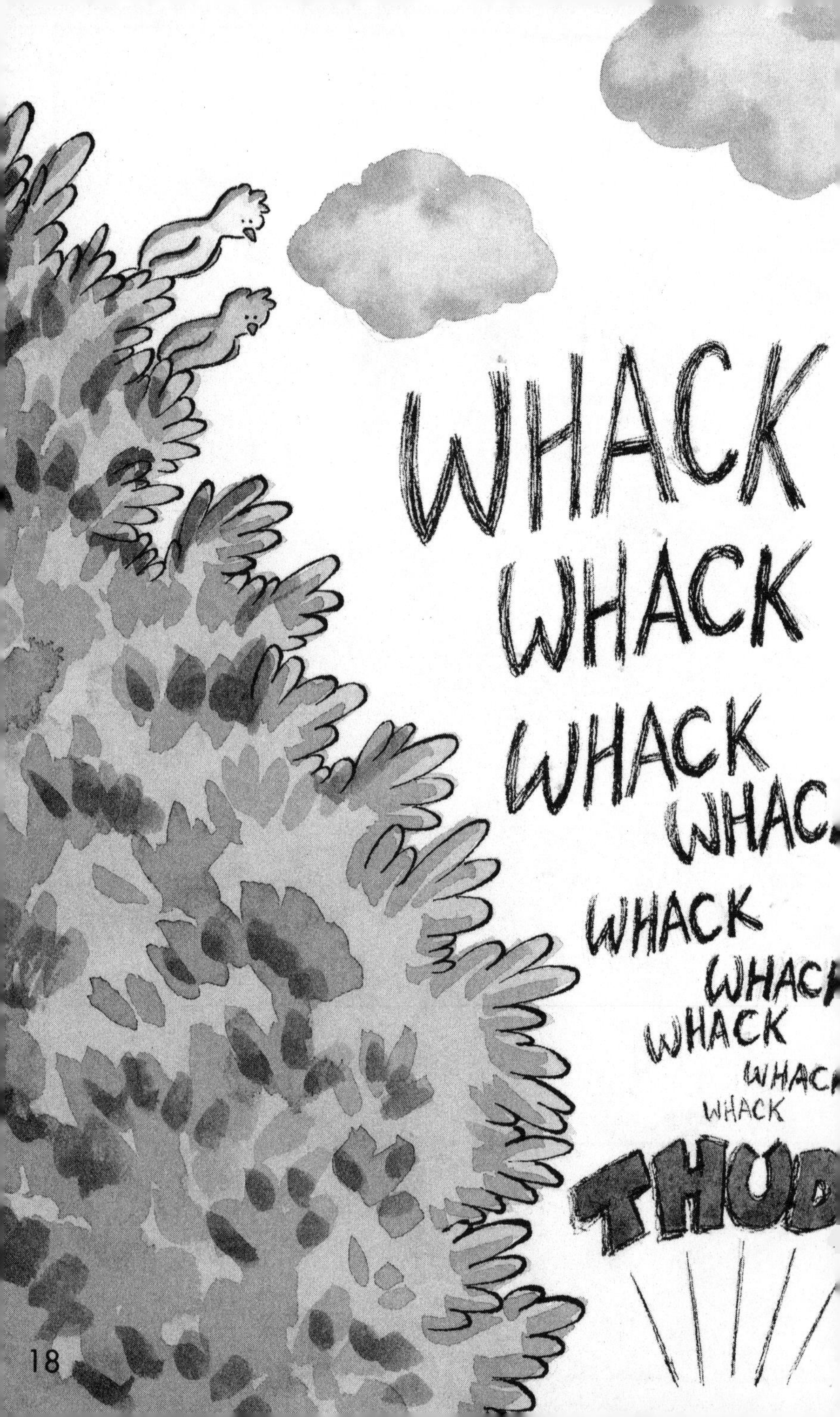
WHACK
WHACK
WHACK
WHAC
WHACK
WHAC
WHACK
WHAC
WHACK
THUD

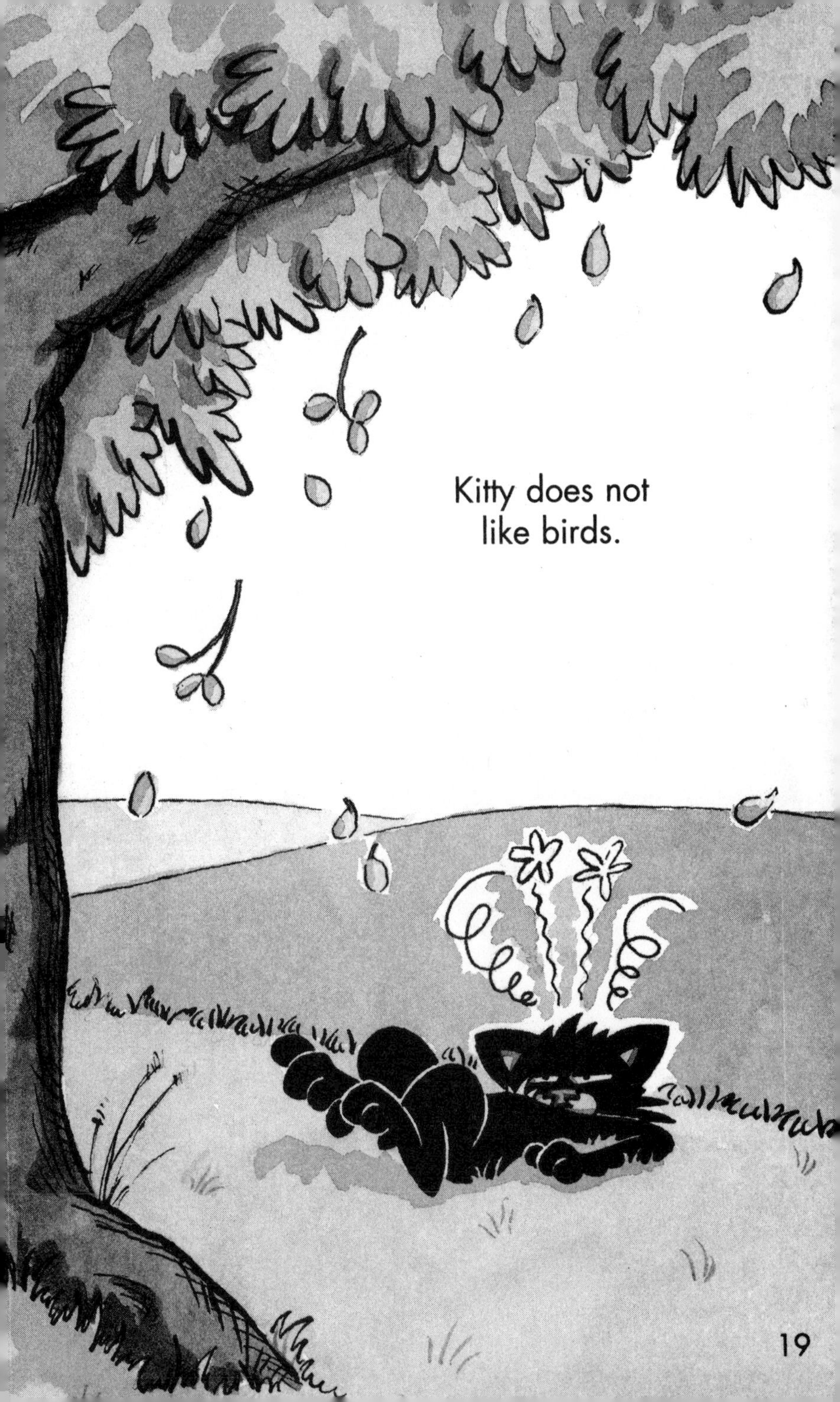

Kitty does not
like birds.

•CHAPTER TWO•

THE NEXT DAY

Good morning, Kitty.

The mail's here, and it looks like you have a certified letter from the Society of Cat Aptitude Management. I've never heard of them. Have you?

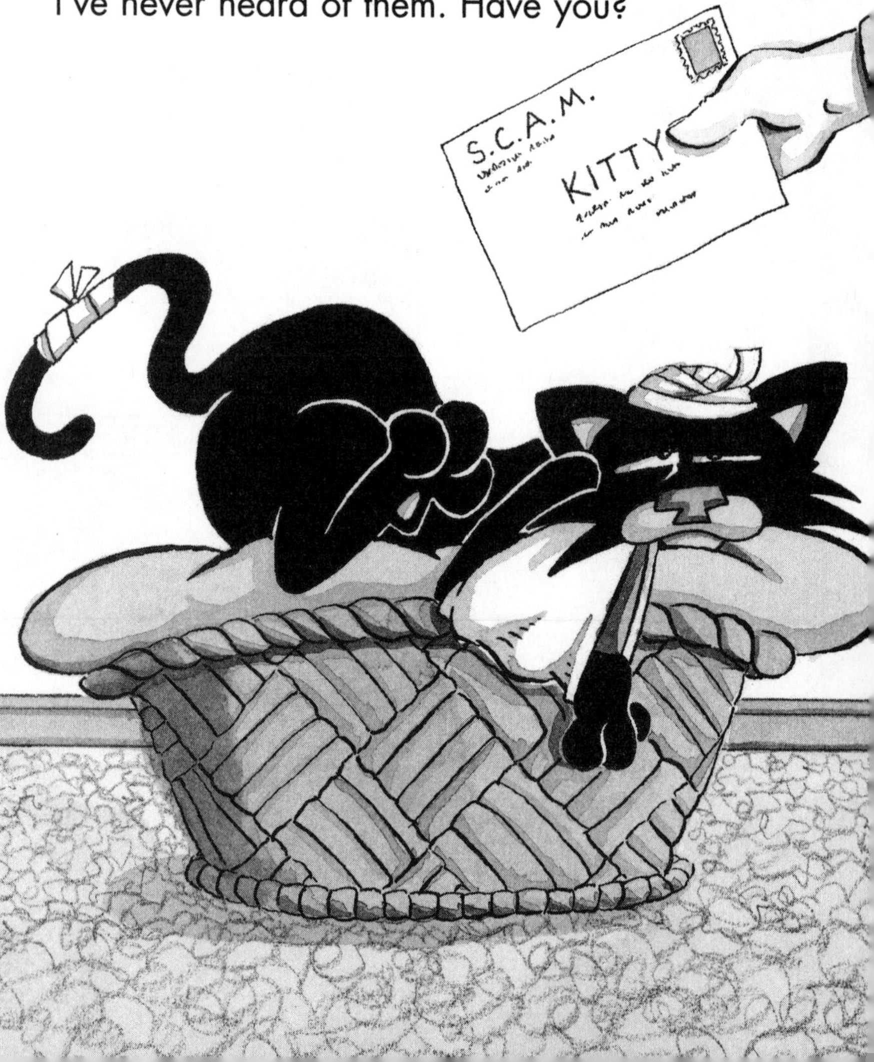
S.C.A.M.
KITTY

Uh-oh. This doesn't look good.

It looks like they know about your run-in with those birds yesterday. Apparently it's considered the most recent instance in a long line of "shameful un-catlike embarrassments." Others include the time you . . .

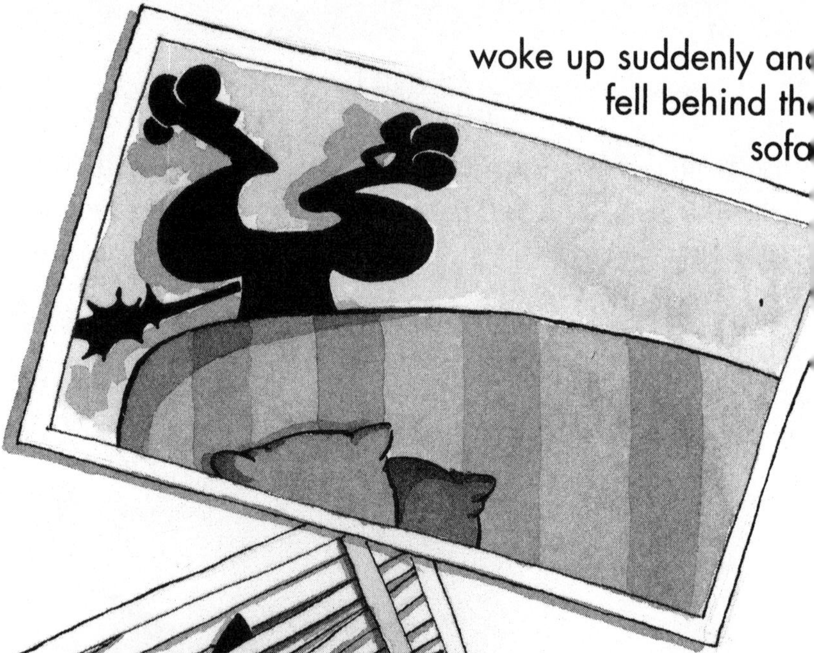

woke up suddenly an
fell behind th
sofa

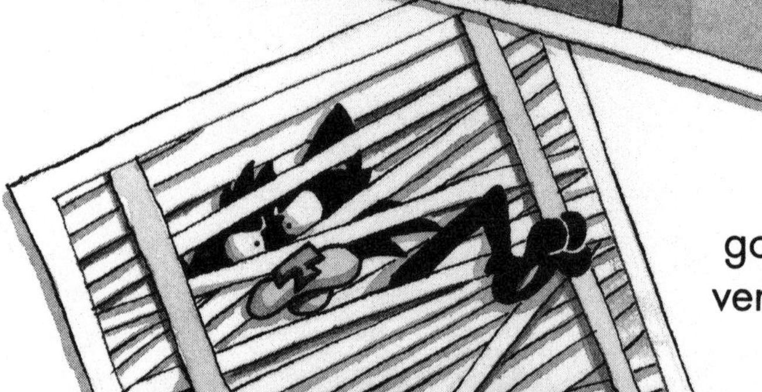

got stuck in the
venetian blinds,

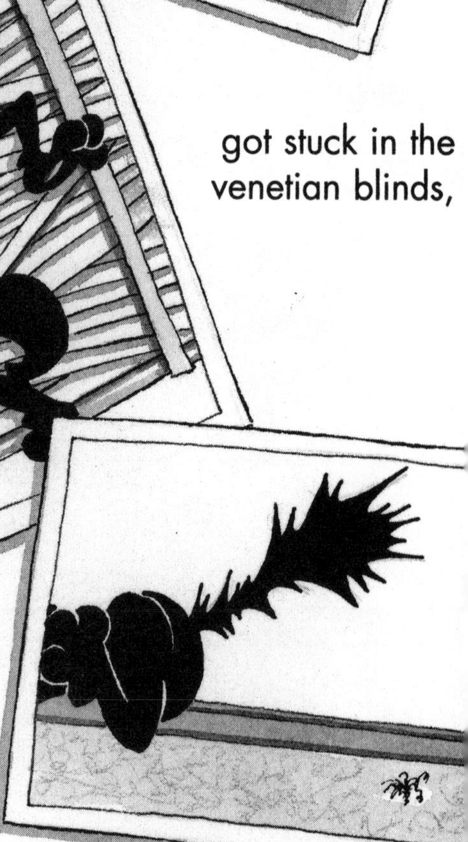

were frightened by
a spider, which
turned out to be
a ball of lint,

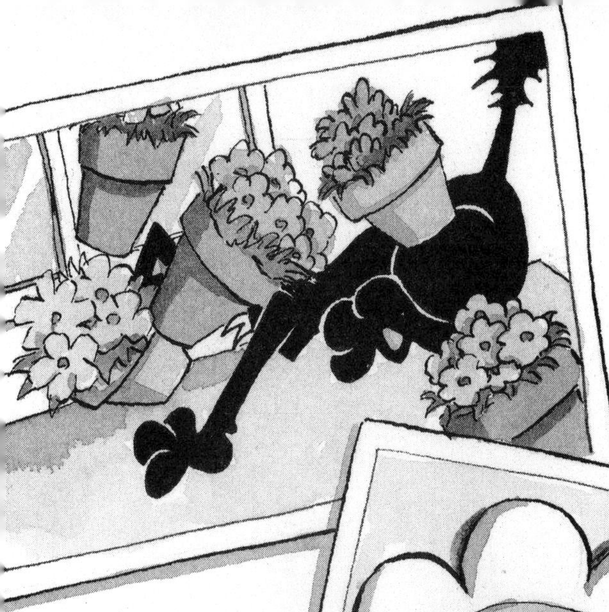

tried to jump
on the desk
but landed
in the
plants,

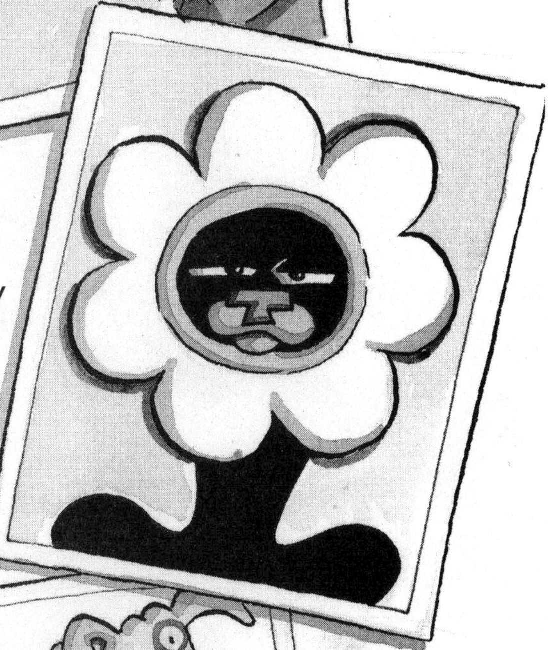

allowed the baby
to dress you up
for Halloween,

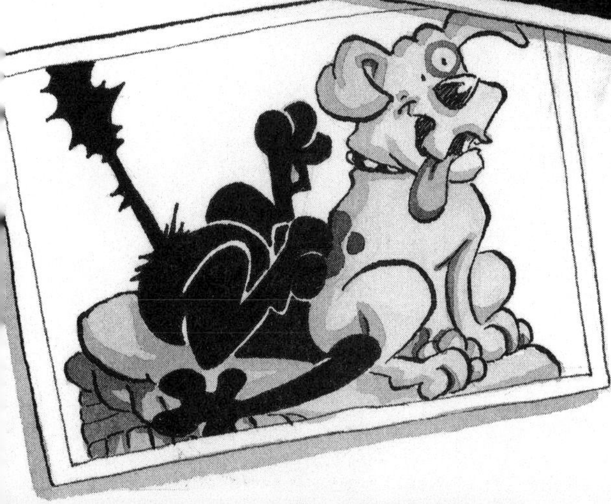

and let the
dog sit on
you while
you were
sleeping.

So apparently because of this recent string
embarrassing behavior, your cat license has bee
REVOKED.

I didn't even know there was such a thing.

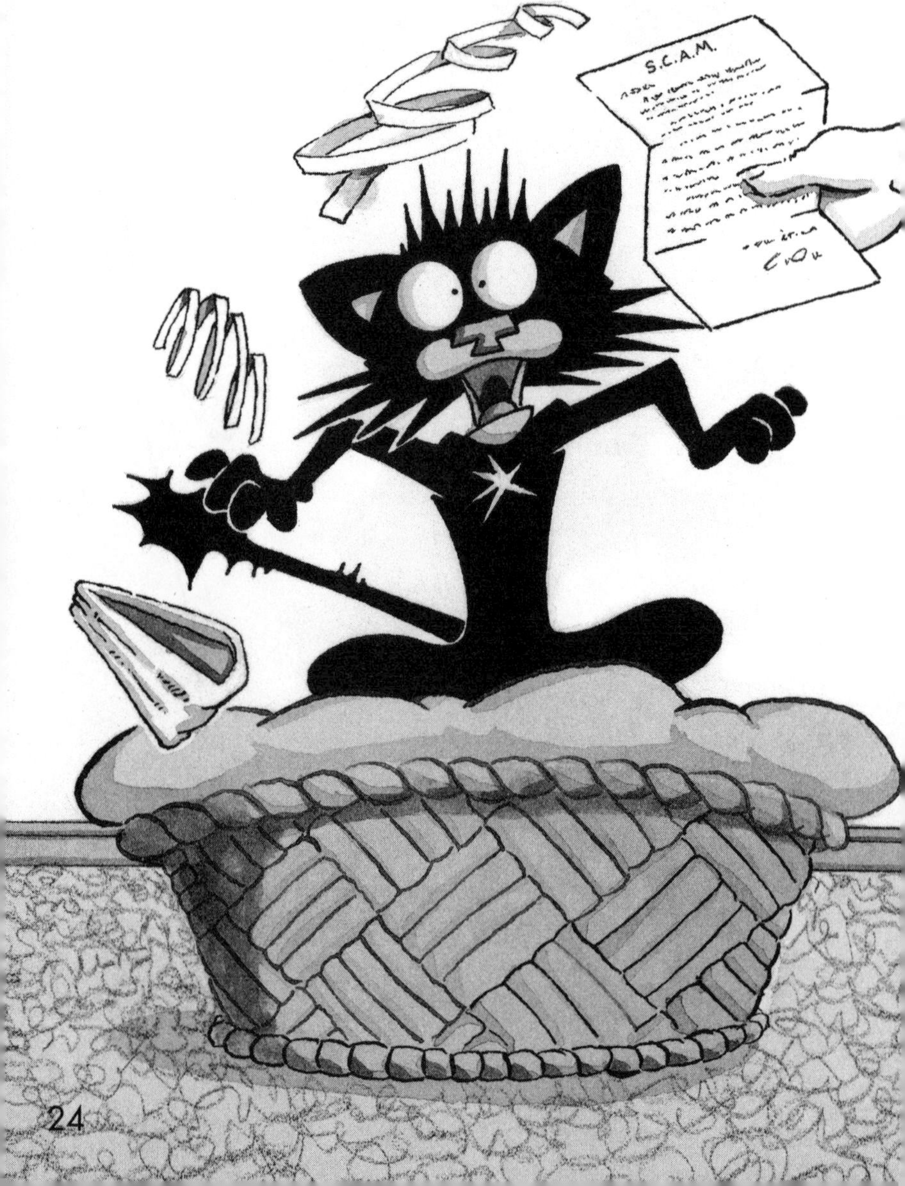
S.C.A.M.

The letter goes on.

In order to renew your cat license, you have to take a special course on being a cat, followed by a TEST. This all happens tomorrow!

A test? Well, Kitty, a test is a process you go through to make sure you understand everything you've learned.

Now pay attention, Kitty. Here's the important part. If you PASS the test, then you'll get your license back.

I didn't even know you had one to begin with.

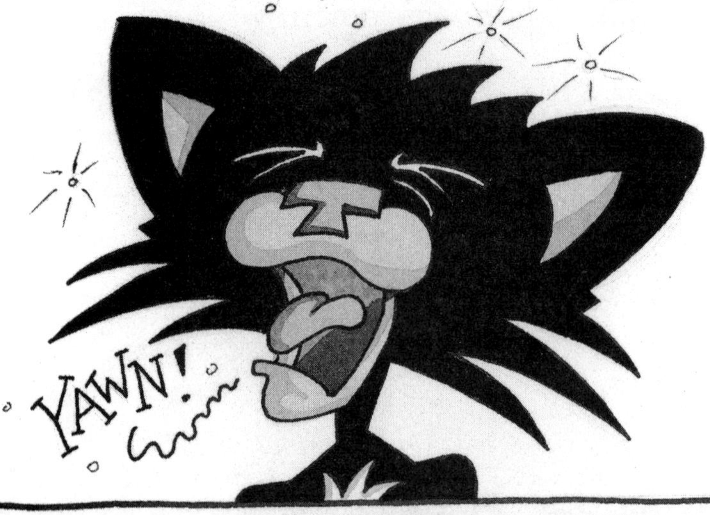
YAWN!

But if you DON'T pass the test . . . well . . . according to this letter, then you won't get your license and then apparently you won't . . . gosh . . . you won't be allowed to be a cat anymore!

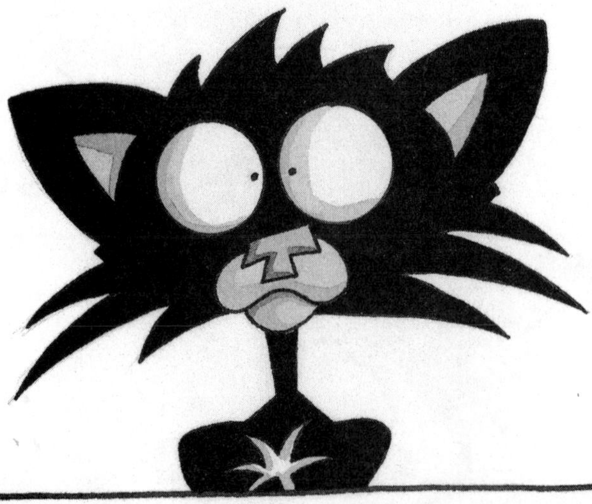

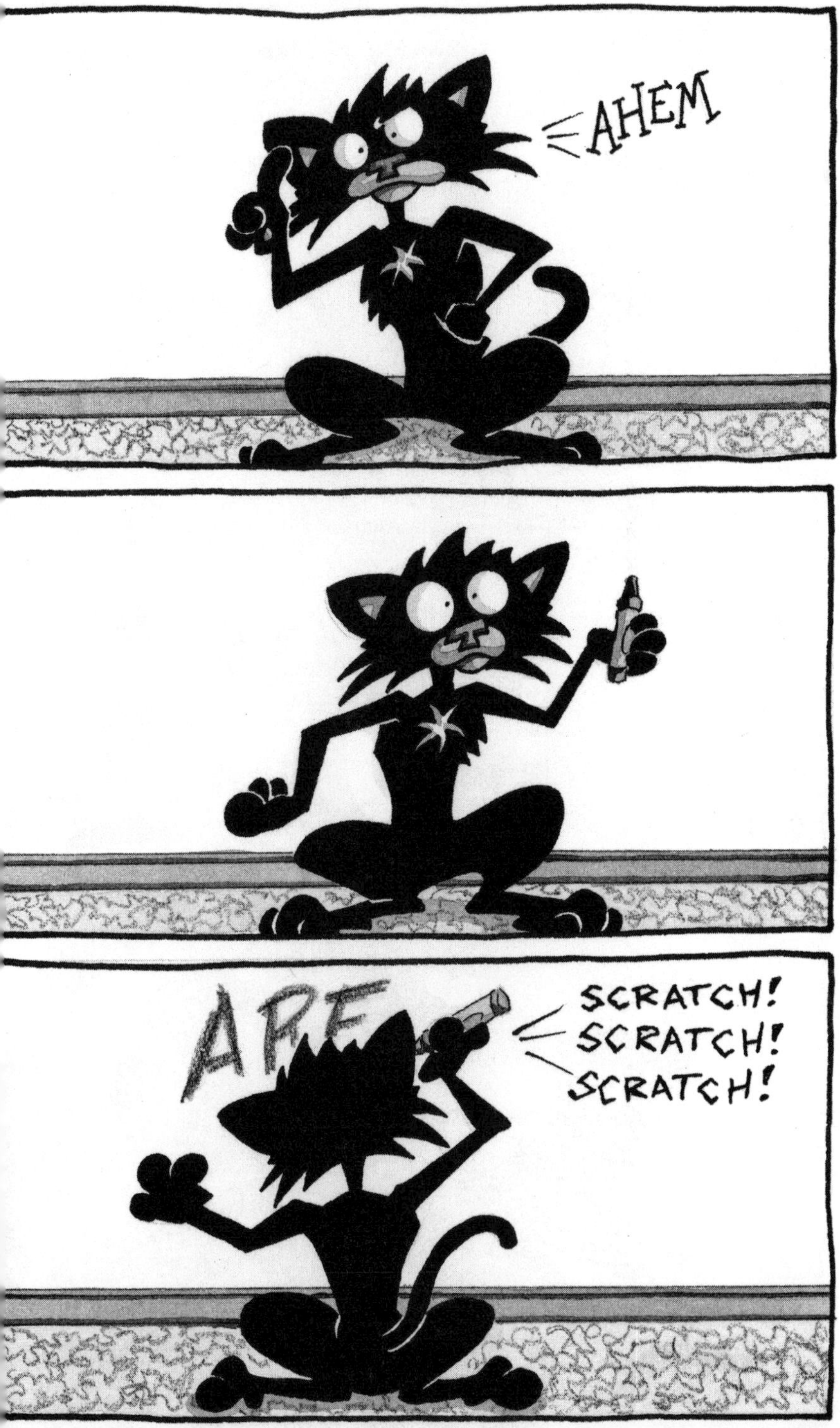
AHEM
ARE
SCRATCH!
SCRATCH!
SCRATCH!

Kitty, I don't make the rules. All I know is that you nee
to take this test tomorrow whether you like it or not.
have the address. I'll bring you there in the morning

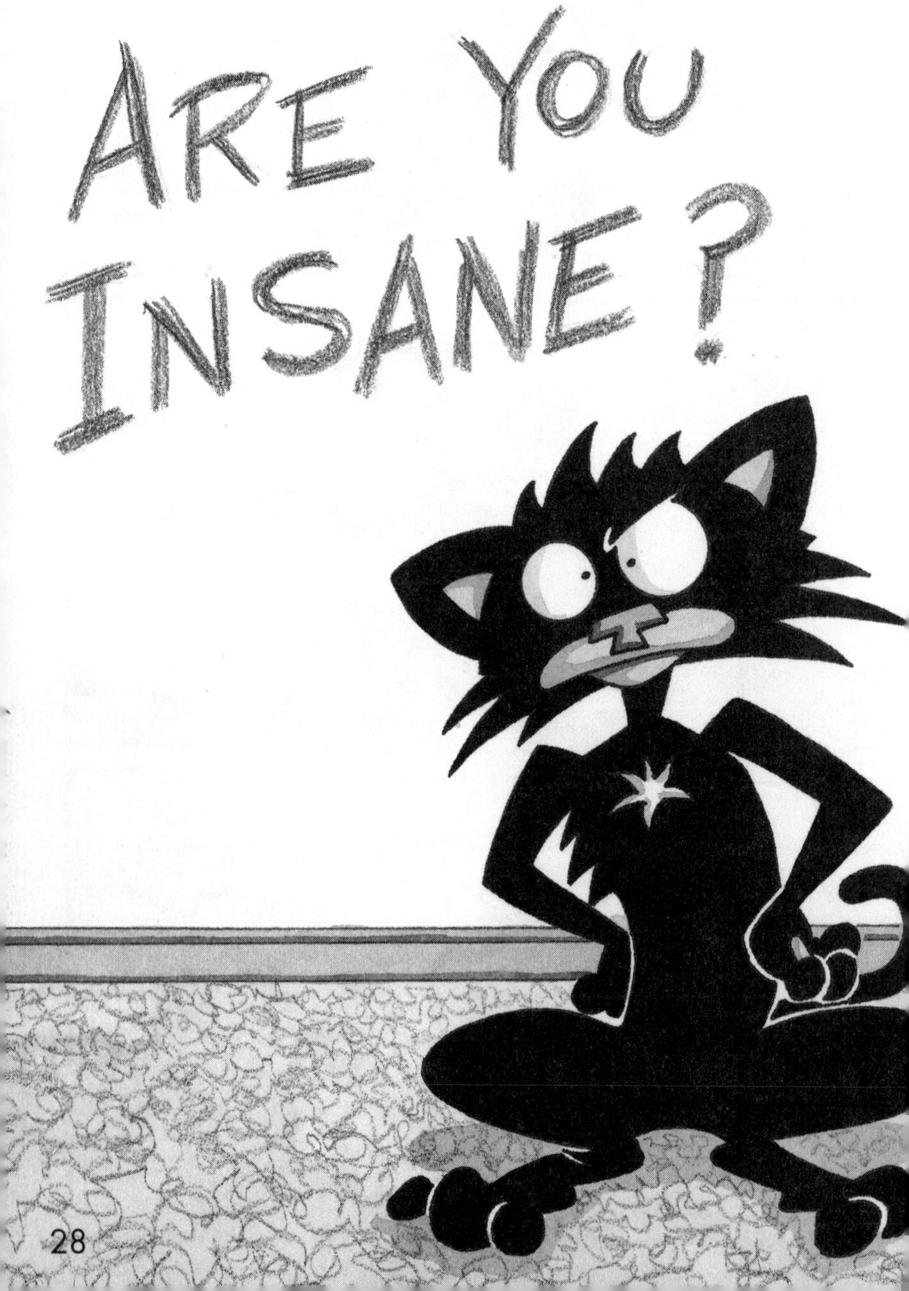
ARE YOU INSANE?

…nd will you please stop writing on the walls?! I've …ad to call the painters 14 times this month.

Kitty?! **KITTY!!!**
Sigh.

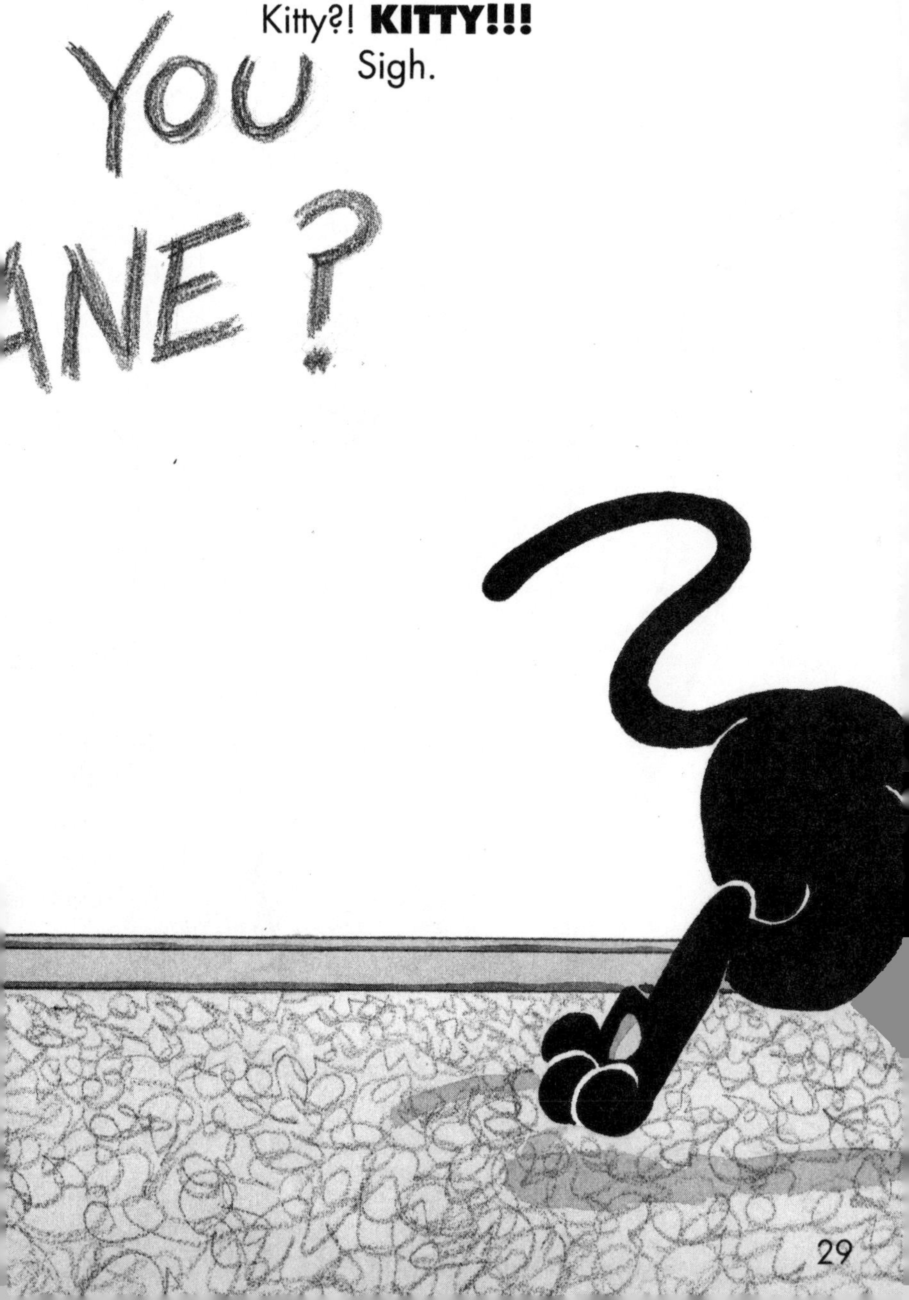
YOU
ANE?

•CHAPTER THREE•

THE NEXT, NEXT DAY

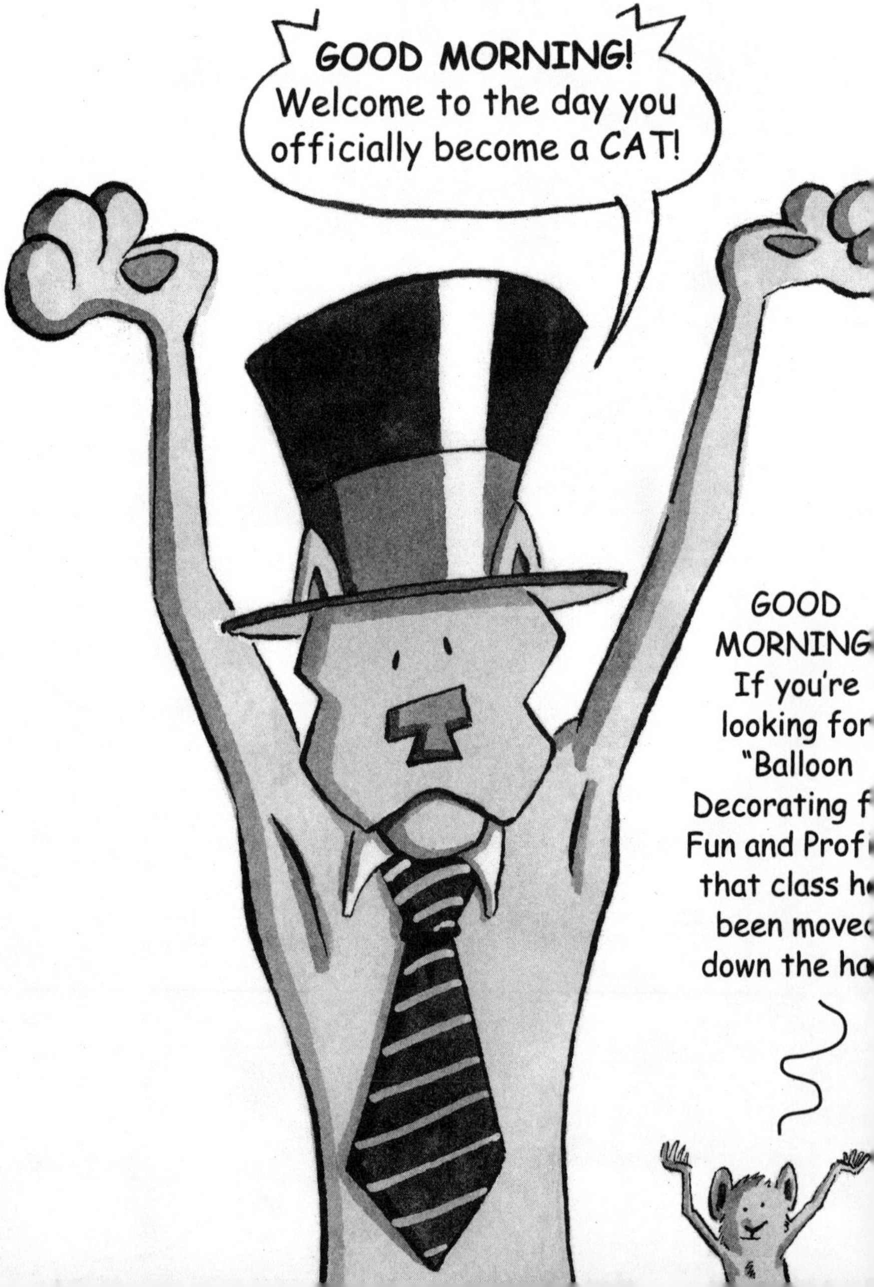

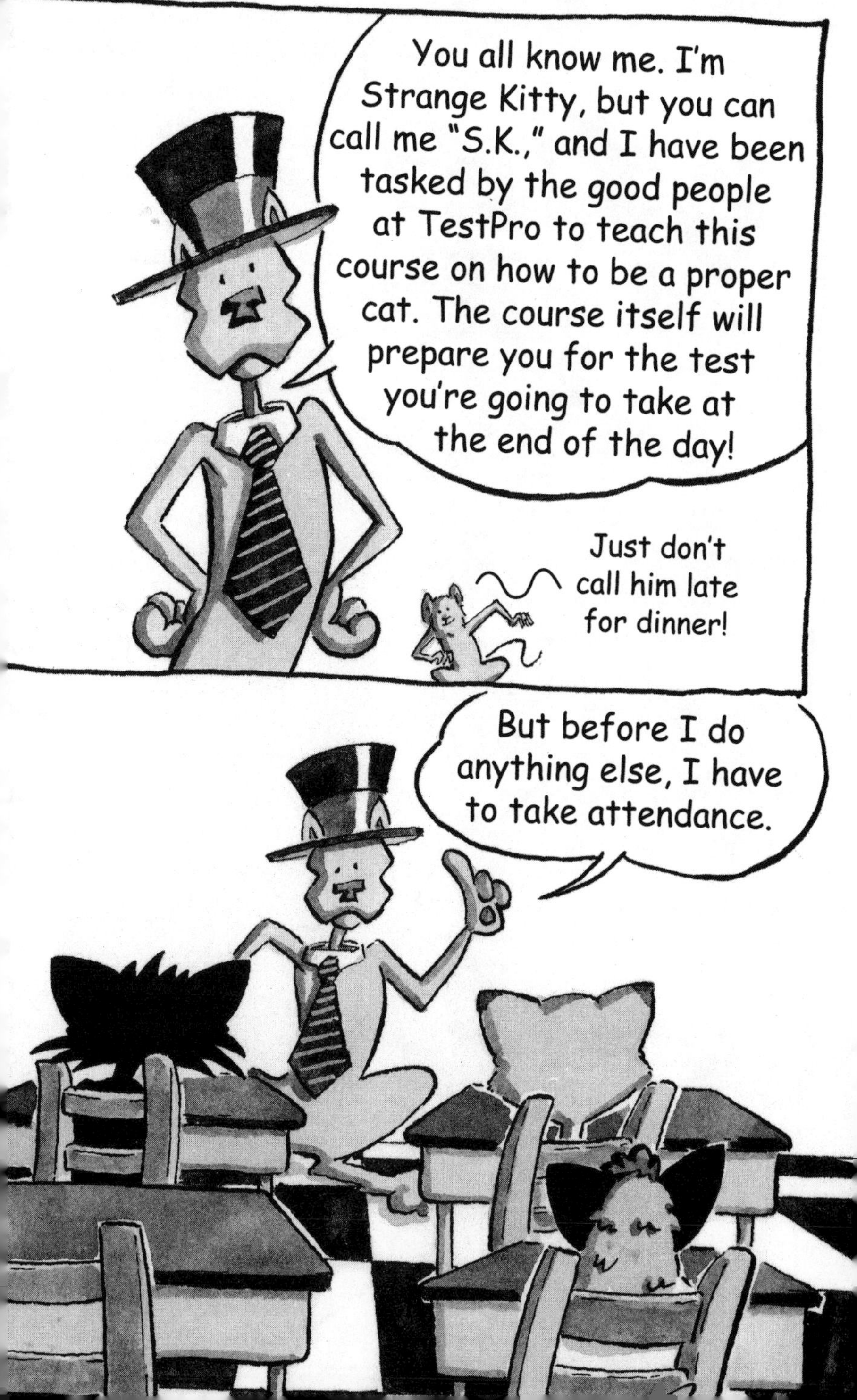
You all know me. I'm Strange Kitty, but you can call me "S.K.," and I have been tasked by the good people at TestPro to teach this course on how to be a proper cat. The course itself will prepare you for the test you're going to take at the end of the day!
Just don't call him late for dinner!
But before I do anything else, I have to take attendance.

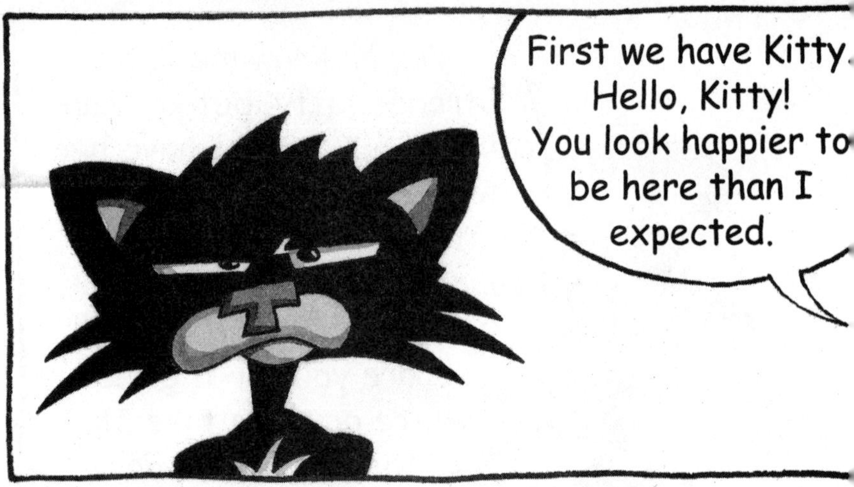
First we have Kitty.
Hello, Kitty!
You look happier to
be here than I
expected.

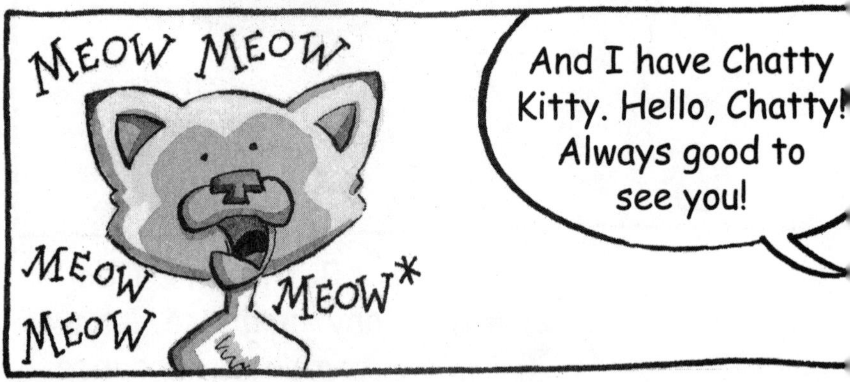
MEOW MEOW
And I have Chatty
Kitty. Hello, Chatty!
Always good to
see you!
MEOW
MEOW
MEOW*

* I HAVE to pass this test! I NEED to pass this test. If I don't pass this test, then won't be a cat. I don't know what I'd be. Maybe I'd be a walrus. I don't want to be walrus. I'm sensitive to cold weather. I haven't slept in three days.

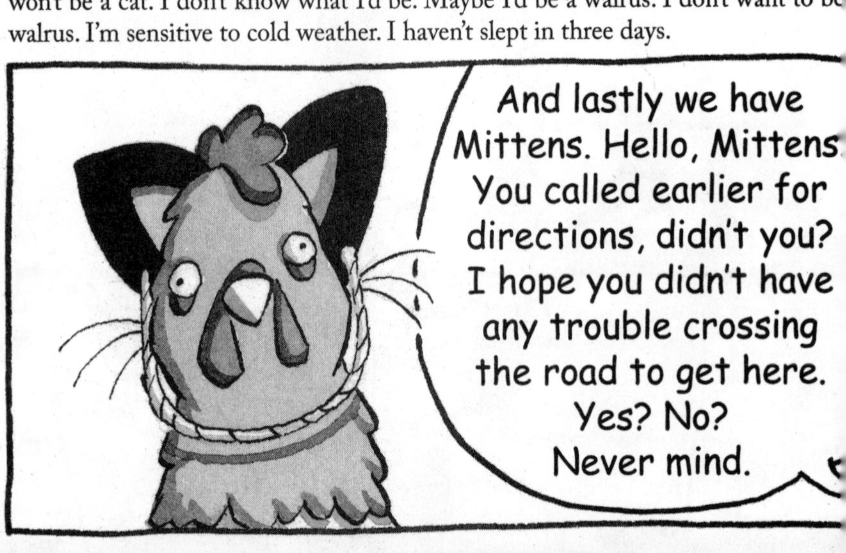
And lastly we have
Mittens. Hello, Mittens.
You called earlier for
directions, didn't you?
I hope you didn't have
any trouble crossing
the road to get here.
Yes? No?
Never mind.

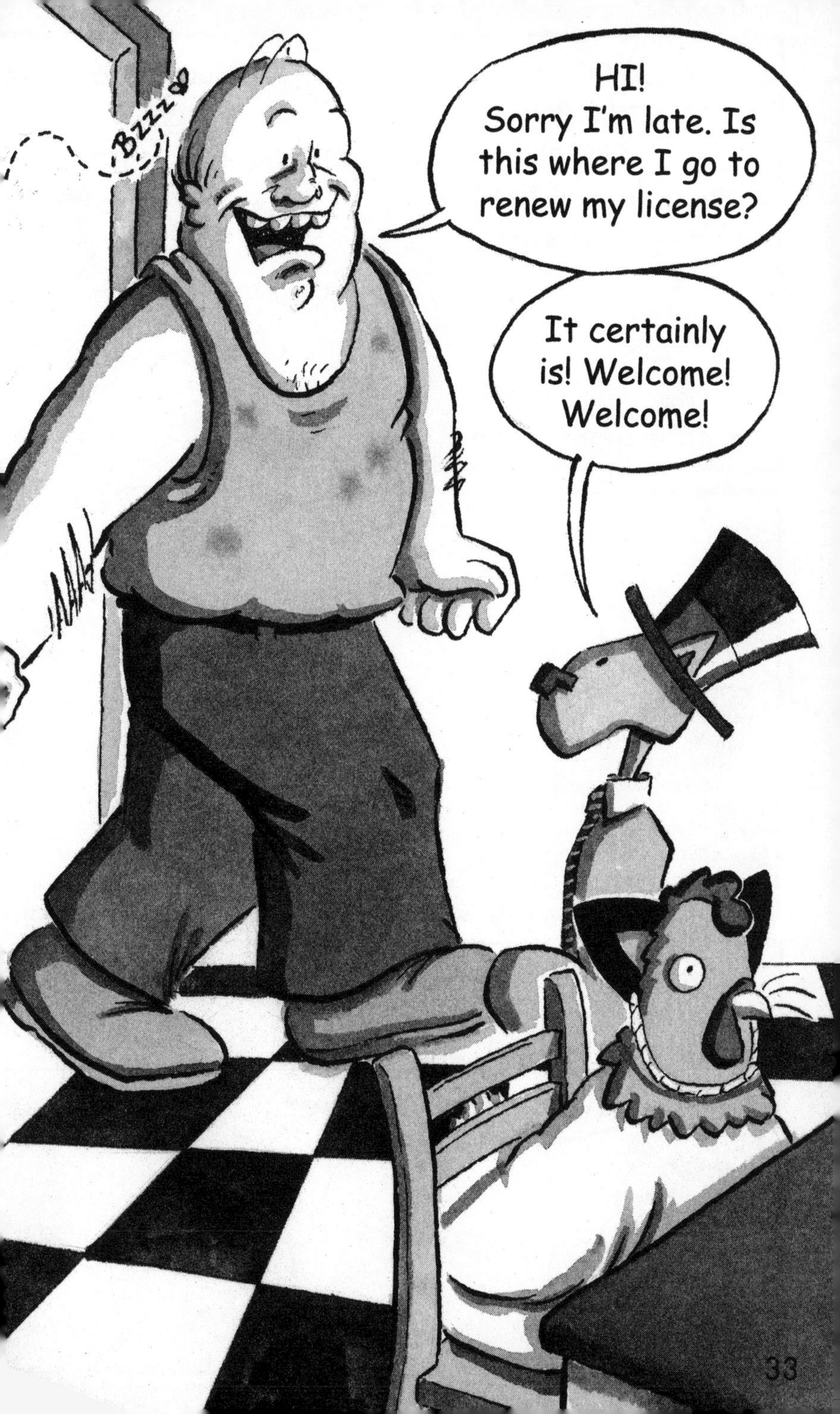
Bzzzd
HI! Sorry I'm late. Is this where I go to renew my license?
It certainly is! Welcome! Welcome!

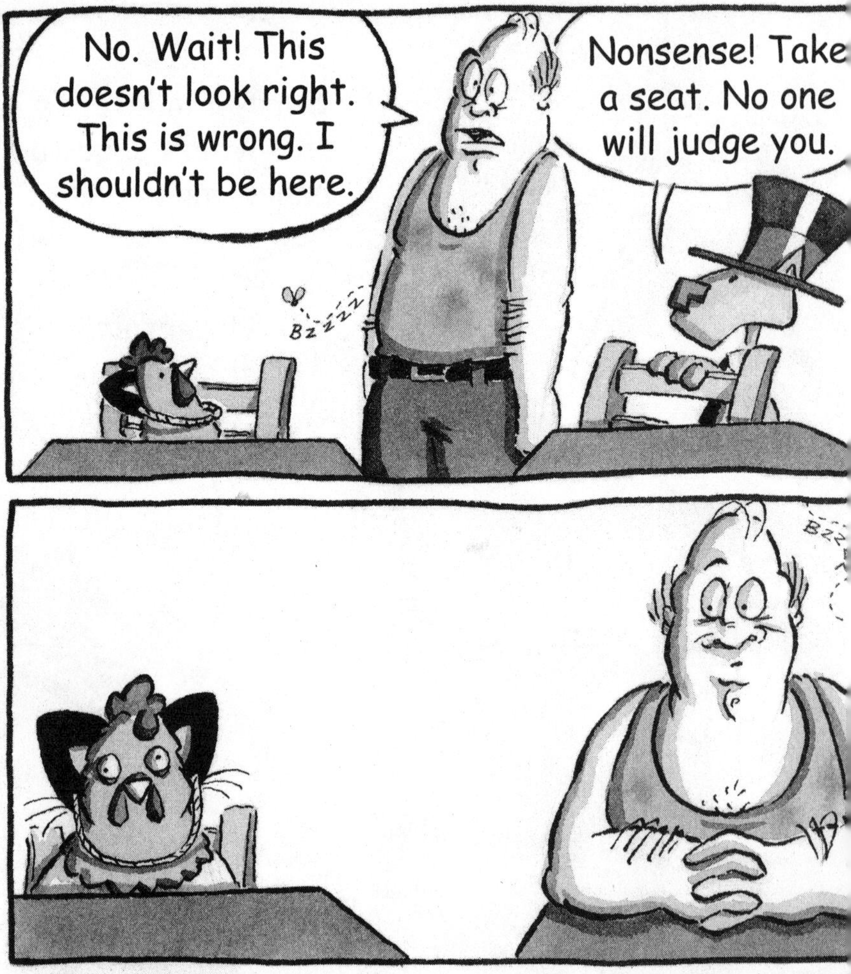
No. Wait! This doesn't look right. This is wrong. I shouldn't be here.
Nonsense! Take a seat. No one will judge you.
Bzzzz
Bzz
Uh . . . Hi. My name's Murray. But everyone calls me Uncle Murray. It's kind of a thing everyone does.
BUK!

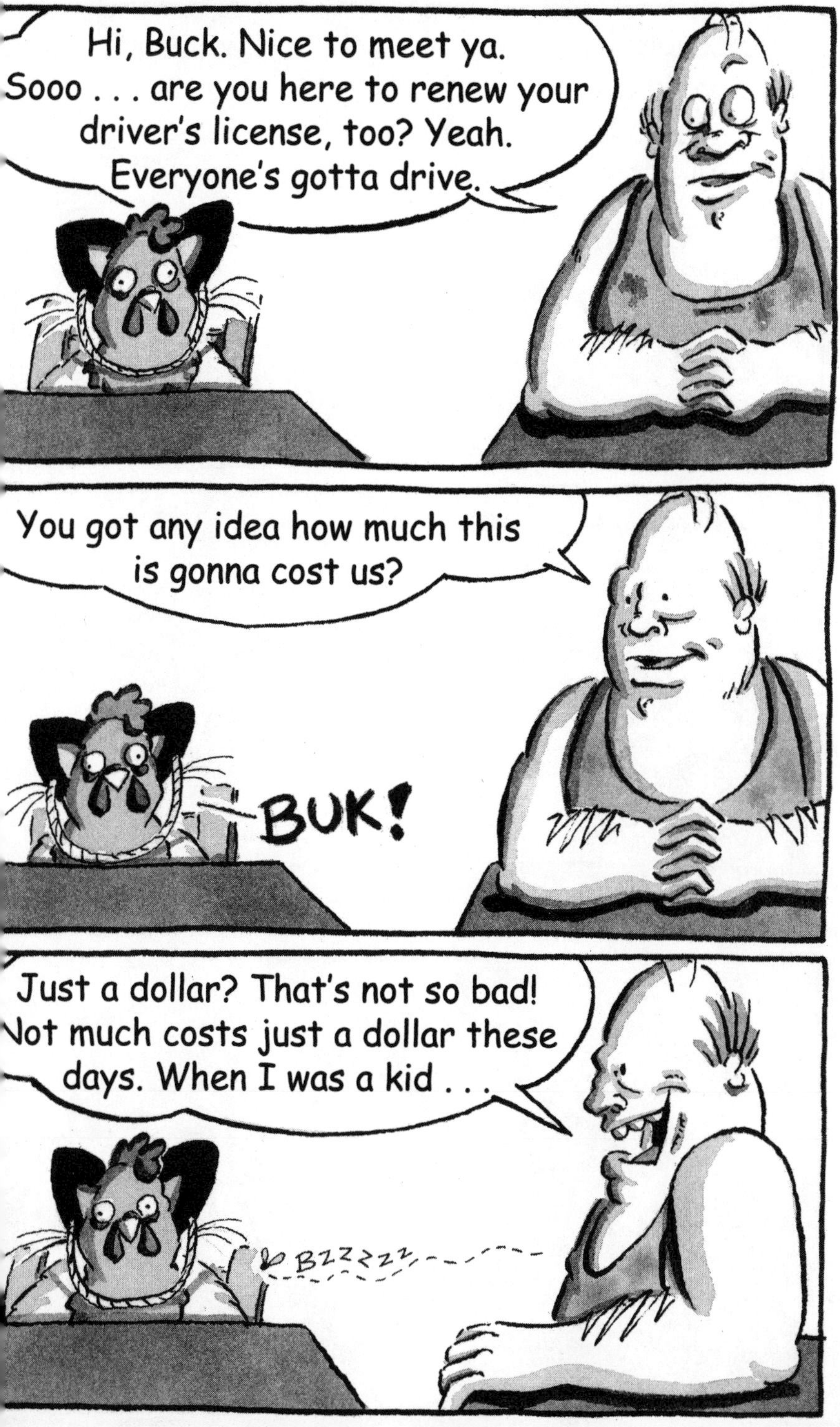
Hi, Buck. Nice to meet ya. Sooo . . . are you here to renew your driver's license, too? Yeah. Everyone's gotta drive.
You got any idea how much this is gonna cost us?
BUK!
Just a dollar? That's not so bad! Not much costs just a dollar these days. When I was a kid . . .
BZZZZZZ

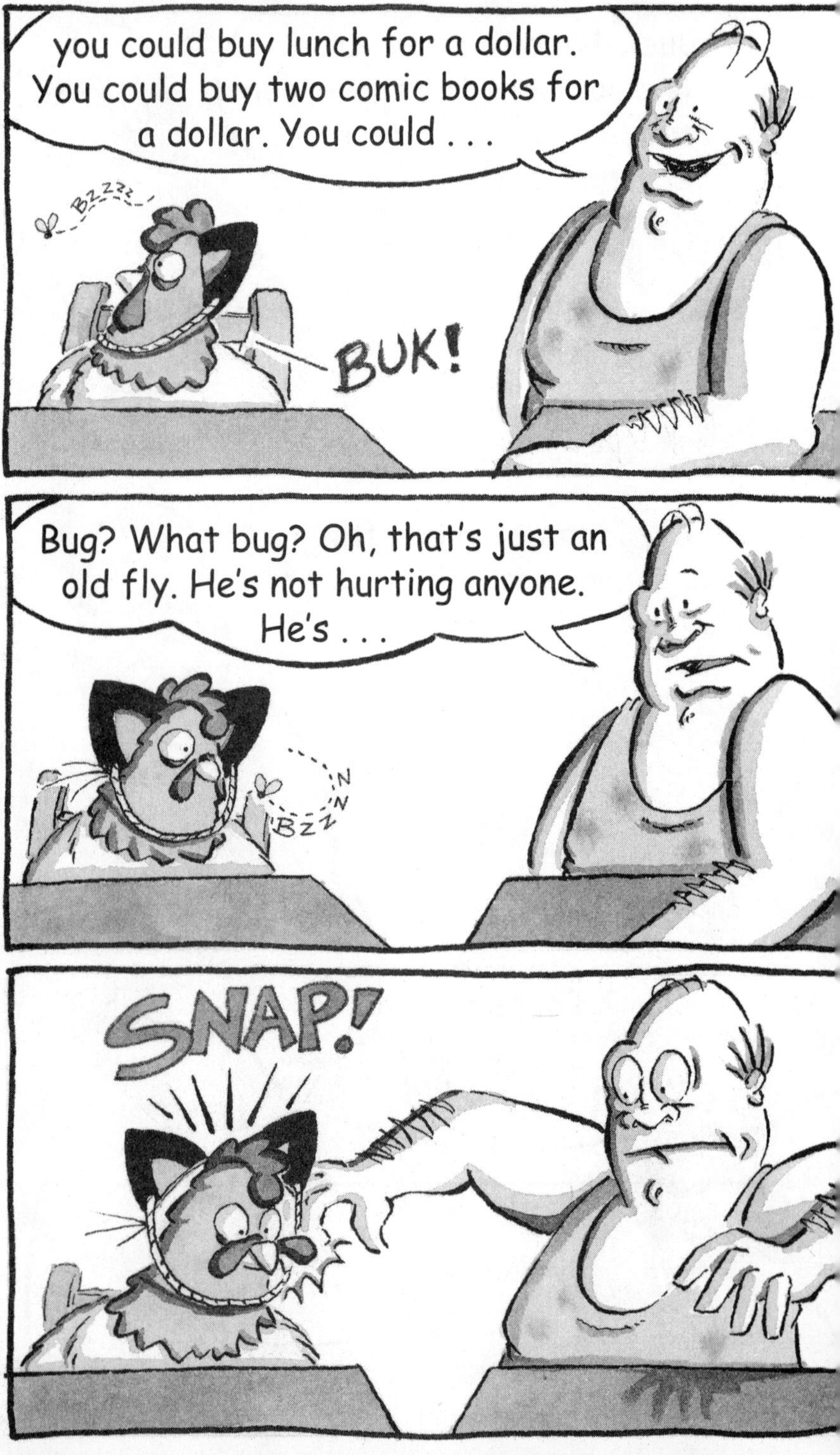
you could buy lunch for a dollar. You could buy two comic books for a dollar. You could . . .
BZZZZ
BUK!
Bug? What bug? Oh, that's just an old fly. He's not hurting anyone. He's . . .
BZZNN
SNAP!

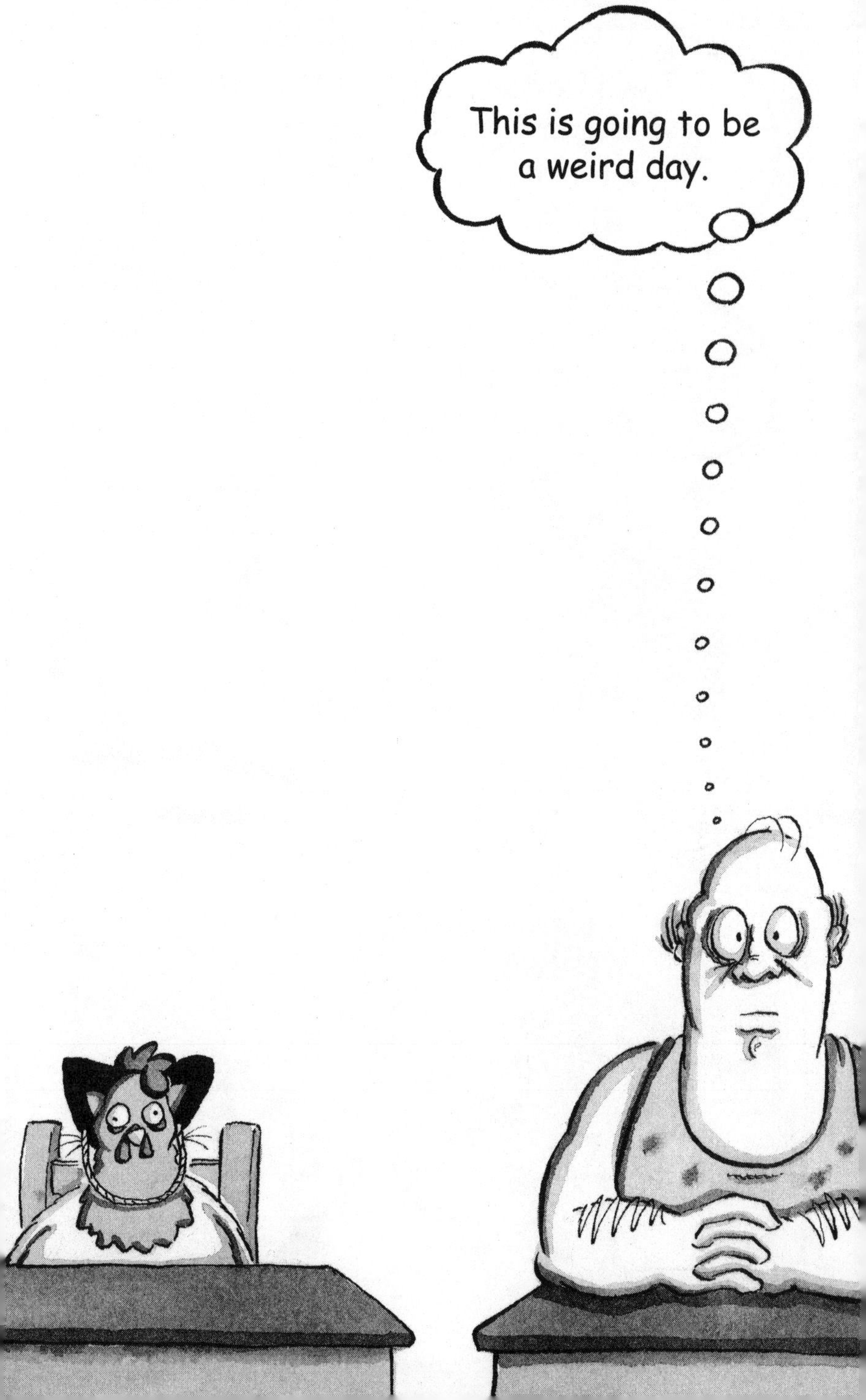
This is going to be a weird day.

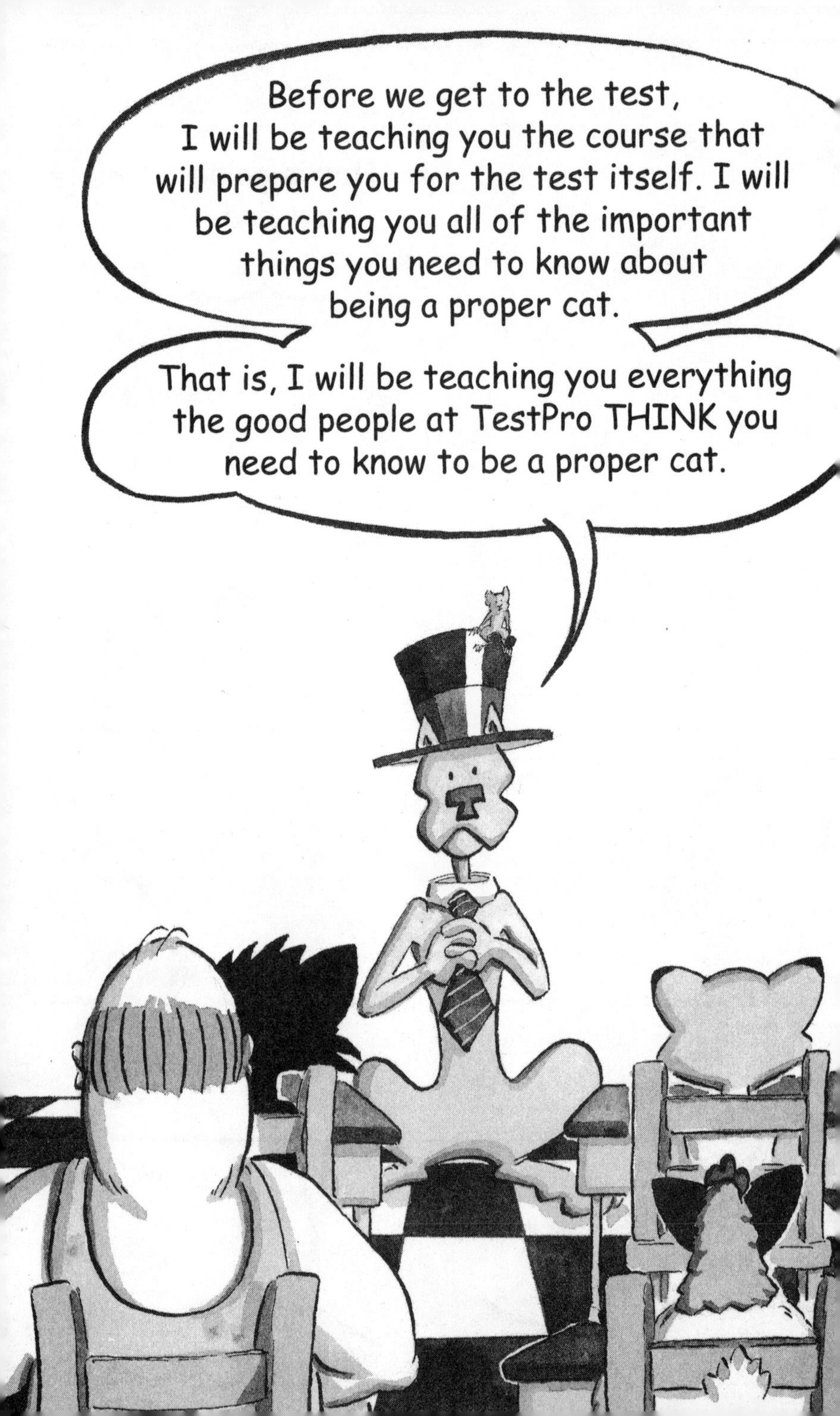
Before we get to the test, I will be teaching you the course that will prepare you for the test itself. I will be teaching you all of the important things you need to know about being a proper cat.
That is, I will be teaching you everything the good people at TestPro THINK you need to know to be a proper cat.

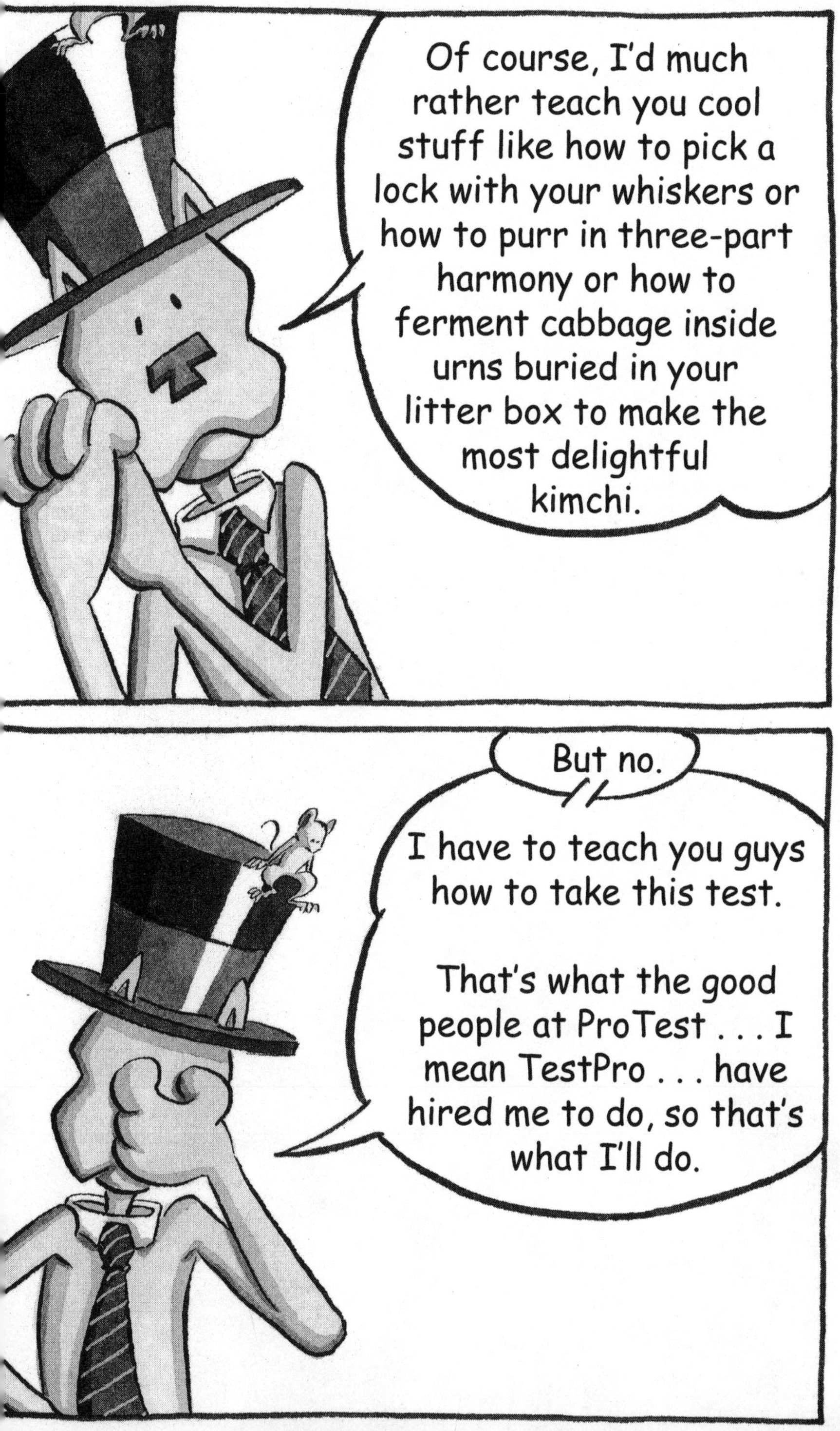
Of course, I'd much rather teach you cool stuff like how to pick a lock with your whiskers or how to purr in three-part harmony or how to ferment cabbage inside urns buried in your litter box to make the most delightful kimchi.
But no.
I have to teach you guys how to take this test.
That's what the good people at ProTest . . . I mean TestPro . . . have hired me to do, so that's what I'll do.

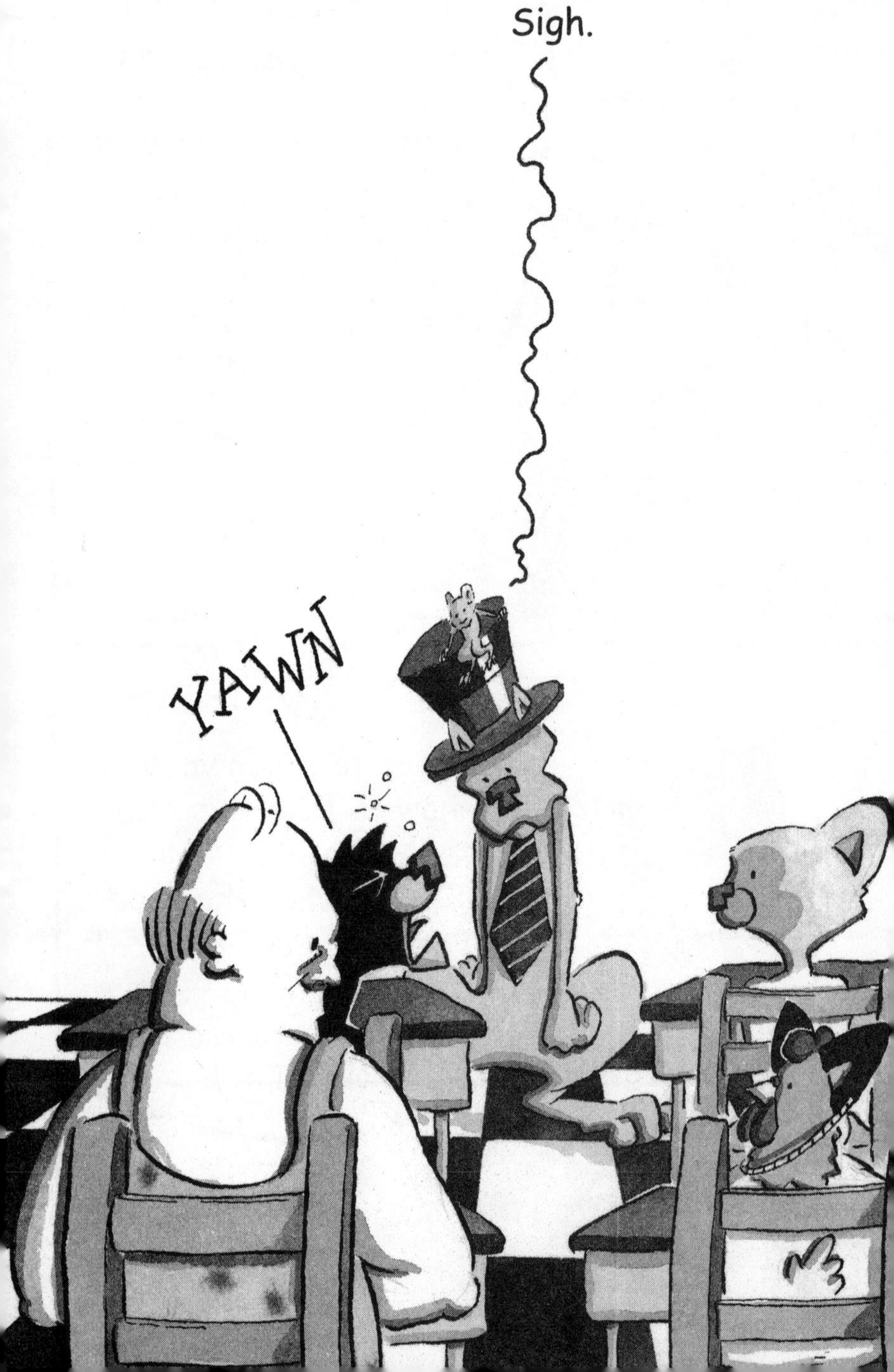
Sigh.
YAWN

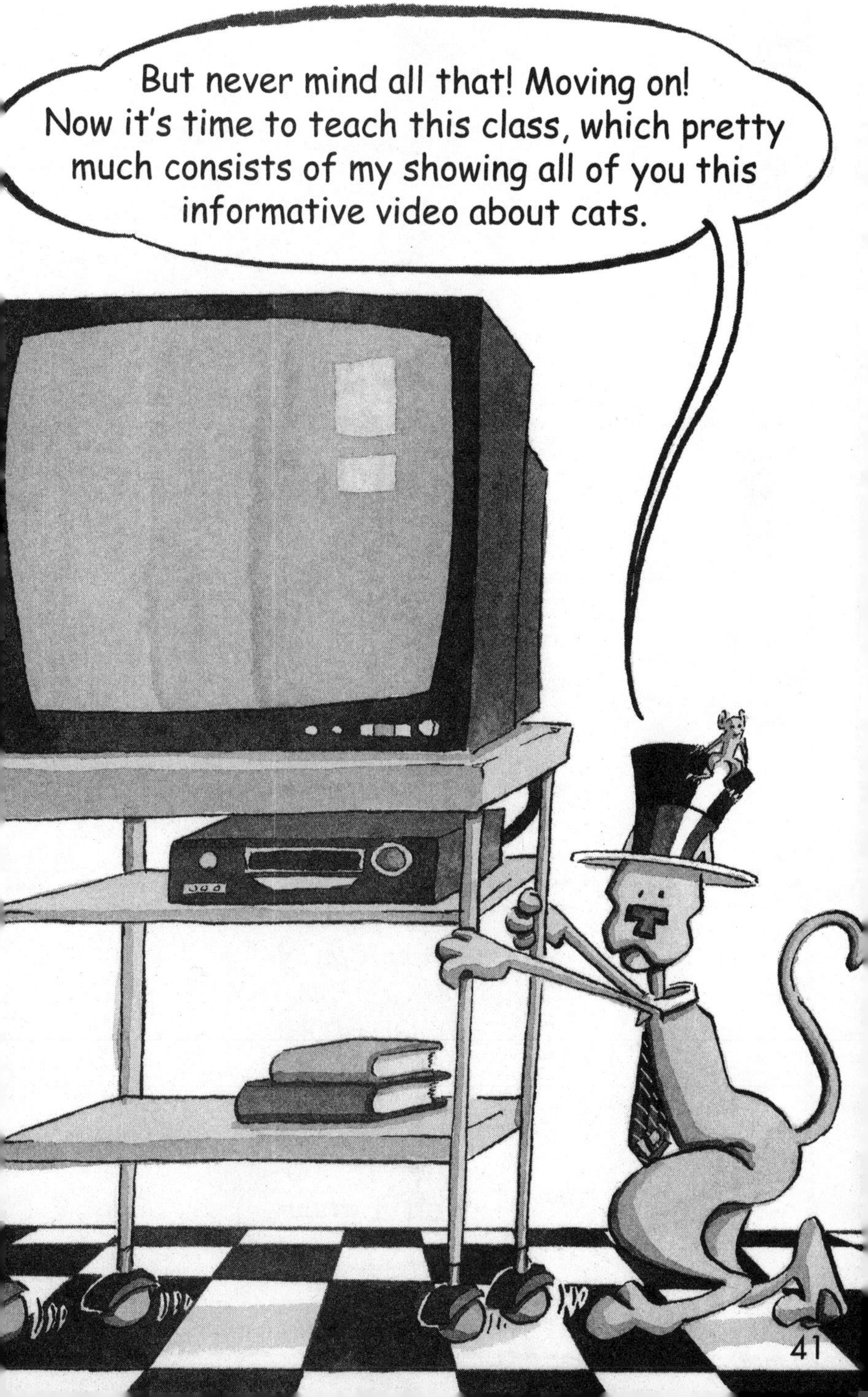
But never mind all that! Moving on! Now it's time to teach this class, which pretty much consists of my showing all of you this informative video about cats.

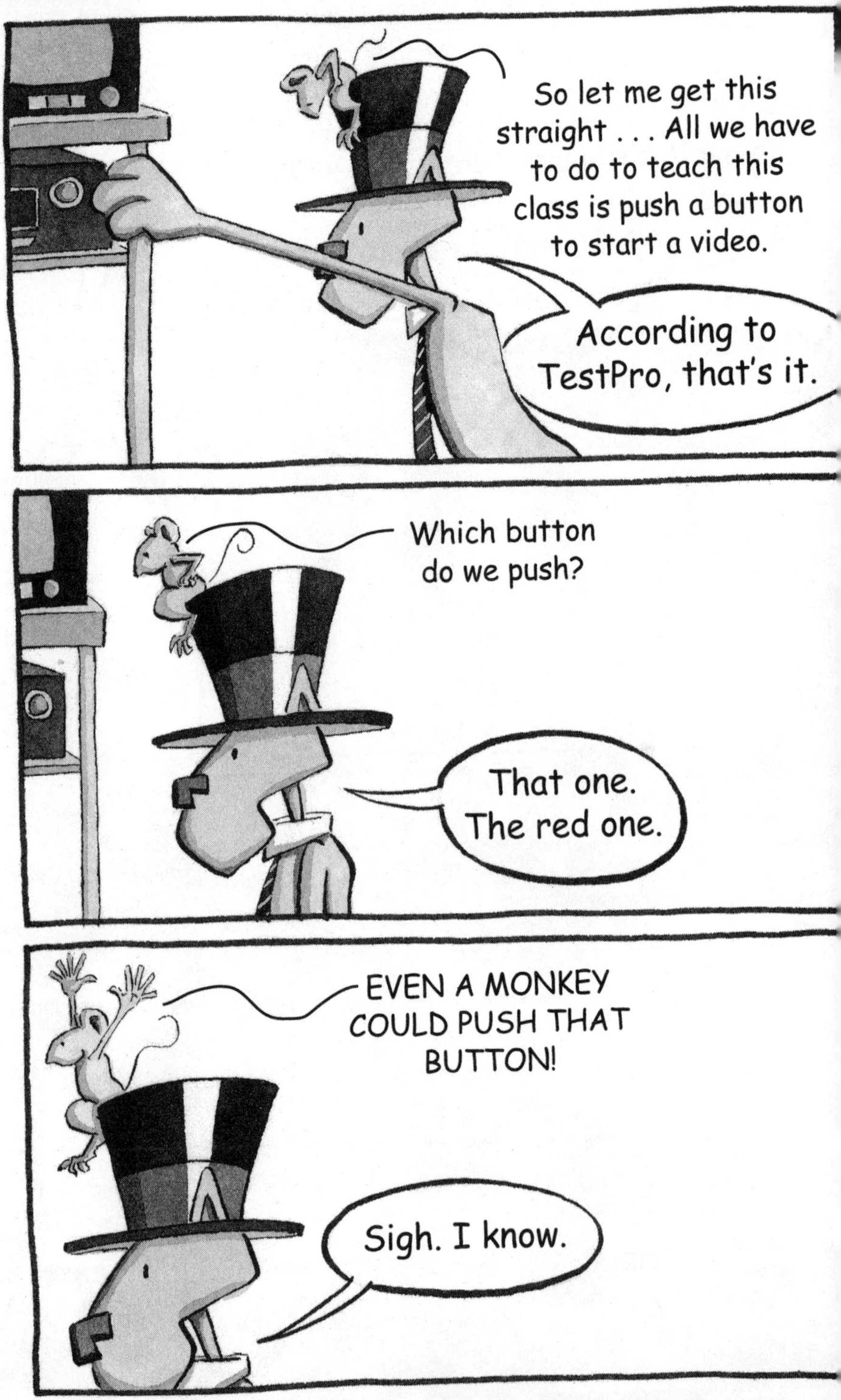

So let me get this straight . . . All we have to do to teach this class is push a button to start a video.
According to TestPro, that's it.
Which button do we push?
That one. The red one.
EVEN A MONKEY COULD PUSH THAT BUTTON!
Sigh. I know.

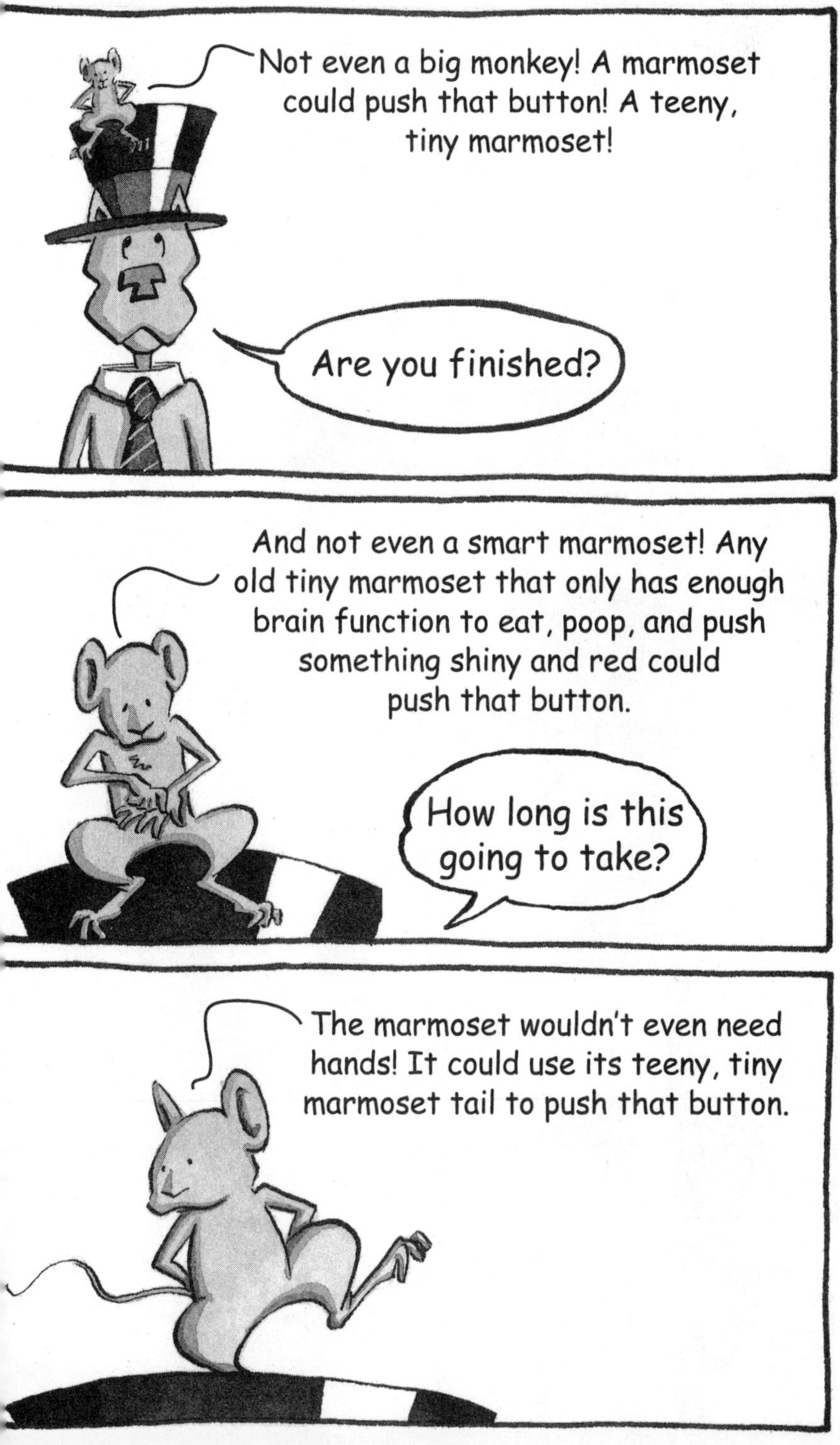
Not even a big monkey! A marmoset could push that button! A teeny, tiny marmoset!
Are you finished?
And not even a smart marmoset! Any old tiny marmoset that only has enough brain function to eat, poop, and push something shiny and red could push that button.
How long is this going to take?
The marmoset wouldn't even need hands! It could use its teeny, tiny marmoset tail to push that button.

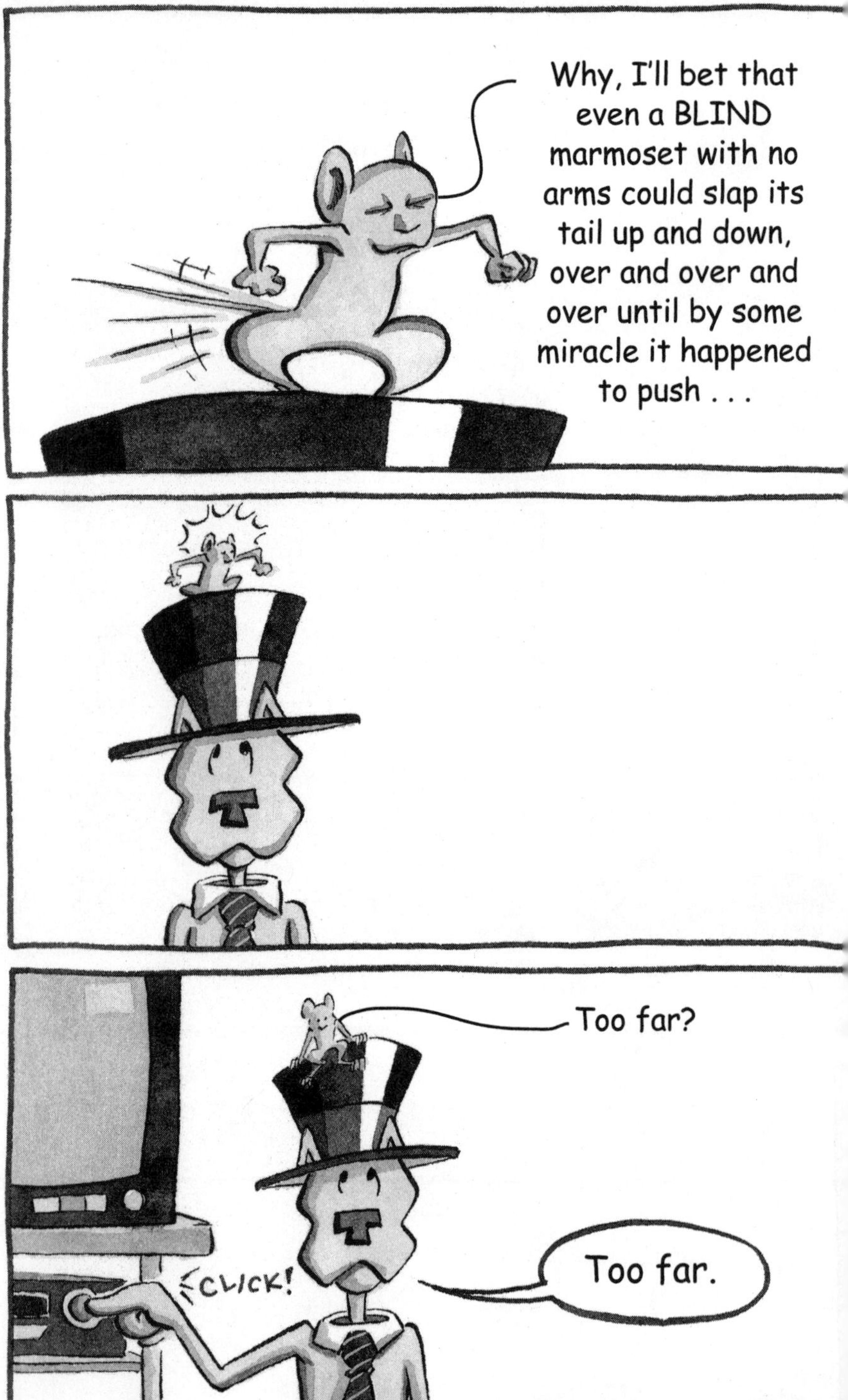
Why, I'll bet that even a BLIND marmoset with no arms could slap its tail up and down, over and over and over until by some miracle it happened to push . . .
Too far?
CLICK!
Too far.

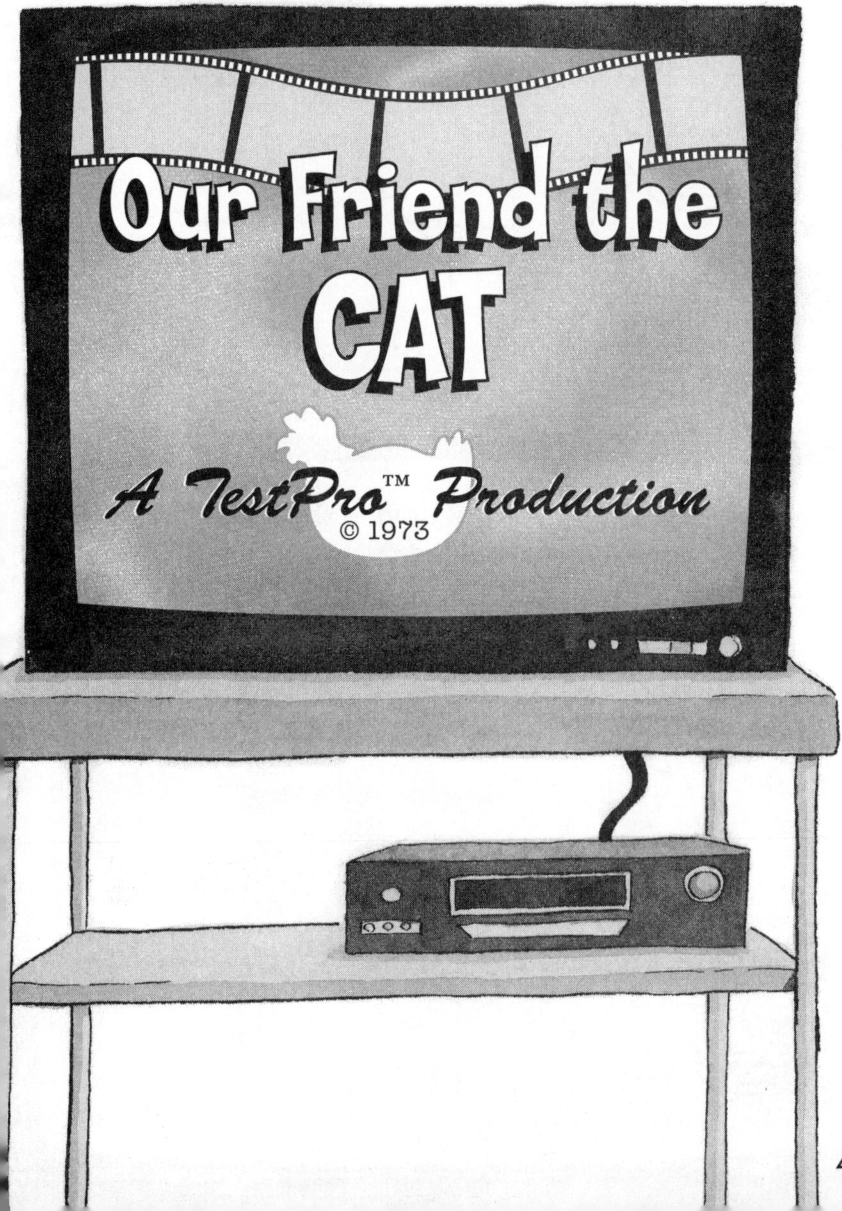
Our Friend the
CAT
A TestPro™ Production
© 1973

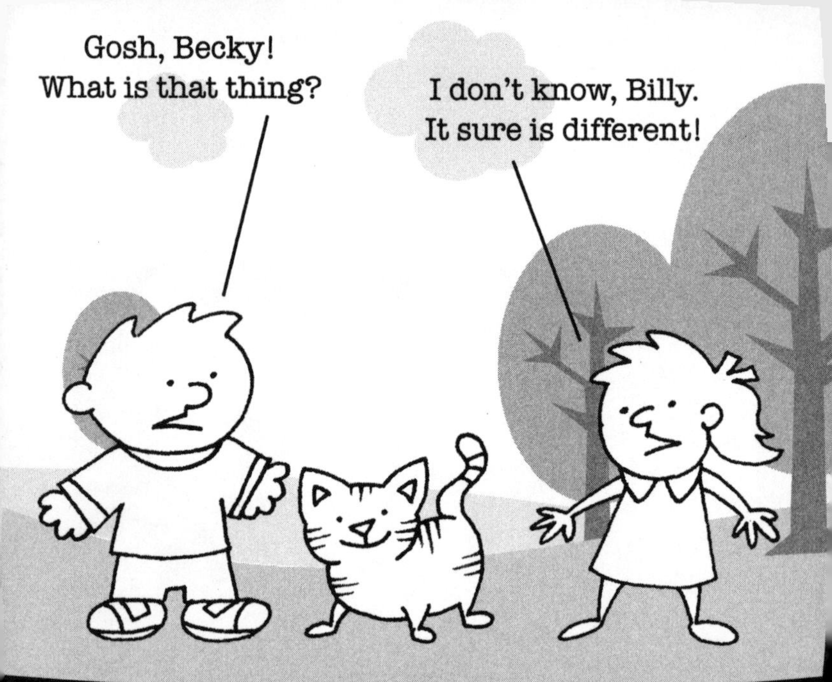
Gosh, Becky!
What is that thing?
I don't know, Billy.
It sure is different!

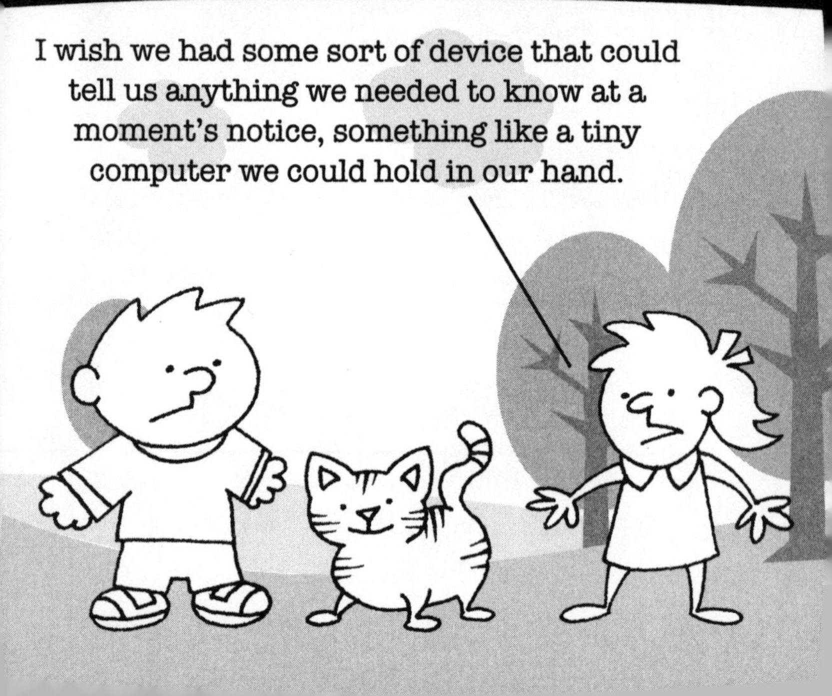
I wish we had some sort of device that could tell us anything we needed to know at a moment's notice, something like a tiny computer we could hold in our hand.

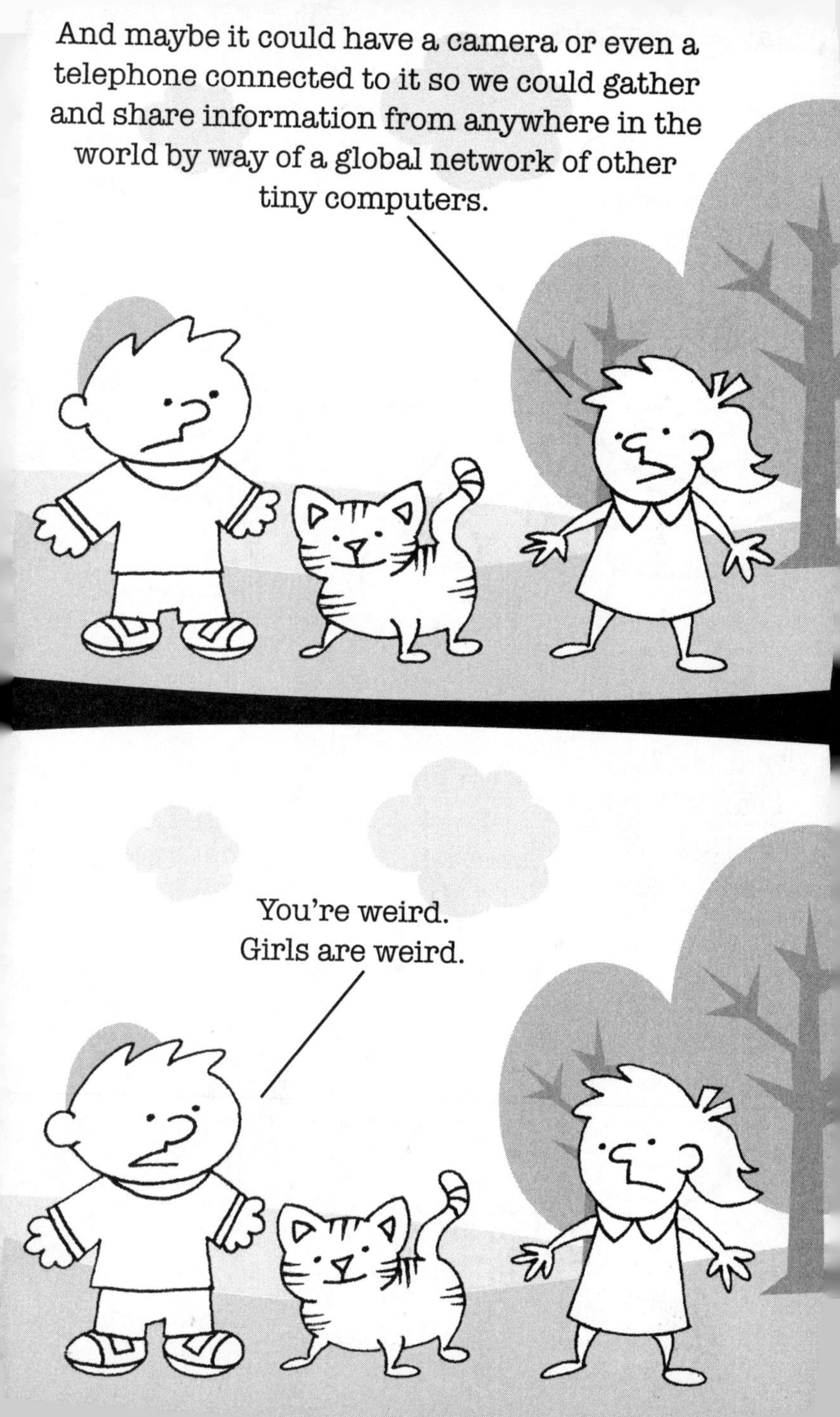
And maybe it could have a camera or even a telephone connected to it so we could gather and share information from anywhere in the world by way of a global network of other tiny computers.
You're weird. Girls are weird.

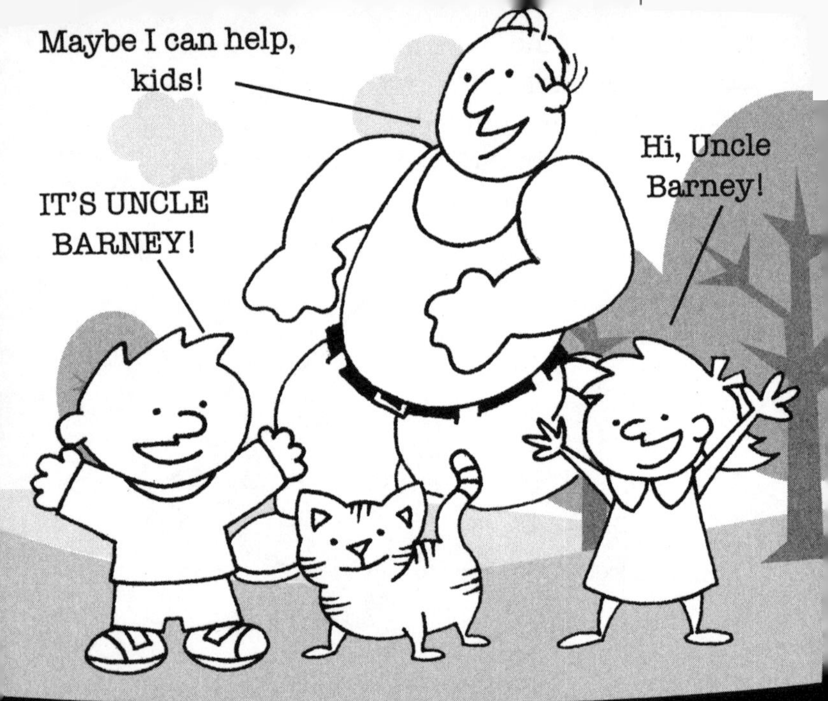
Maybe I can help, kids!
IT'S UNCLE BARNEY!
Hi, Uncle Barney!
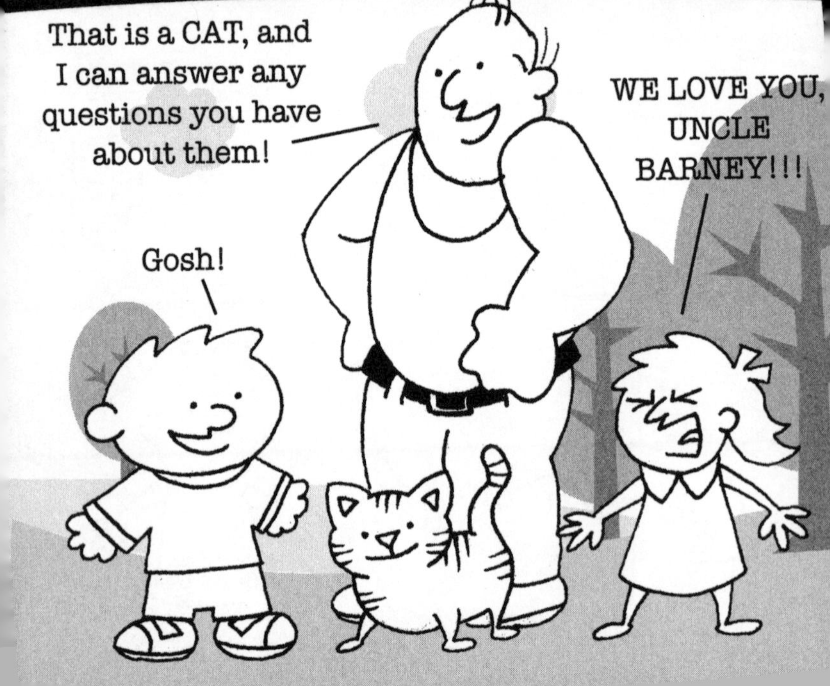
That is a CAT, and I can answer any questions you have about them!
WE LOVE YOU, UNCLE BARNEY!!!
Gosh!

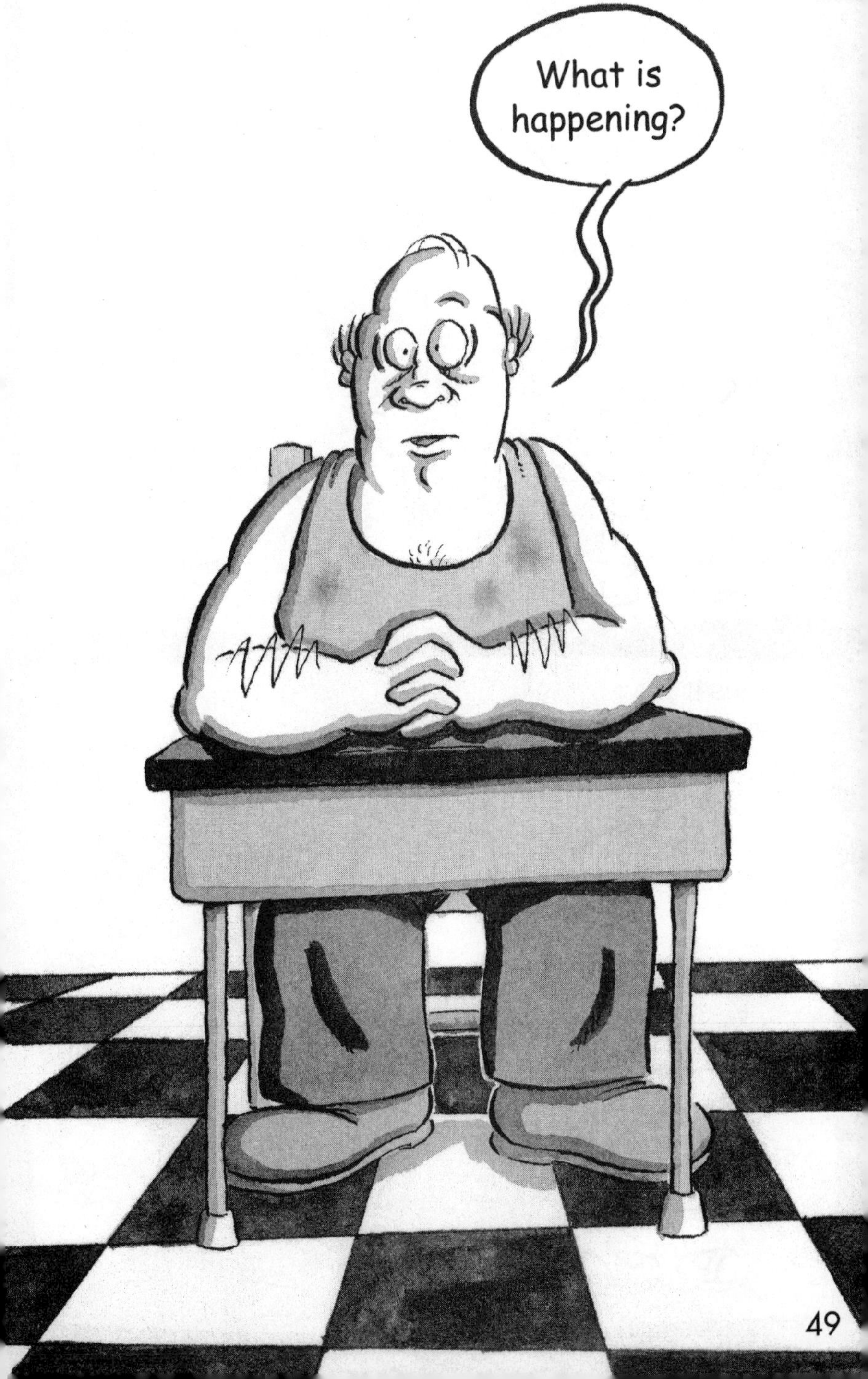
What is happening?

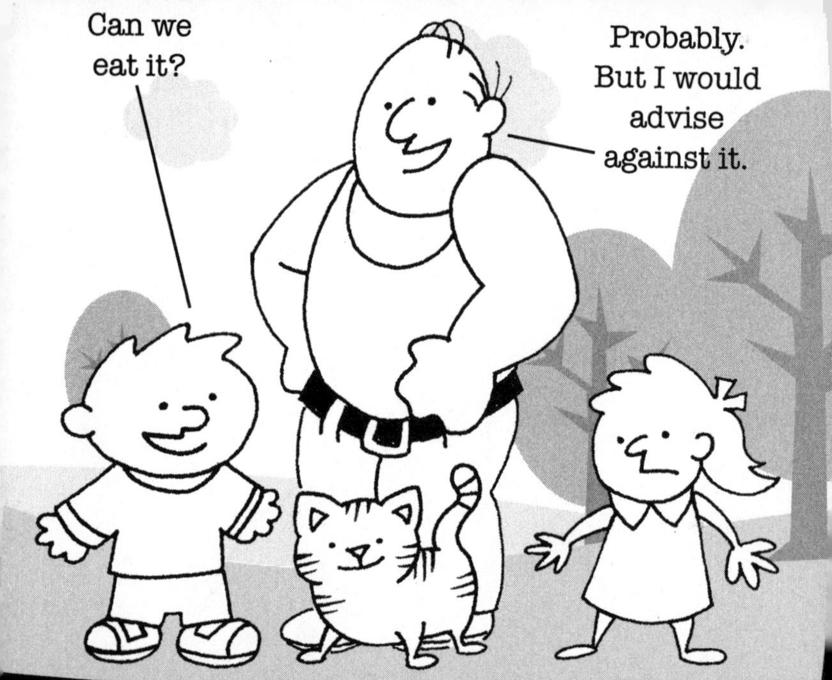
Can we eat it?
Probably. But I would advise against it.

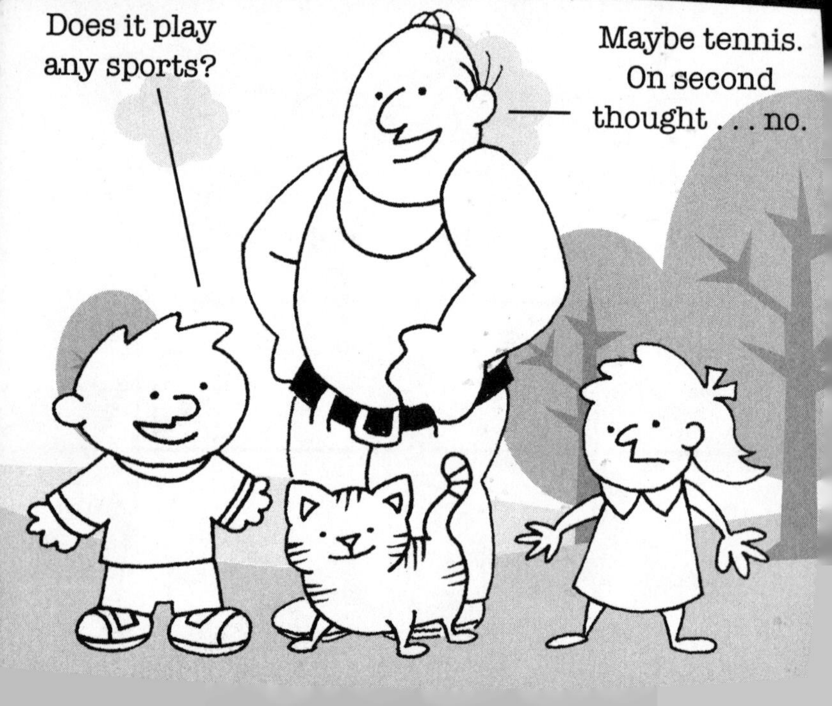
Does it play any sports?
Maybe tennis. On second thought . . . no.

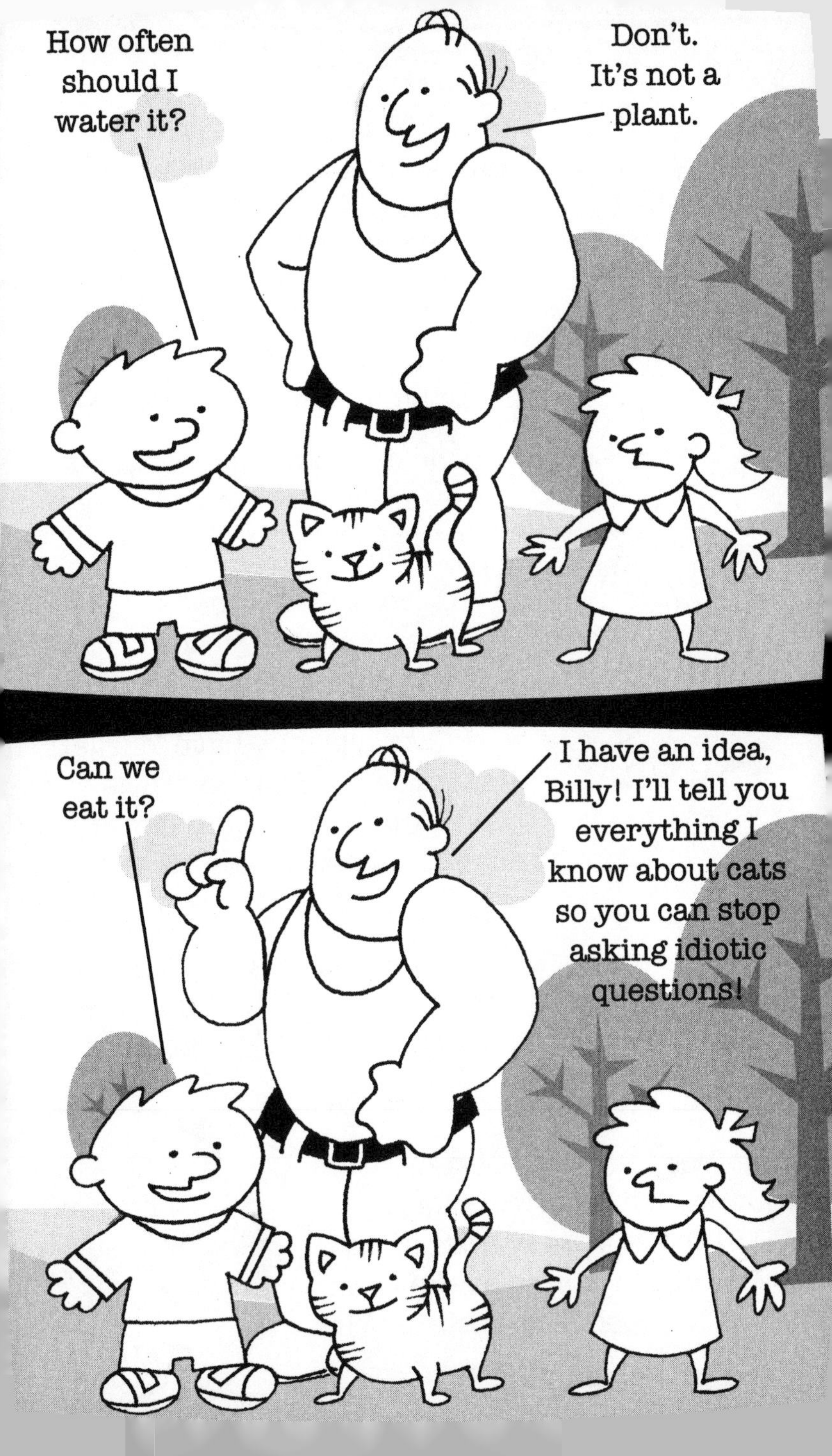
How often should I water it?
Don't. It's not a plant.
Can we eat it?
I have an idea, Billy! I'll tell you everything I know about cats so you can stop asking idiotic questions!

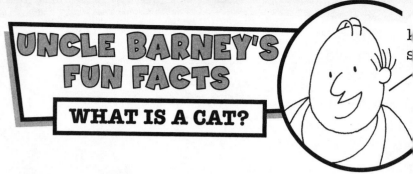

UNCLE BARNEY'S FUN FACTS

WHAT IS A CAT?

- A cat is an animal.

- A giant squid is also an animal. It has tentacles.

NOT A CAT

- Cats do not have tentacles, therefore they are rarely mistaken for giant squids.

- Other animals that are not cats are squirrels, giraffes, lobsters, and porcupines.

- Cats typically have four legs. If a cat has less than four legs or more than four legs, then something is wrong and medical attention may be required.

- In 1963, the French sent the first cat into space, a black-and-white Parisian street cat named Félicette who traveled 100 miles above the Earth in a capsule before descending safely back to the ground by parachute.

- "Cat" in Vietnamese is *con mèo*.

- The World Health Organization estimates that approximately 400,000 people are bitten by cats in the United States every year. No one has died from their injuries.

- "Cat" in Swahili is *paka*.

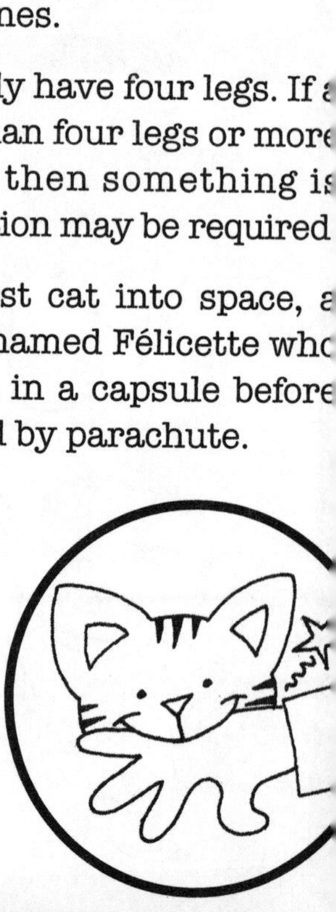

Legend has it that Sir Isaac
ewton, the scientist and math-
matician who discovered gravi-
itional mechanics and created
alculus, also invented the cat
lap on doors because he was
red of constantly getting up
om his experiments to let his cat,
pithead, in and out of his study.

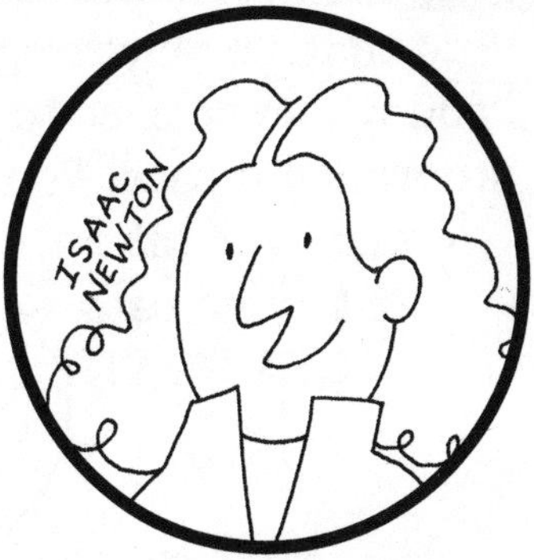
ISAAC NEWTON

That's right . . . Sir Isaac Newton named his cat Spit-
ead.

"Cat" in Icelandic is *köttur*.

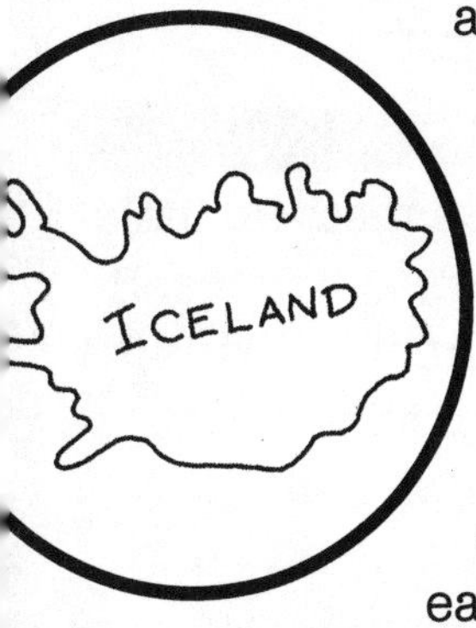
ICELAND

- "Cat" spelled backward is "tac," which are the first three letters in the word "taco," which is a delicious food that cats will sometimes eat when dropped on the floor.

- In the early 1960s, the CIA launched Operation Acoustic Kitty, an actual plan to use cats as spies. Cats would be trained to eavesdrop on Russian conversations. hey would be released nearby with microphones mplanted in their ears, transmitters ttached to their collars, and antennae ied to their tails. The first cat gent was deployed and then run ver by a taxi moments later. wenty million dollars was spent n the program that was termi- ated shortly thereafter.

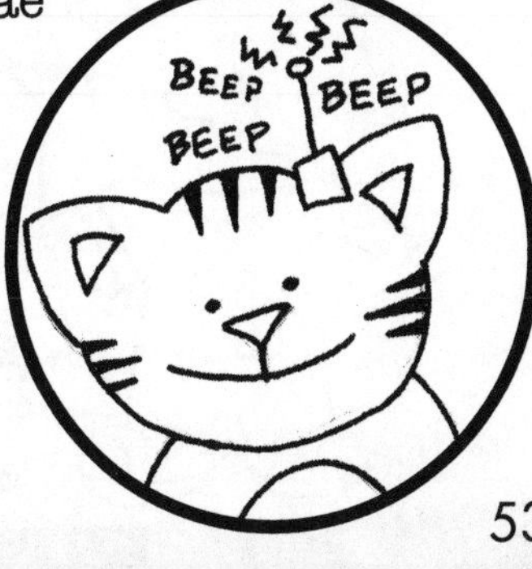
BEEP
BEEP
BEEP

- Spithead.

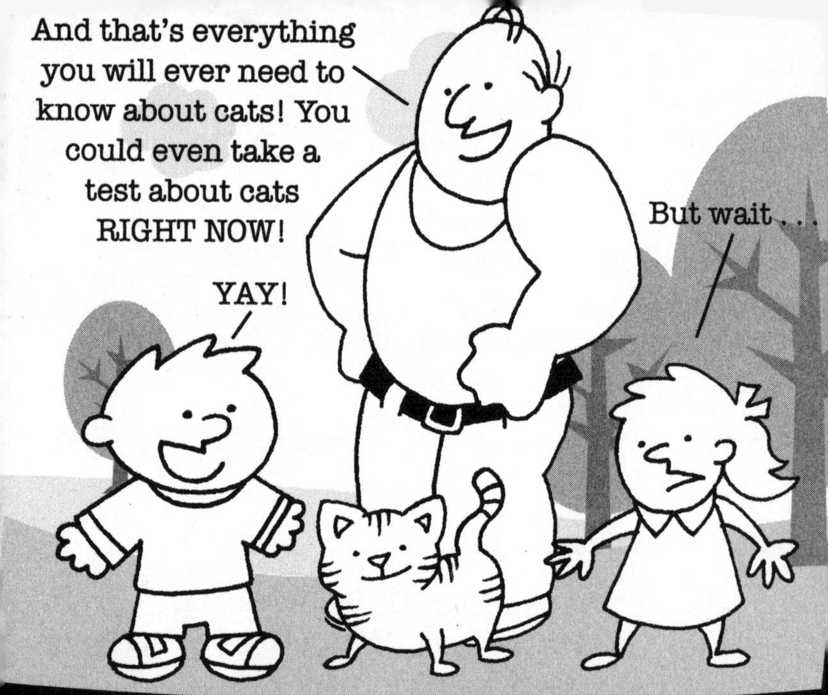
And that's everything you will ever need to know about cats! You could even take a test about cats RIGHT NOW!
YAY!
But wait . . .

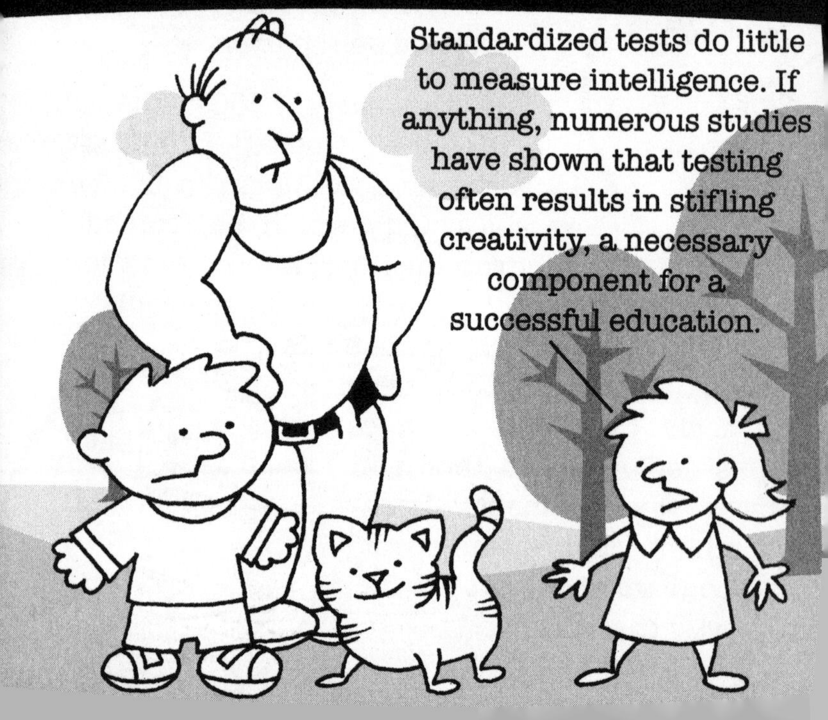
Standardized tests do little to measure intelligence. If anything, numerous studies have shown that testing often results in stifling creativity, a necessary component for a successful education.

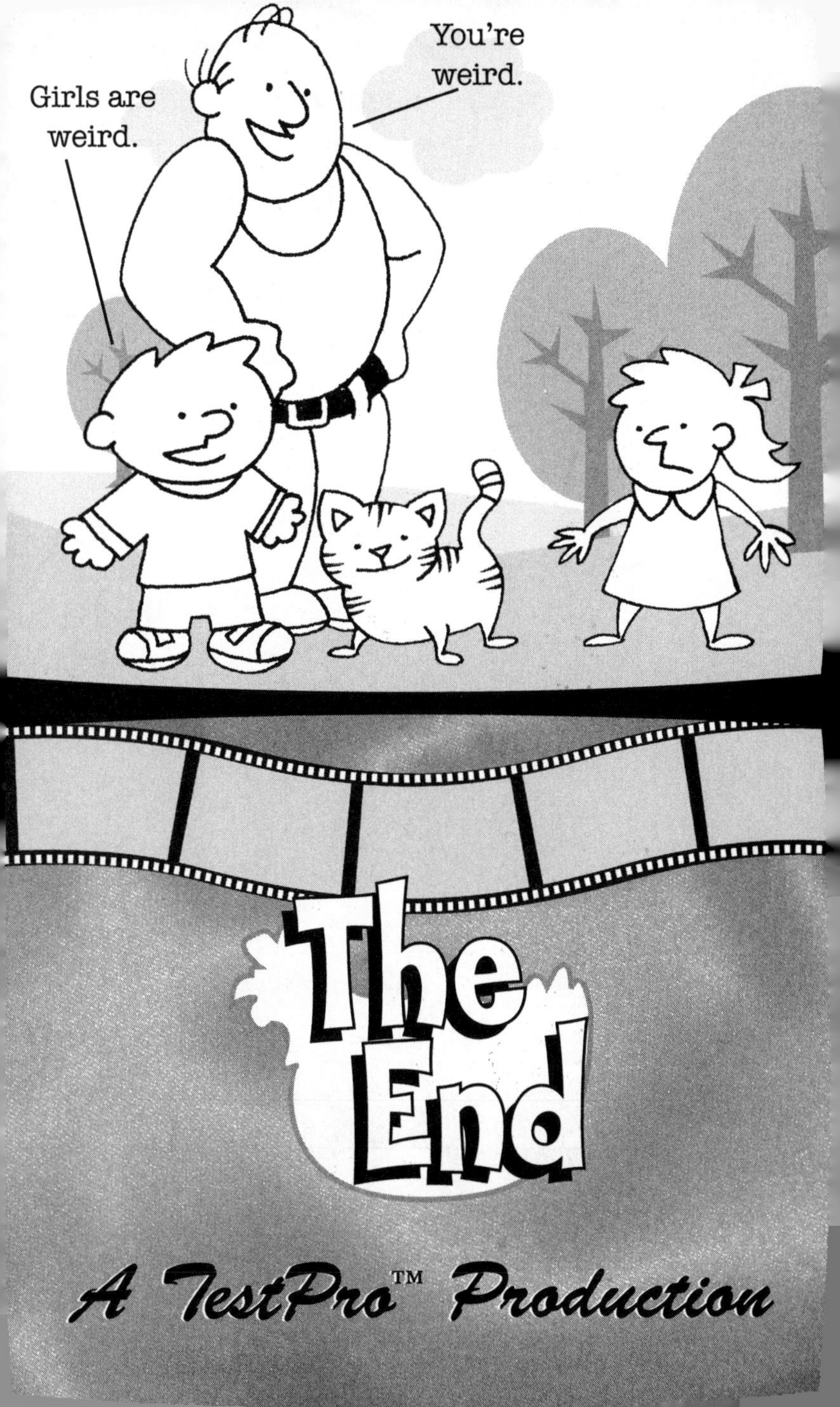
Girls are weird.
You're weird.
The End
A TestPro™ Production

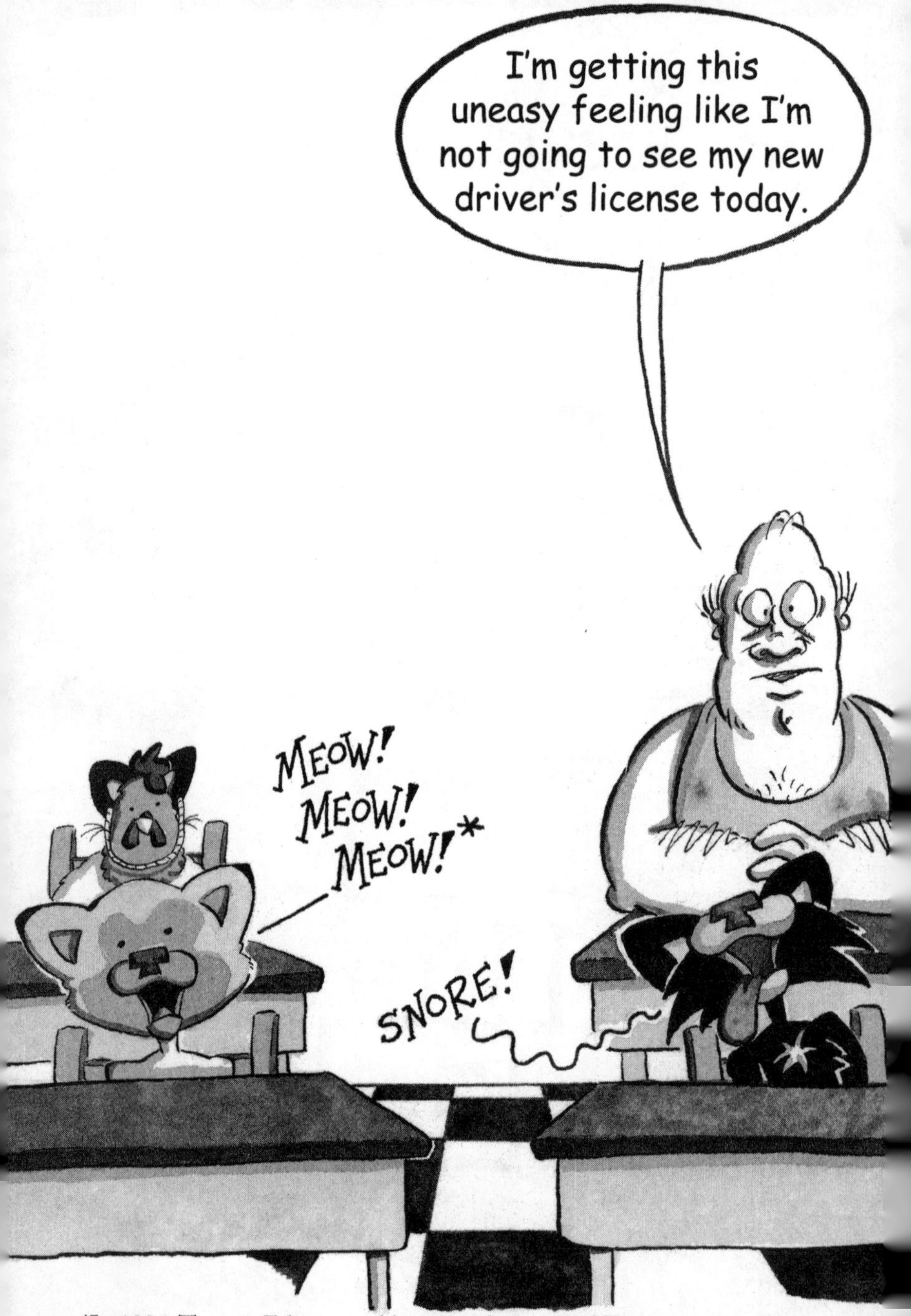
I'm getting this uneasy feeling like I'm not going to see my new driver's license today.
MEOW! MEOW! MEOW!*
SNORE!

*In 1894, Thomas Edison used his recently invented Kinetograph to film two cat
boxing. It is considered to be the very first cat video. I hope THAT'S on the test

•CHAPTER FOUR•

PREPARATION

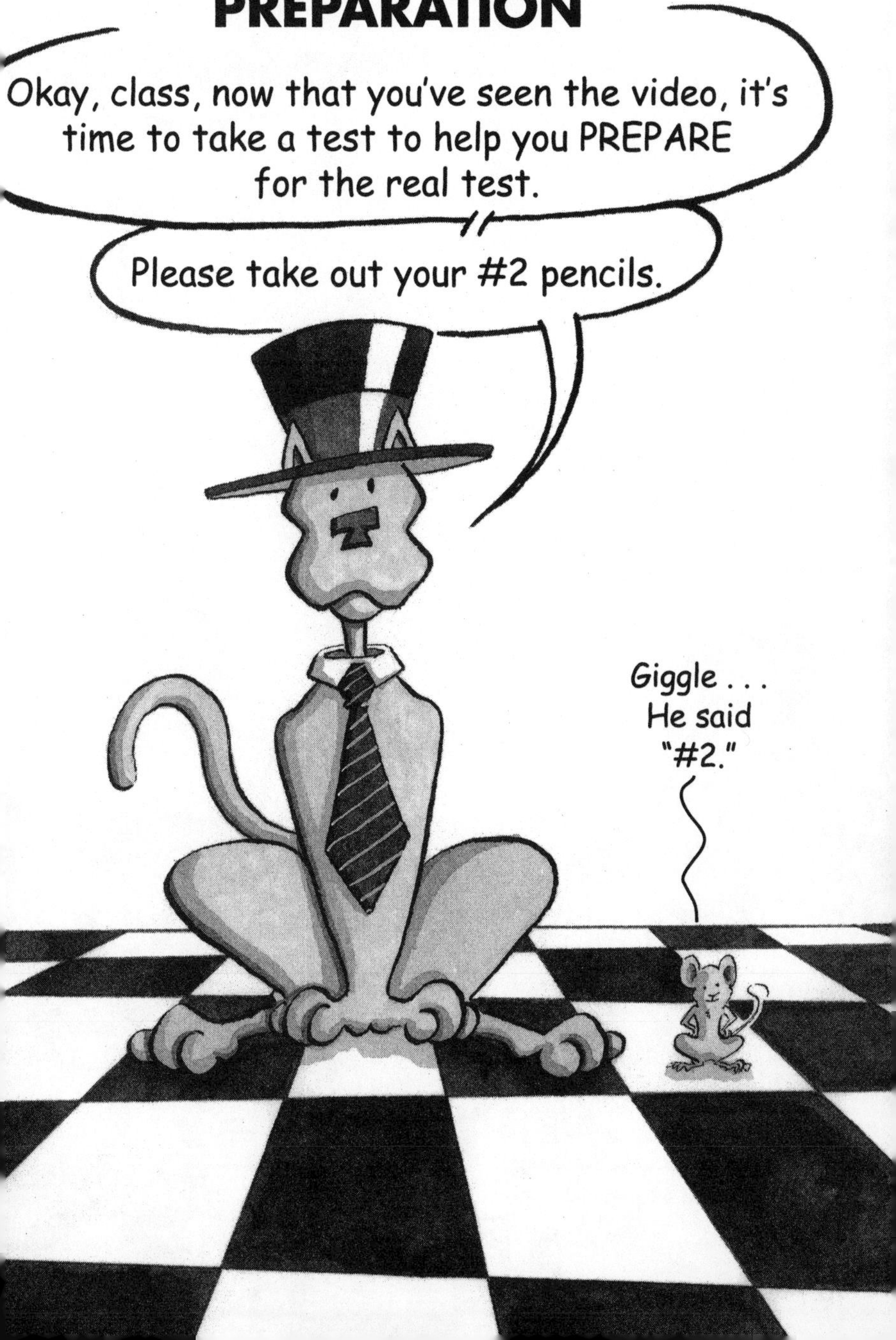
Okay, class, now that you've seen the video, it's time to take a test to help you PREPARE for the real test.
Please take out your #2 pencils.
Giggle . . . He said "#2."

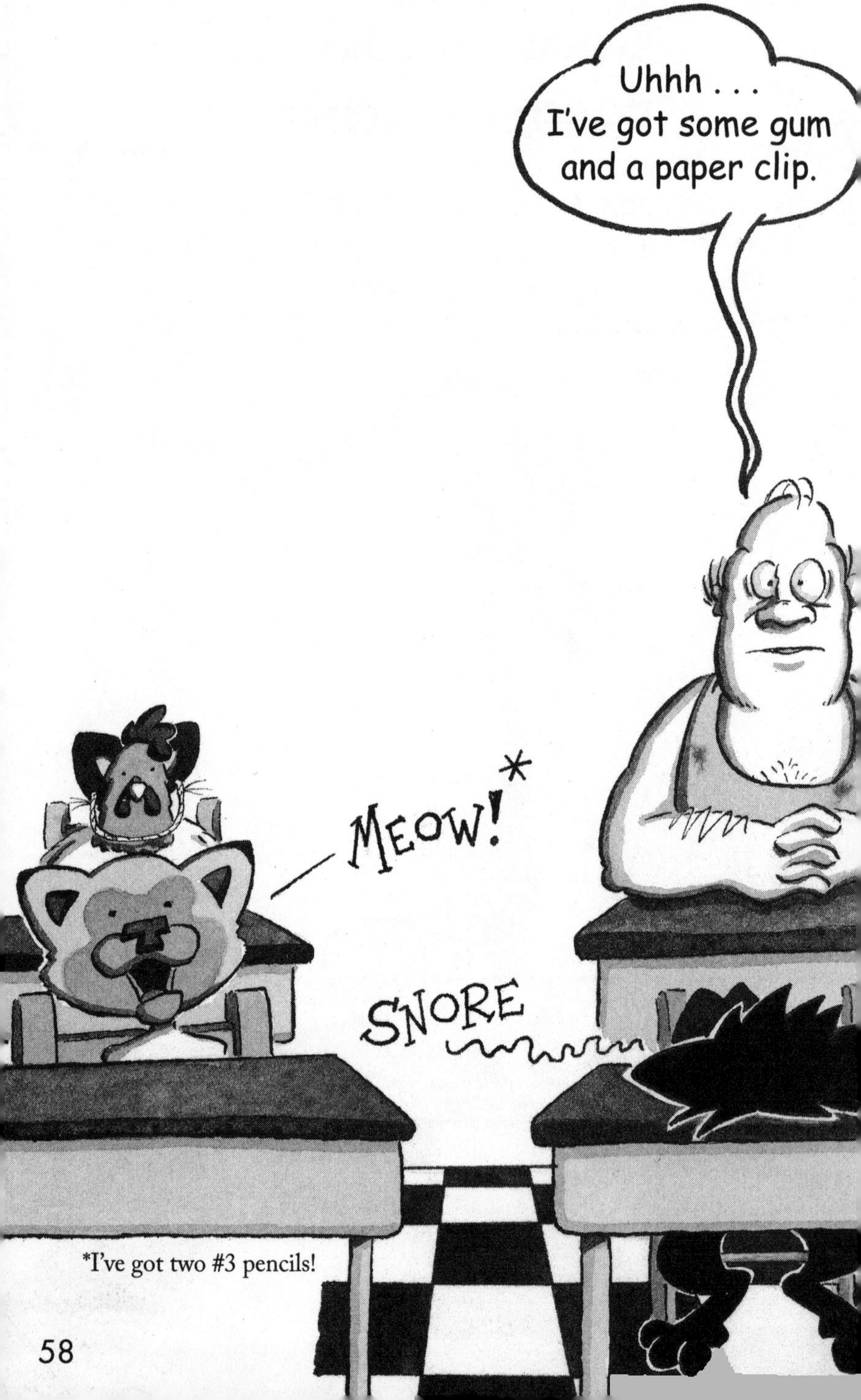
Uhhh . . .
I've got some gum
and a paper clip.
MEOW!*
SNORE

*I've got two #3 pencils!

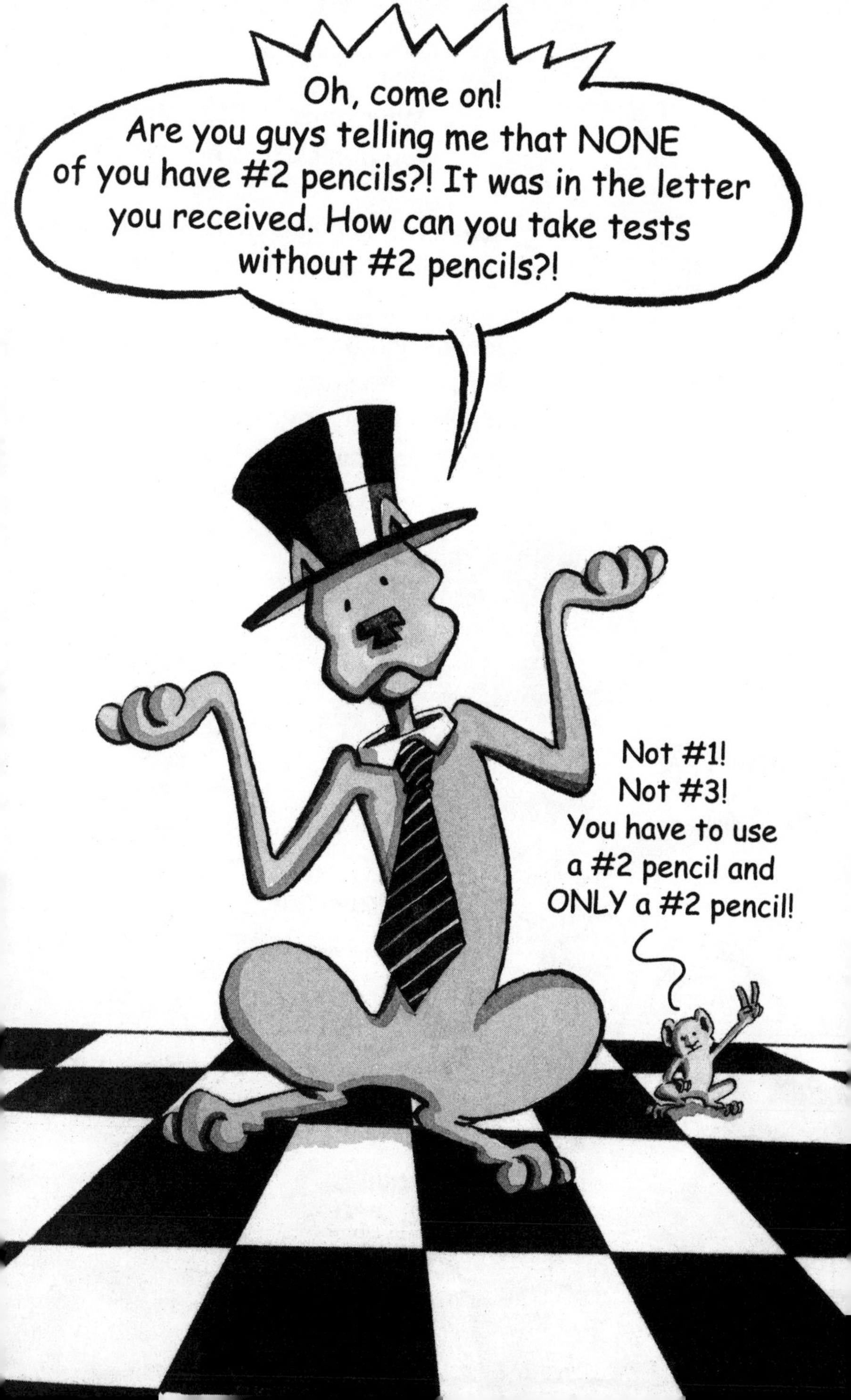

Oh, come on! Are you guys telling me that NONE of you have #2 pencils?! It was in the letter you received. How can you take tests without #2 pencils?!
Not #1! Not #3! You have to use a #2 pencil and ONLY a #2 pencil!

Mountains will crumble
if you don't use a #2 pencil!
Rivers will run red with tomato juice
if you don't use a #2 pencil!
Oceans will become deserts! Deserts
will become shopping malls! The dead
shall rise from their graves to feast a
our all-you-can-eat shrimp buffets if
you don't use a #2 pencil!
Okay, now . . .

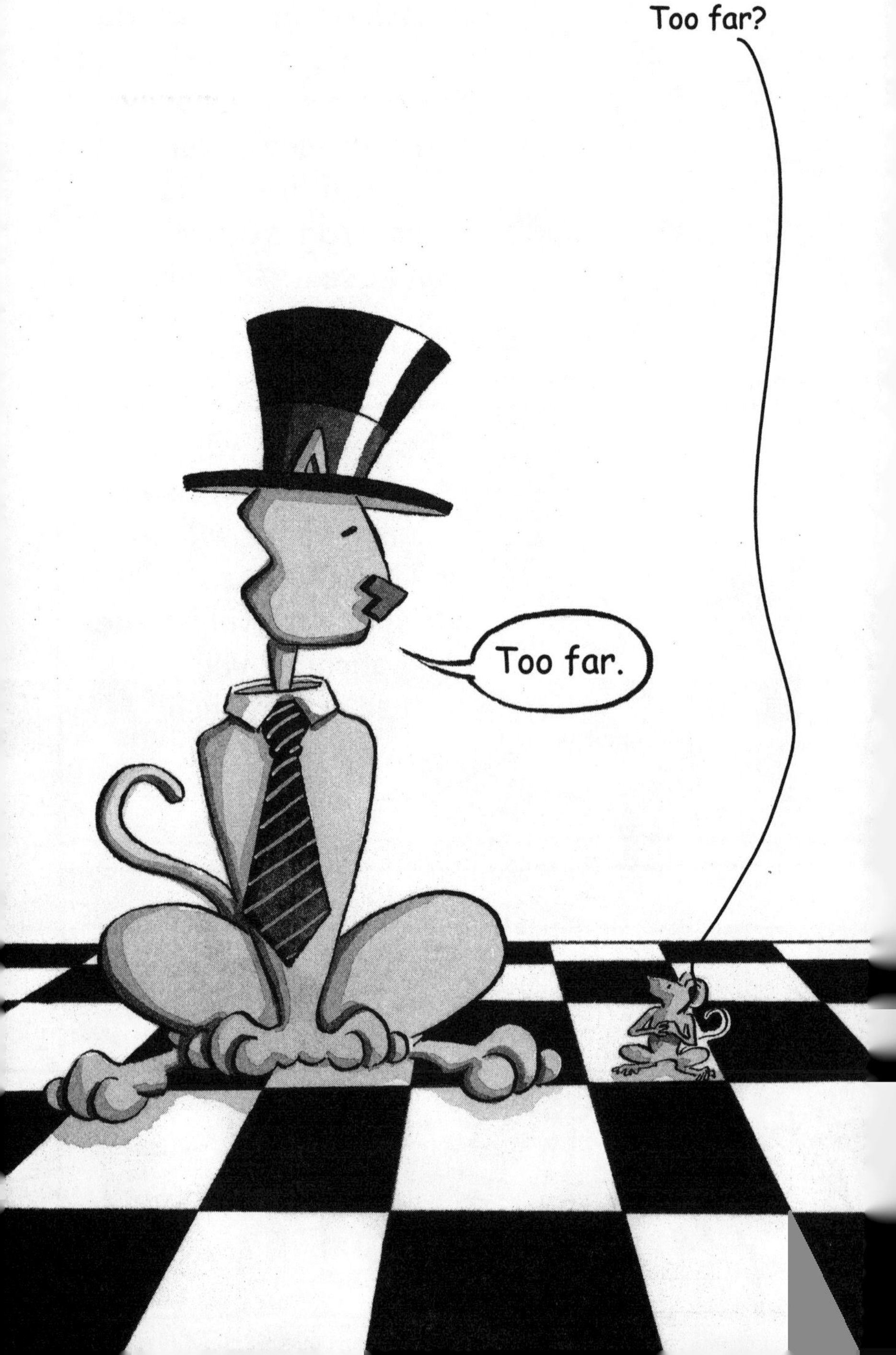
Too far?
Too far.

Okay, class. Now that you all FINALLY have your #2 pencils, we can take the test that will prepare you for the next test. THAT test will prepare you for the next test. THAT test will prepare you for the next test. And THAT test will . . .

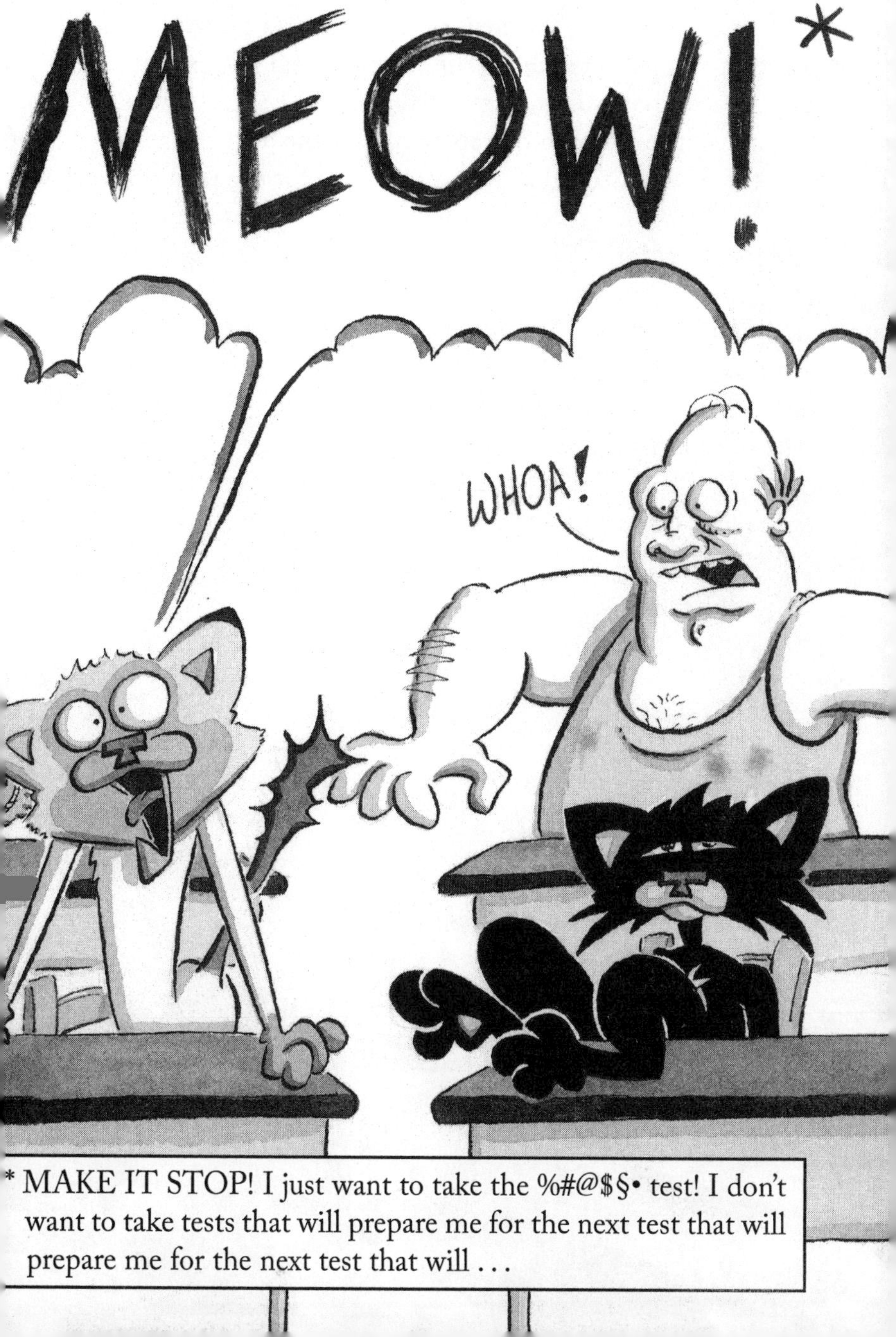
MEOW!*
WHOA!
* MAKE IT STOP! I just want to take the %#@$§• test! I don't want to take tests that will prepare me for the next test that will prepare me for the next test that will . . .

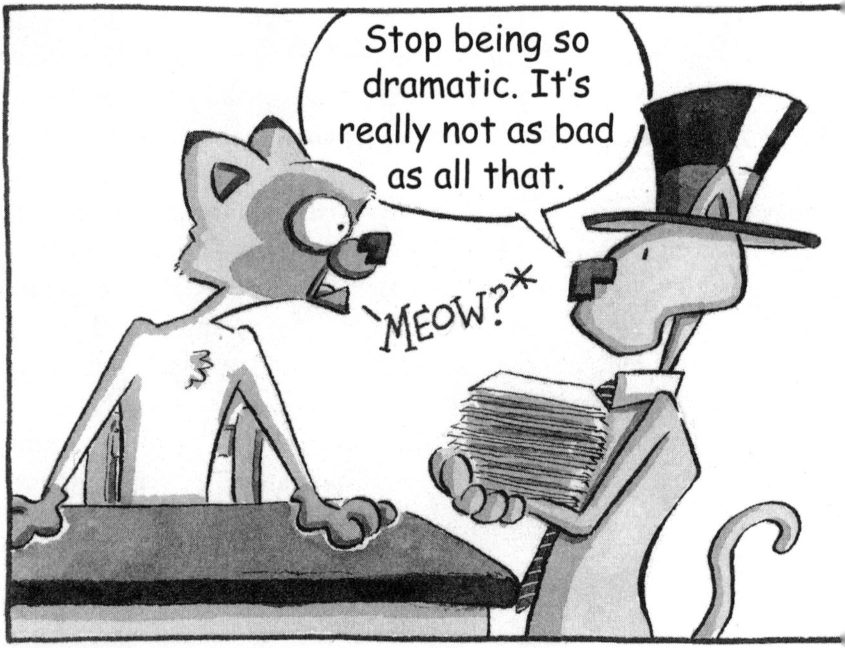
Stop being so dramatic. It's really not as bad as all that.
MEOW?*

* How many tests is it really?

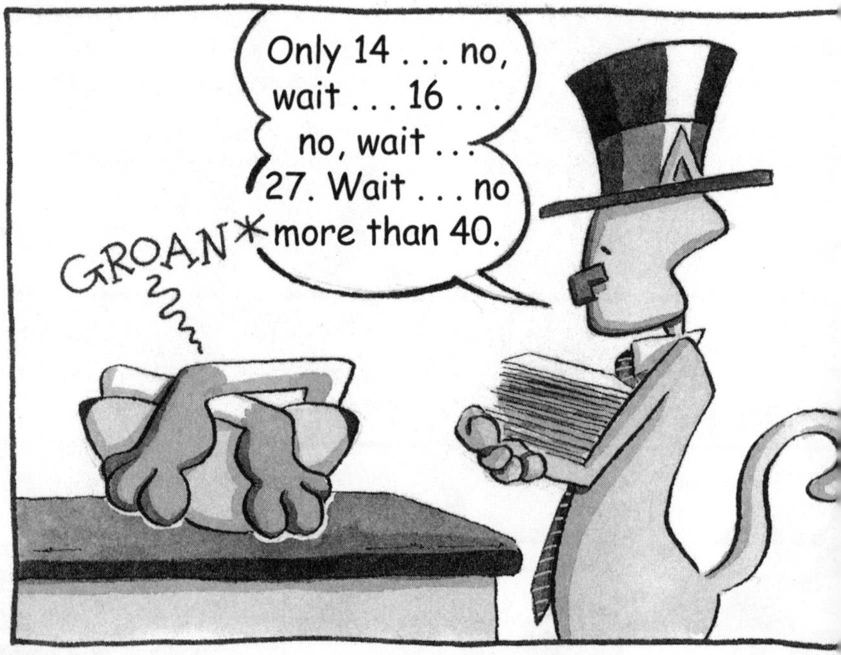
Only 14 . . . no, wait . . . 16 . . . no, wait . . . 27. Wait . . . no more than 40.
GROAN*

* Groan

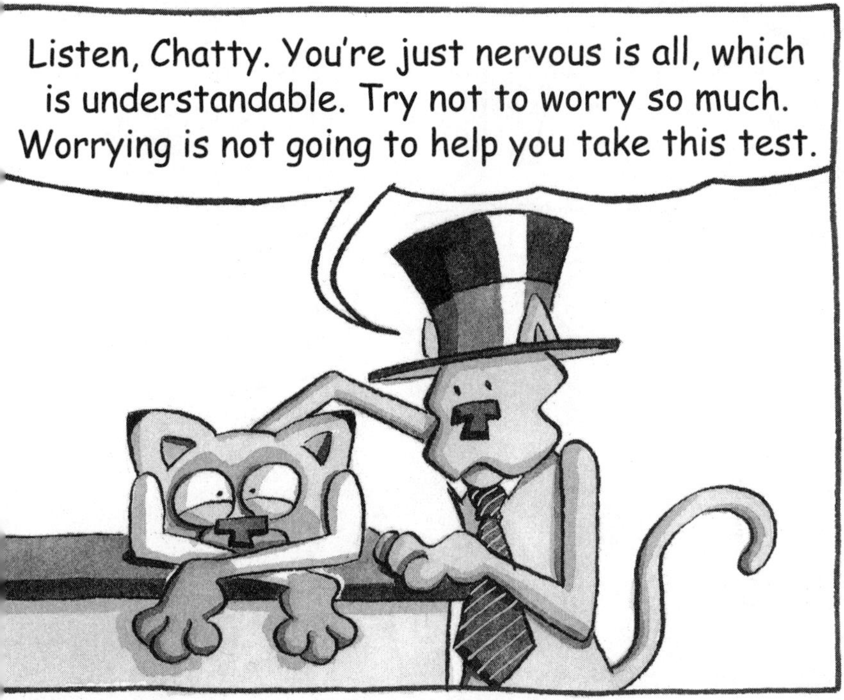
Listen, Chatty. You're just nervous is all, which is understandable. Try not to worry so much. Worrying is not going to help you take this test.

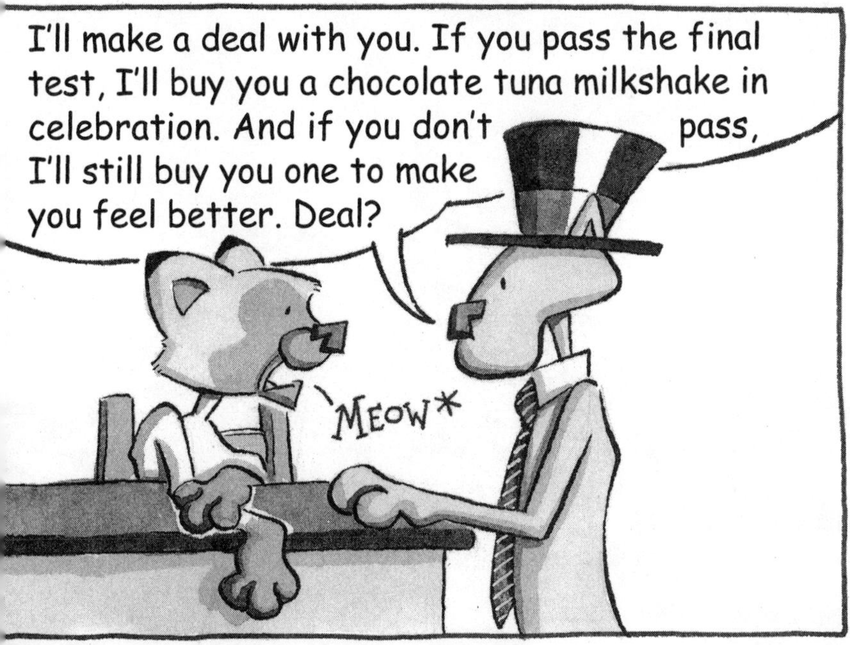
I'll make a deal with you. If you pass the final test, I'll buy you a chocolate tuna milkshake in celebration. And if you don't pass, I'll still buy you one to make you feel better. Deal?
MEOW

That sounds simultaneously disgusting and exquisite.

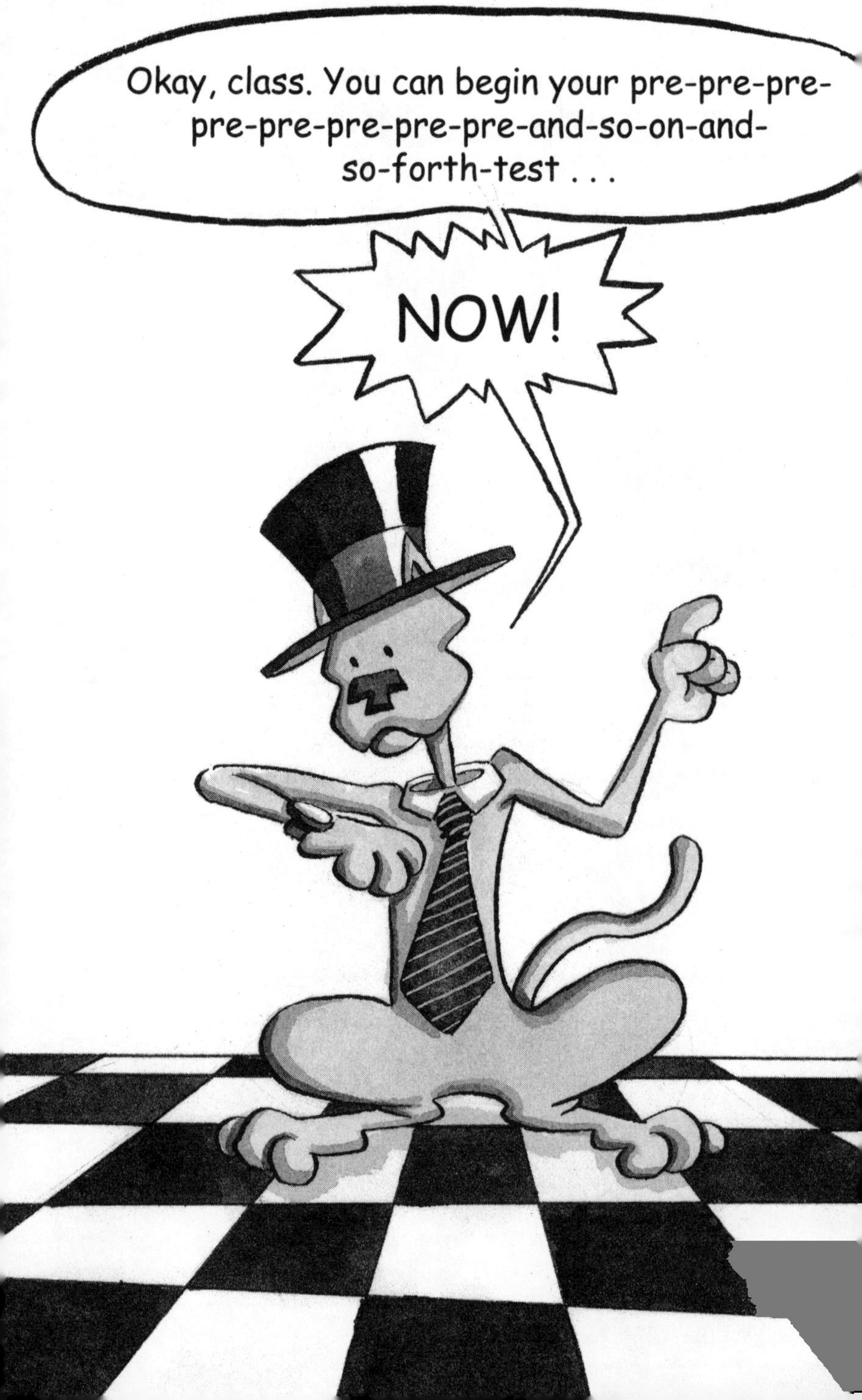
Okay, class. You can begin your pre-pre-pre-pre-pre-pre-pre-pre-pre-pre-and-so-on-and-so-forth-test . . .
NOW!

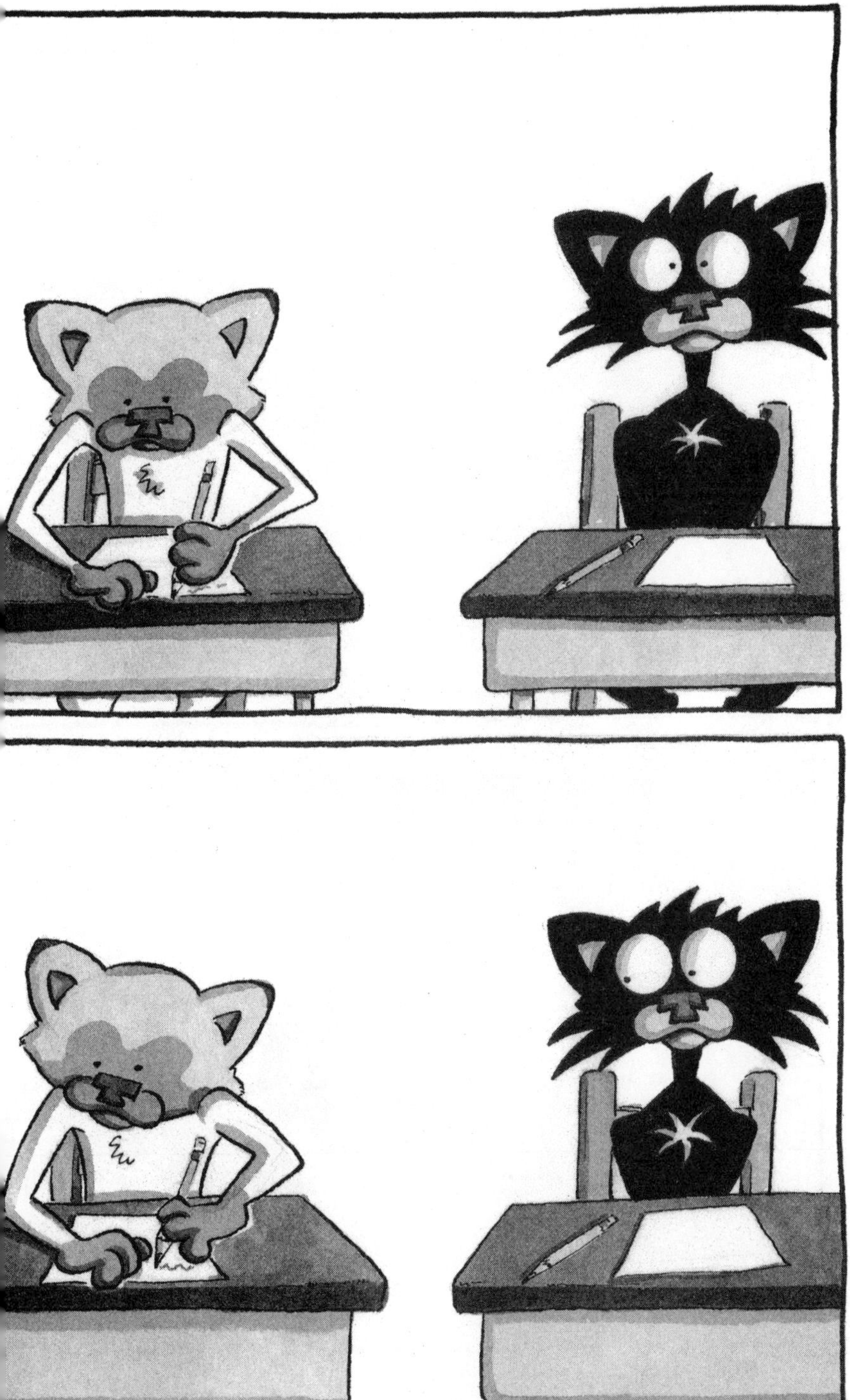

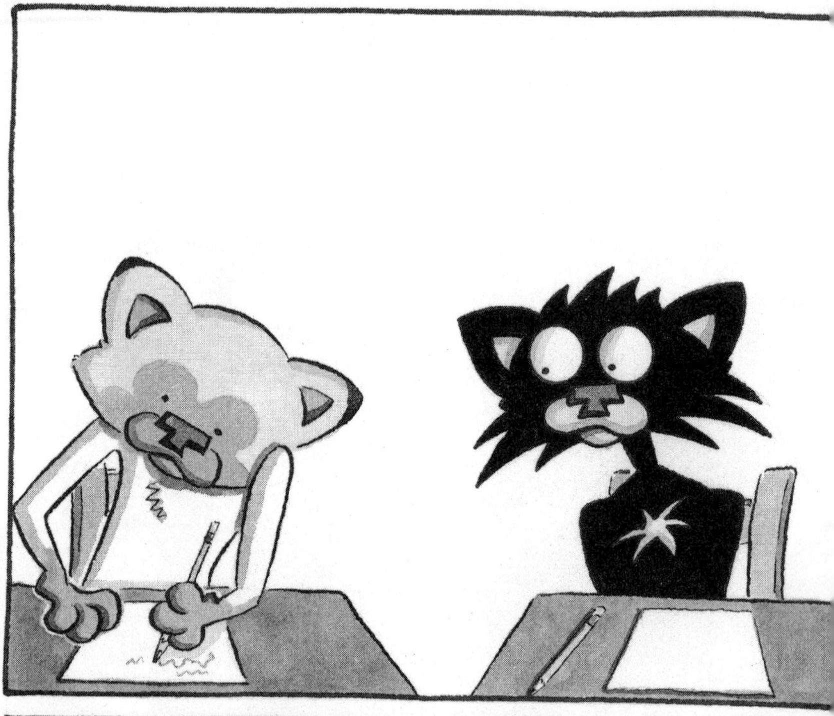

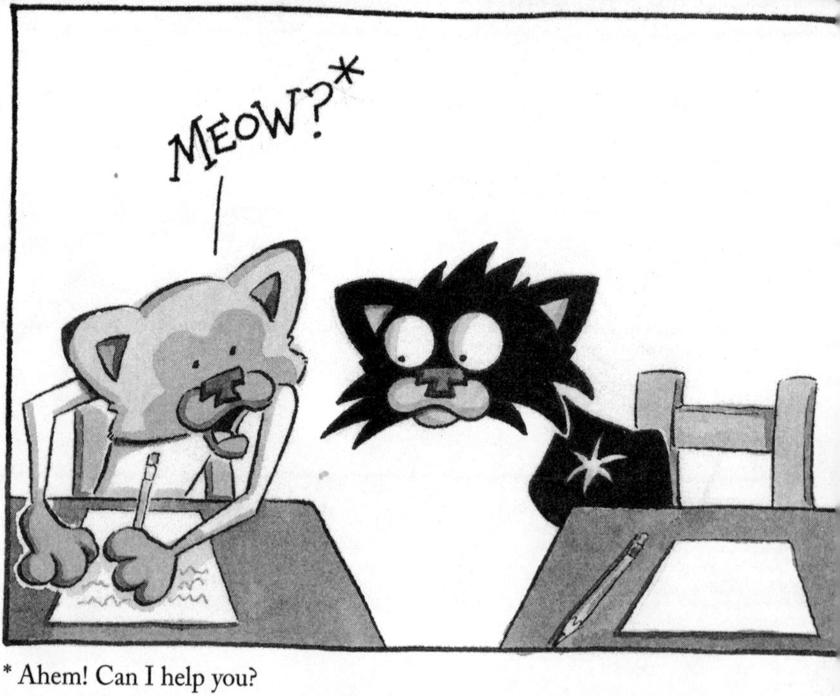
MEOW?*

* Ahem! Can I help you?

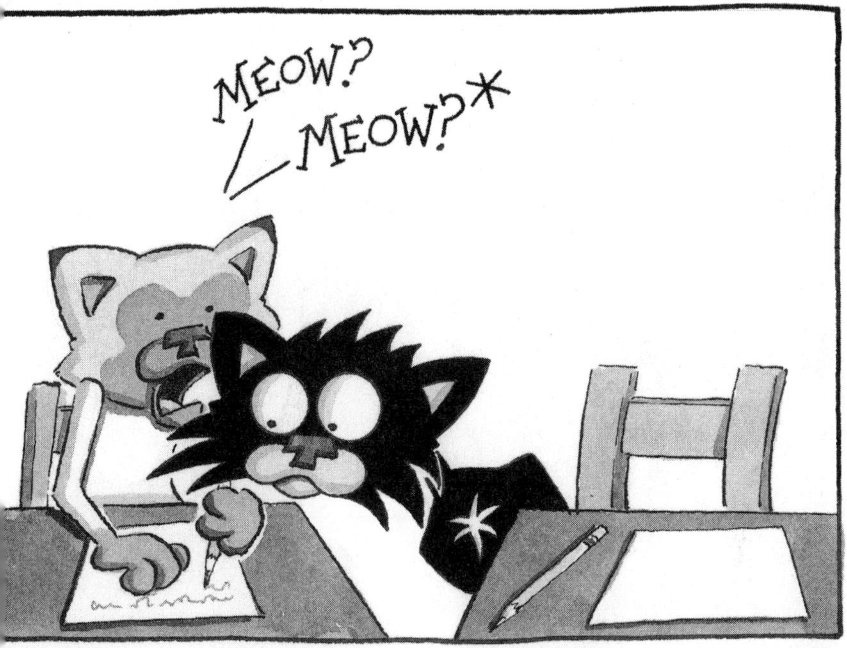
MEOW?
MEOW?*

re you looking for something? Did you lose your pencil? Do you need more paper?

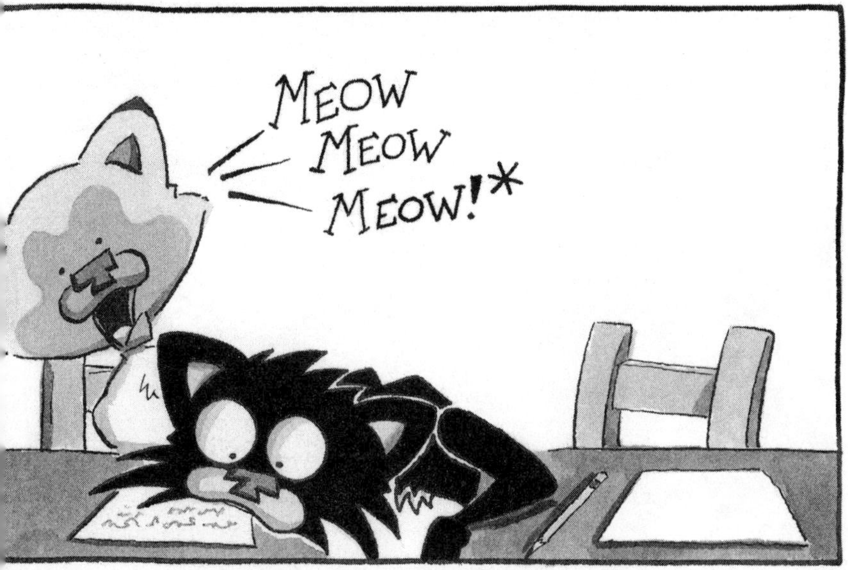
MEOW
MEOW
MEOW!*

Are you aware that psychologists recommend clear personal boundaries be set :tween two individuals in order to ensure an environment wherein their relation-ıip can remain mutually respectful and supportive? And I can smell what you had r lunch.

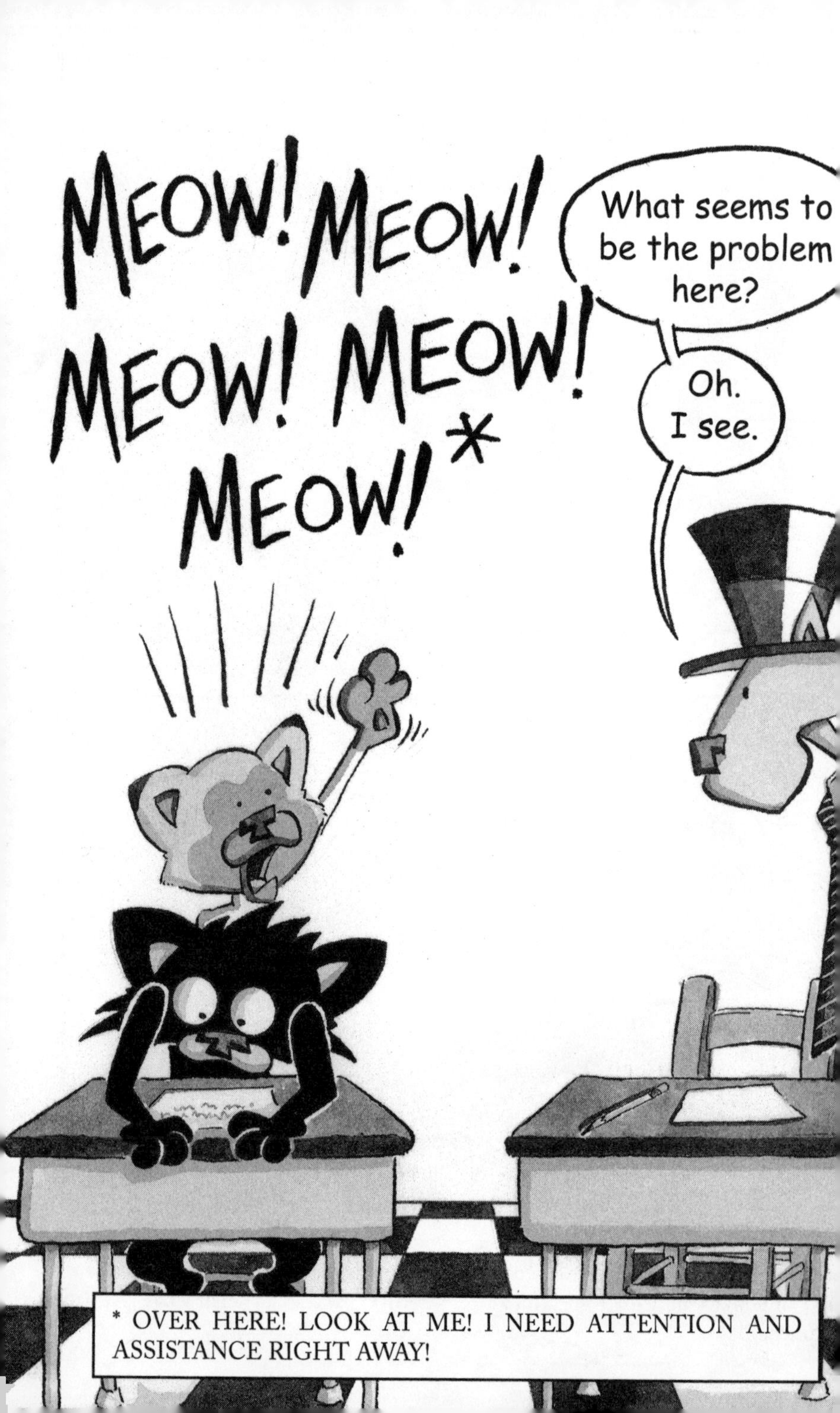

MEOW! MEOW! MEOW! MEOW! MEOW!*
What seems to be the problem here?
Oh. I see.
* OVER HERE! LOOK AT ME! I NEED ATTENTION AND ASSISTANCE RIGHT AWAY!

Kitty, there is one, and only one, rule to taking tests—no cheating.

If you copy from someone else's test, that's cheating. And if you cheat, it means that you're not learning anything. We can't have that.

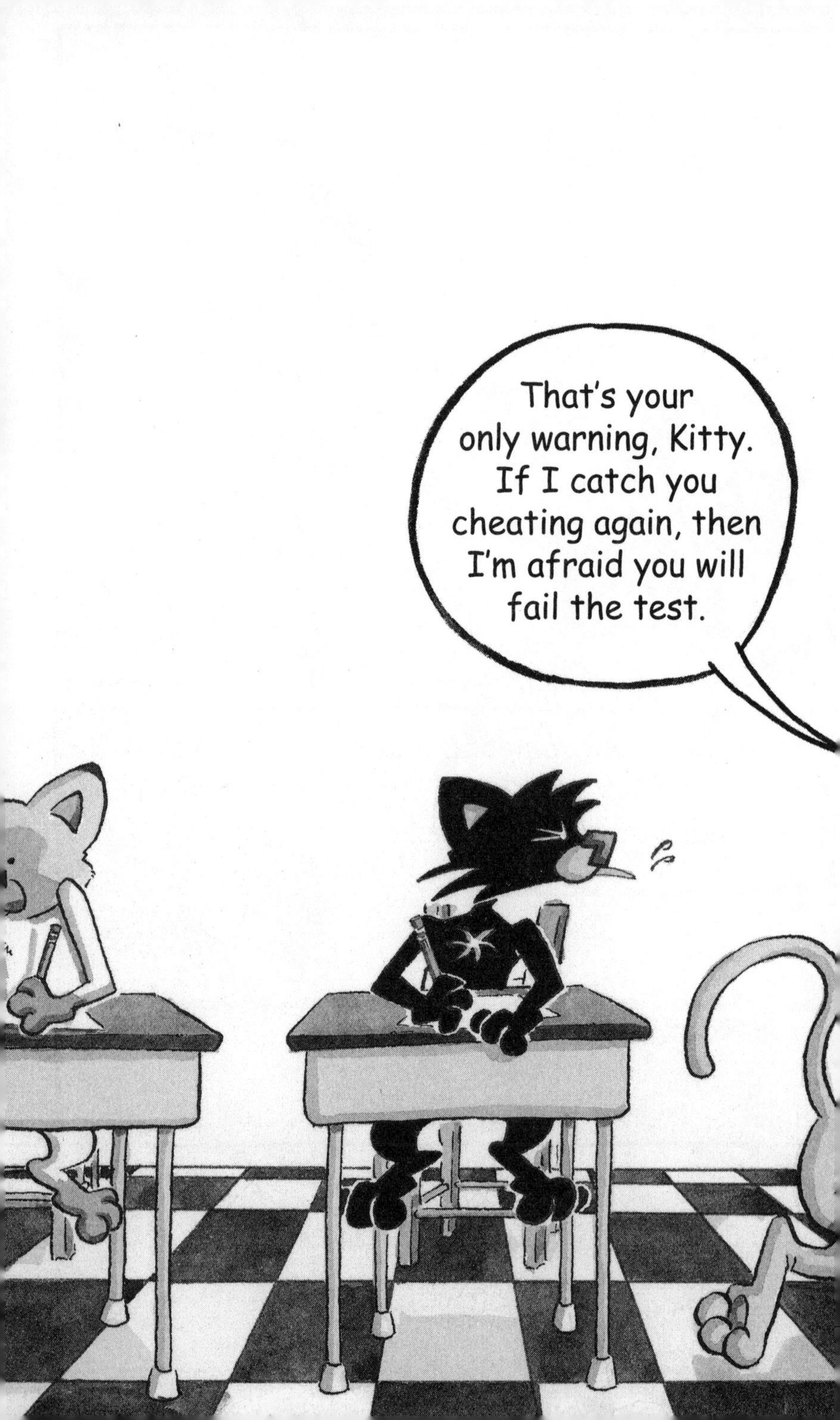
That's your only warning, Kitty. If I catch you cheating again, then I'm afraid you will fail the test.

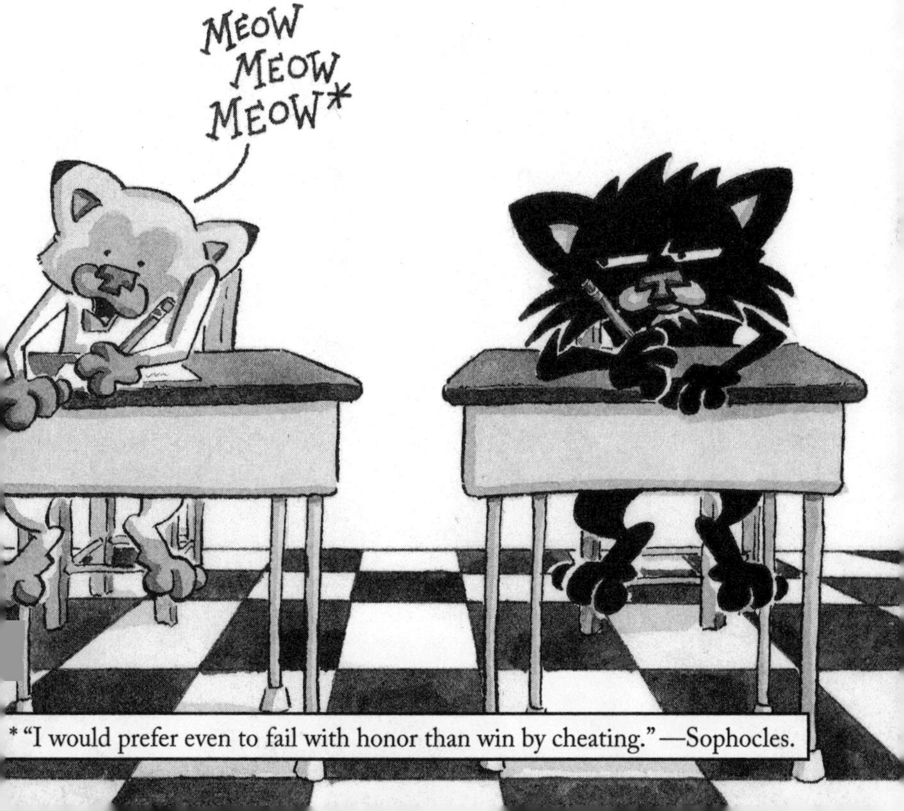
MEOW
MEOW
MEOW*

* "I would prefer even to fail with honor than win by cheating." —Sophocles.

•CHAPTER FIVE•

14 HOURS LATER

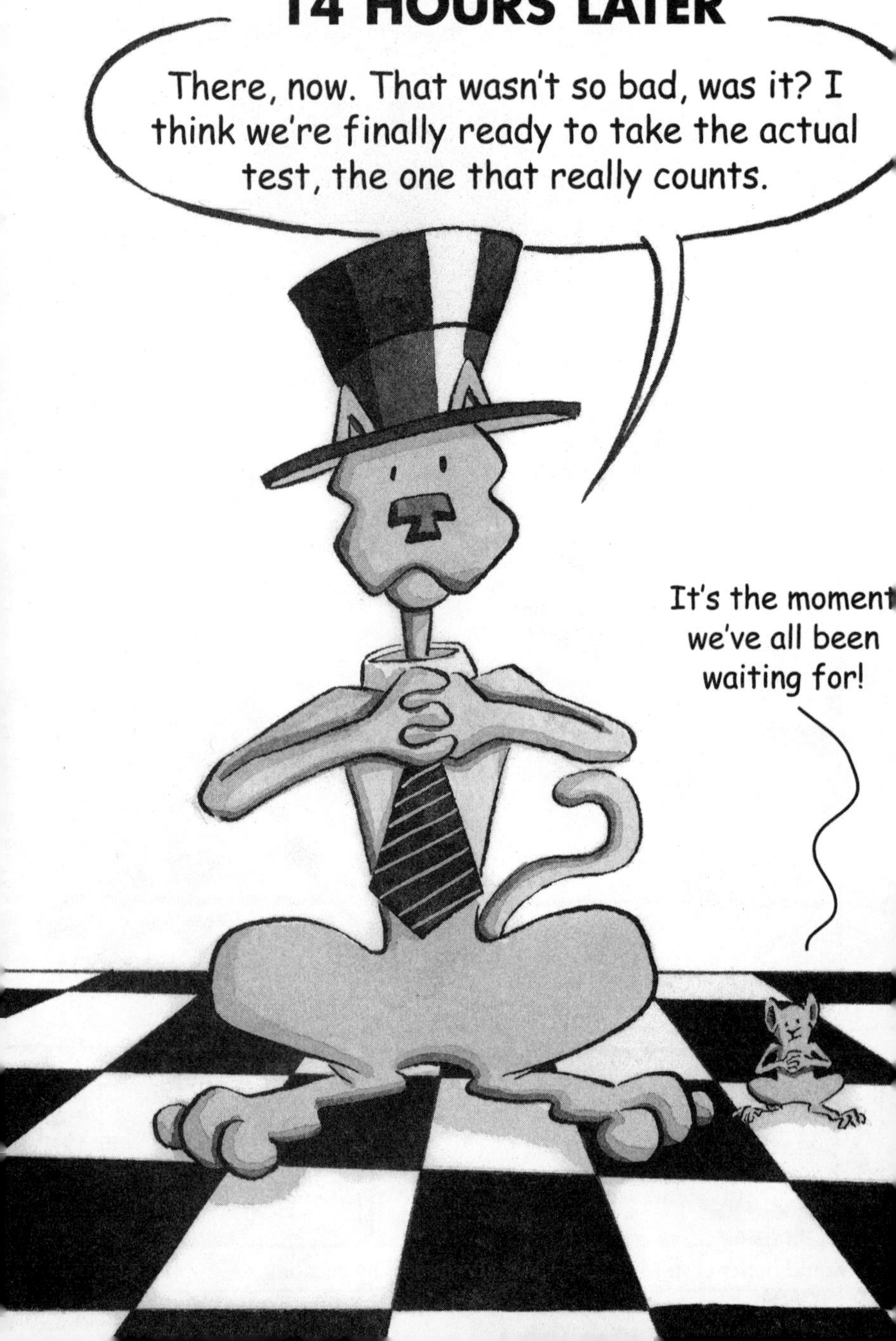

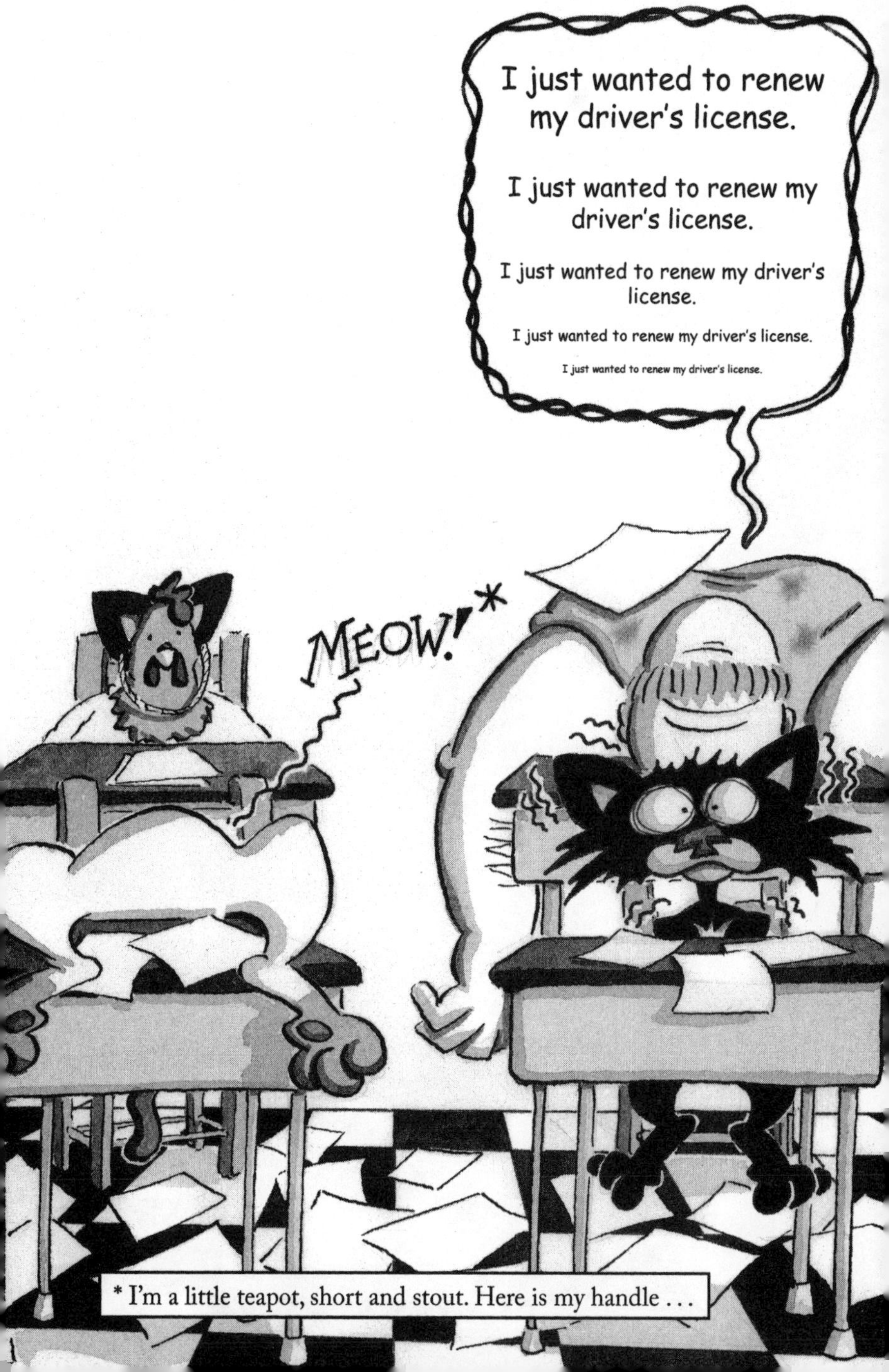
I just wanted to renew my driver's license.
I just wanted to renew my driver's license.
I just wanted to renew my driver's license.
I just wanted to renew my driver's license.
I just wanted to renew my driver's license.
MEOW!*
* I'm a little teapot, short and stout. Here is my handle . . .

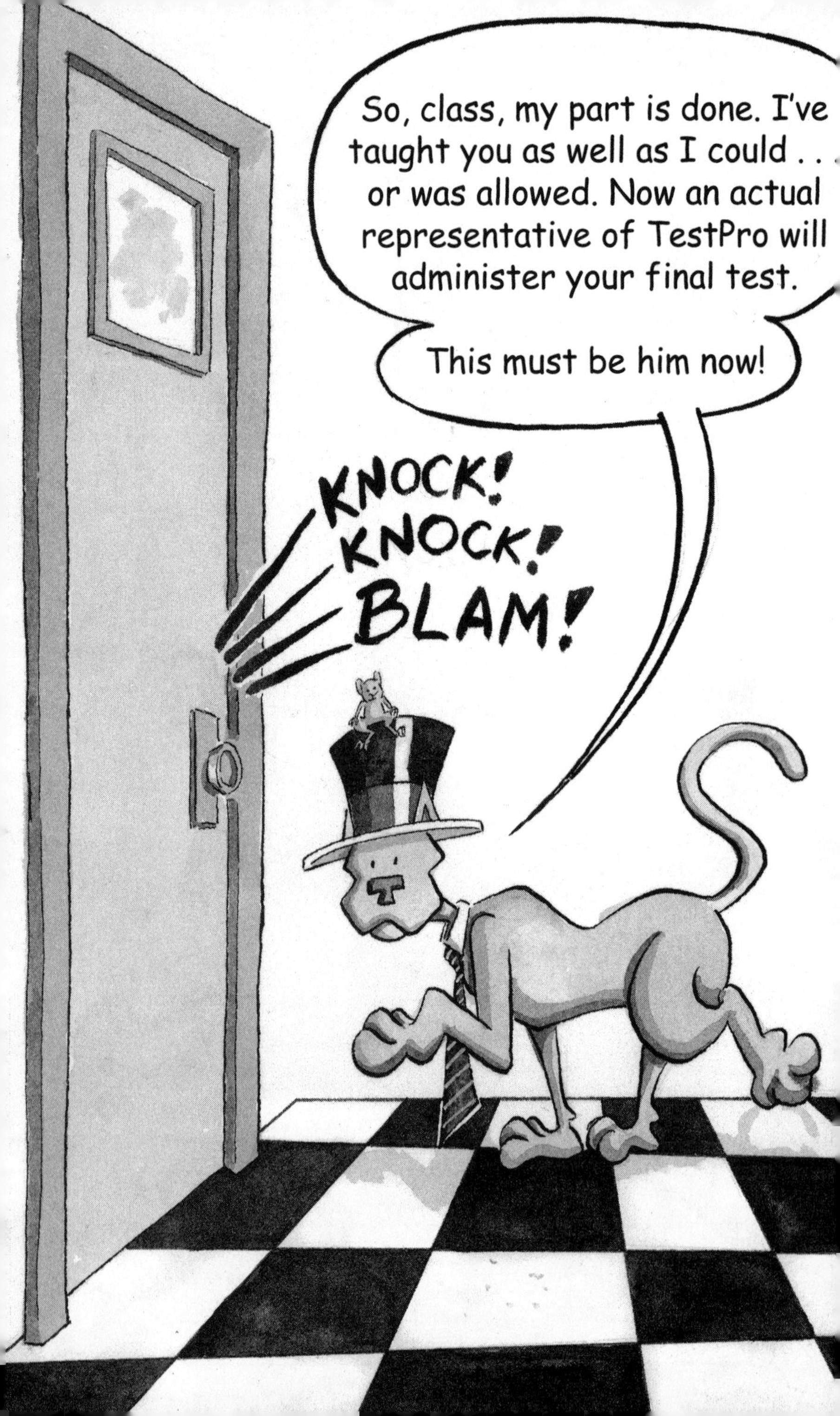
So, class, my part is done. I've taught you as well as I could . . . or was allowed. Now an actual representative of TestPro will administer your final test.
This must be him now!
KNOCK! KNOCK! BLAM!

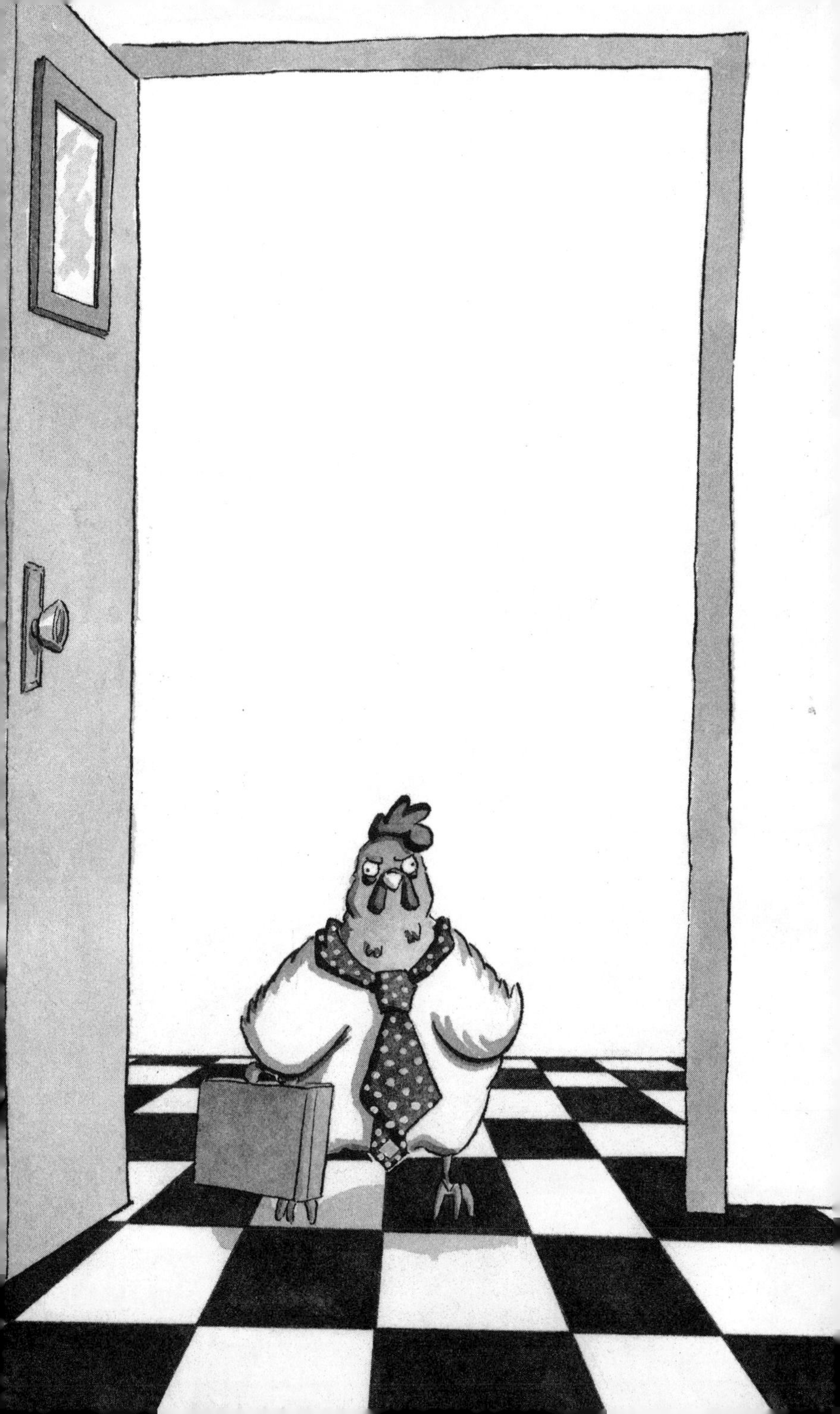

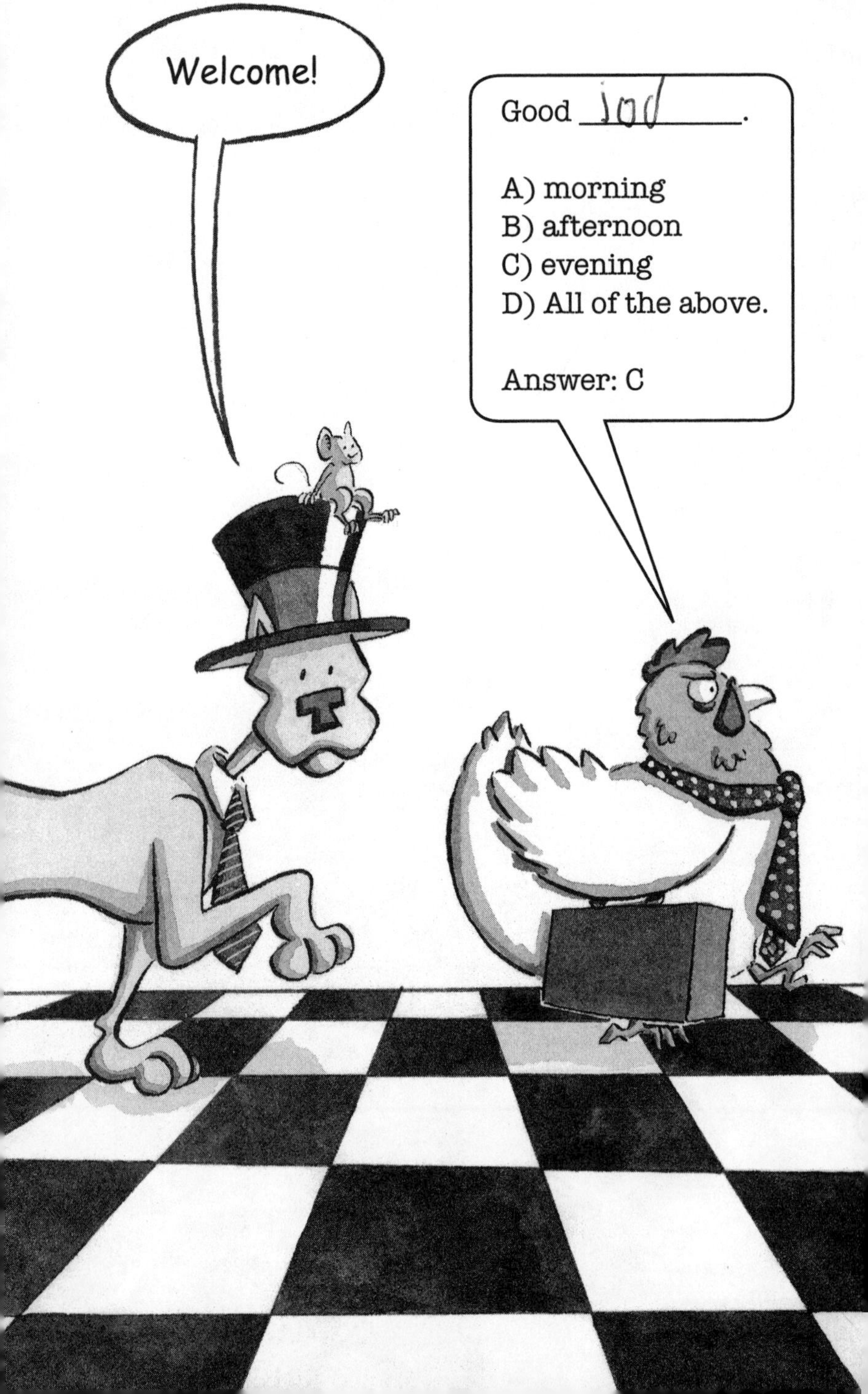
Welcome!
Good jod.
A) morning
B) afternoon
C) evening
D) All of the above.
Answer: C

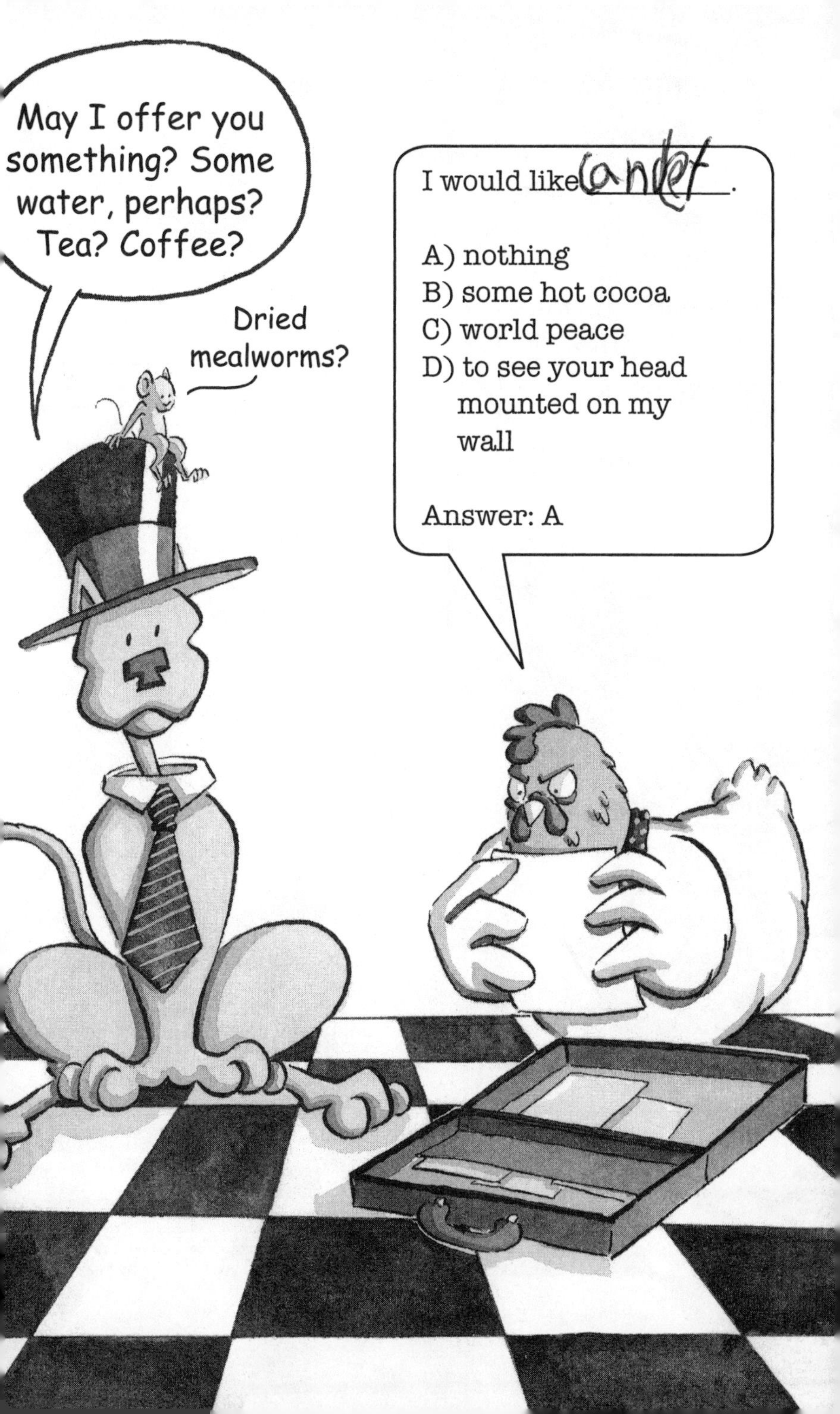
May I offer you something? Some water, perhaps? Tea? Coffee?
Dried mealworms?
I would like ________.
A) nothing
B) some hot cocoa
C) world peace
D) to see your head mounted on my wall
Answer: A

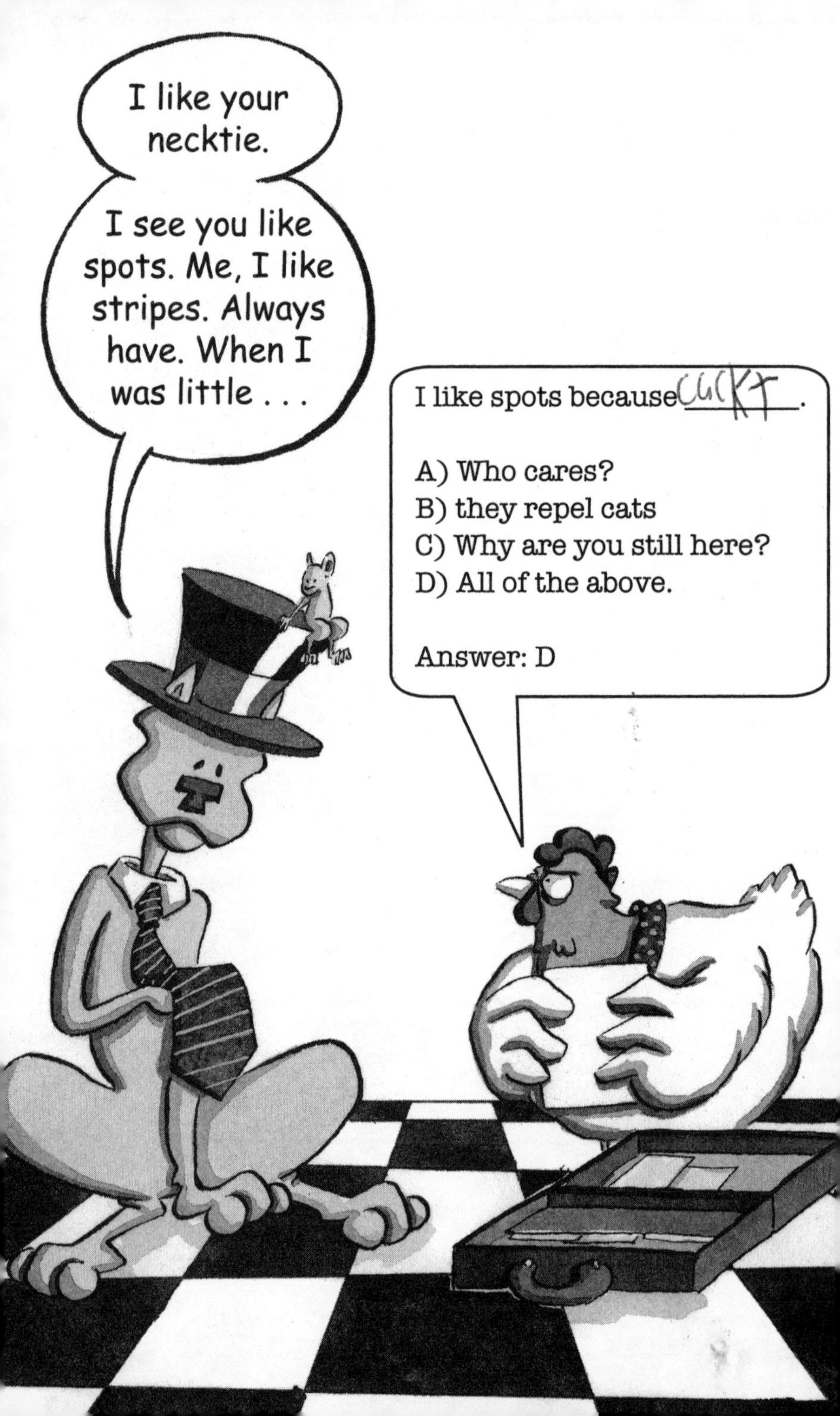
I like your necktie.
I see you like spots. Me, I like stripes. Always have. When I was little . . .
I like spots because CLUCK.
A) Who cares?
B) they repel cats
C) Why are you still here?
D) All of the above.
Answer: D

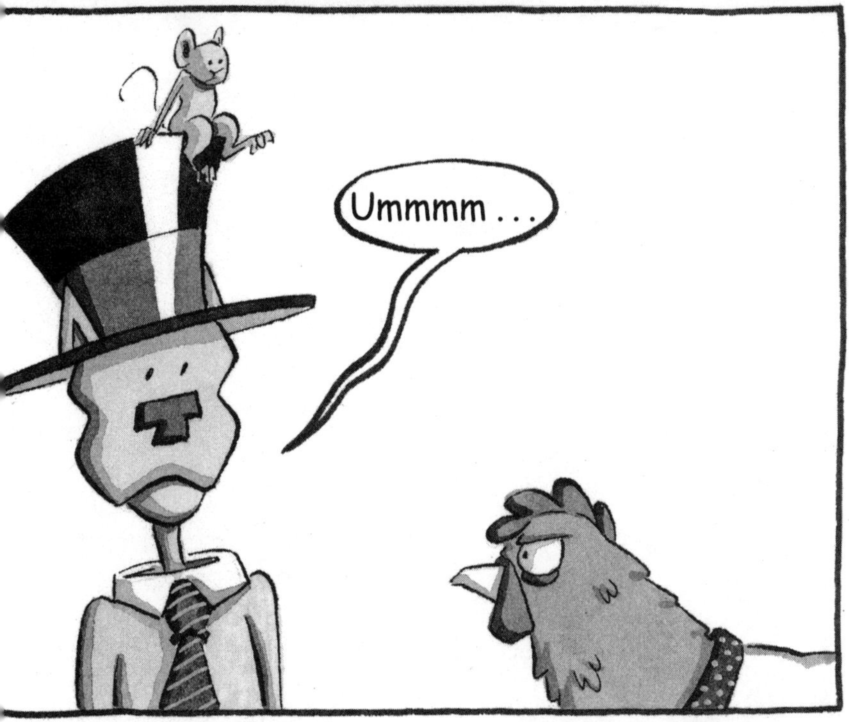
Ummmm . . .

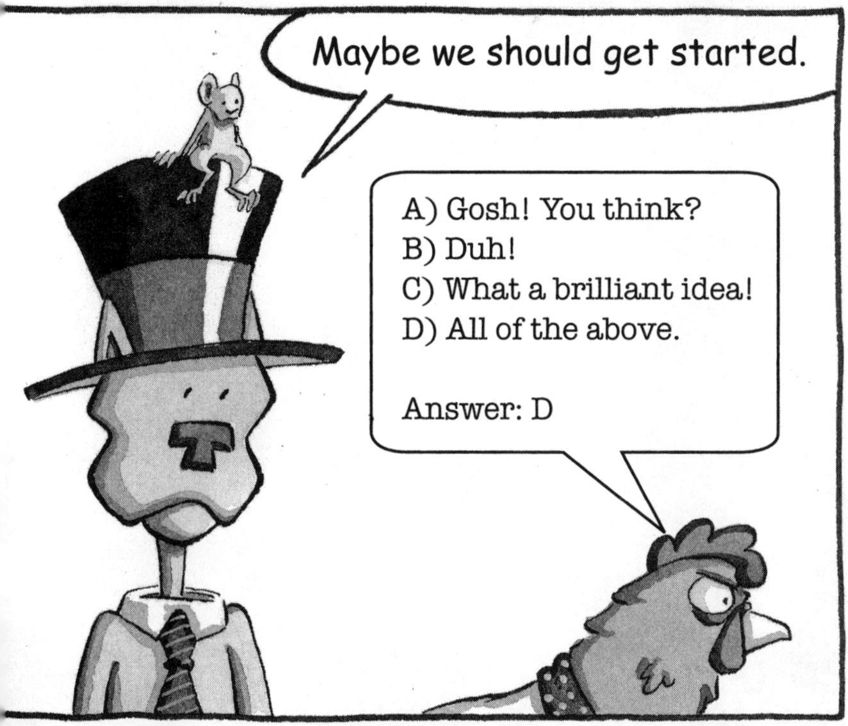
Maybe we should get started.
A) Gosh! You think?
B) Duh!
C) What a brilliant idea!
D) All of the above.
Answer: D

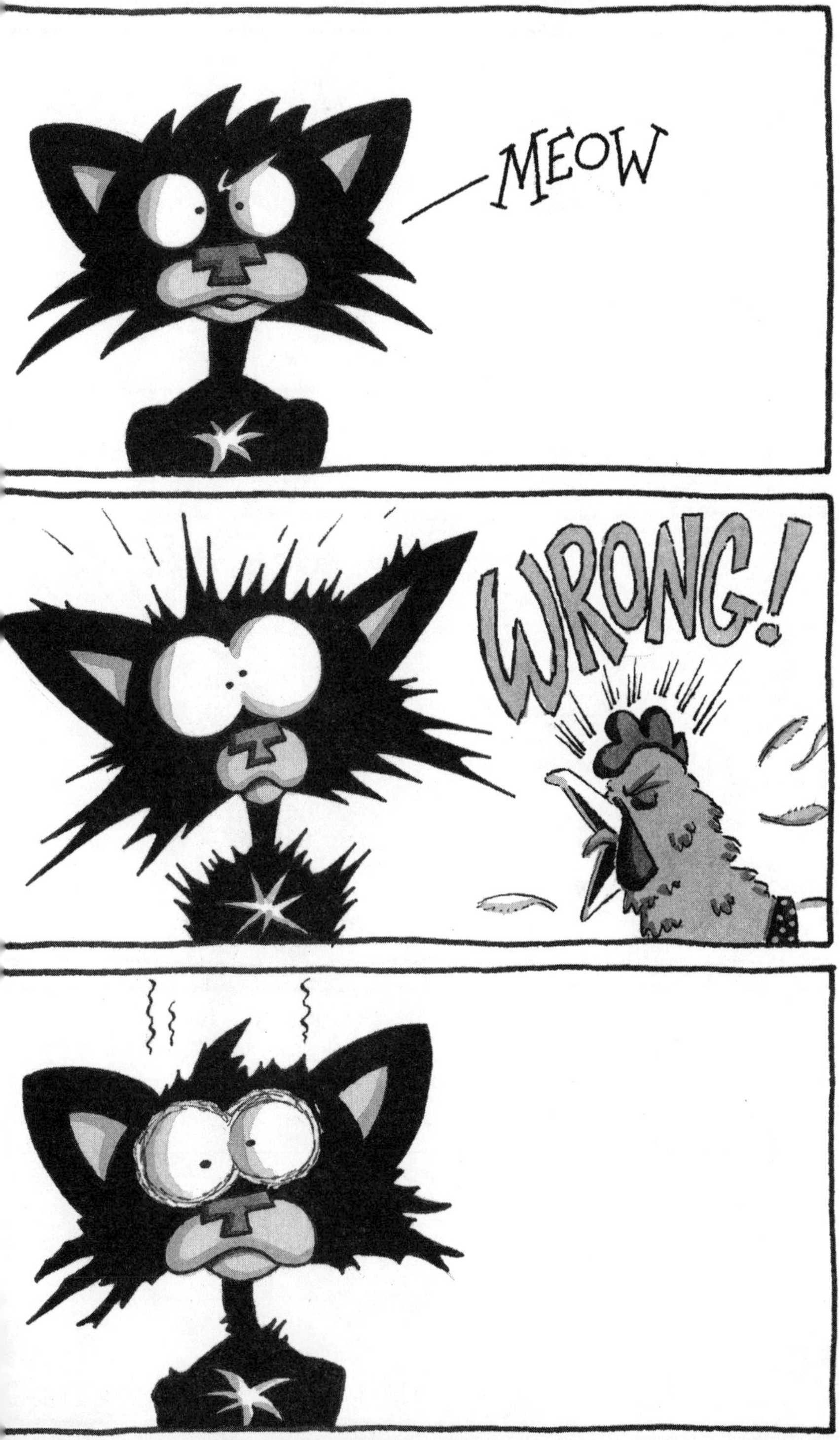
MEOW
WRONG!

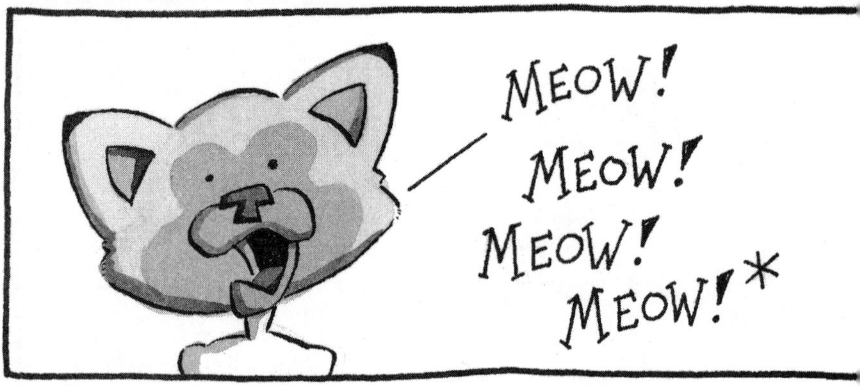
MEOW!
MEOW!
MEOW!
MEOW! *

* Actually, the average cat has around 16 separate vocalizations with which they ca communicate. This does not include body language like tail twitching or the roars tha large cats commonly use . . .

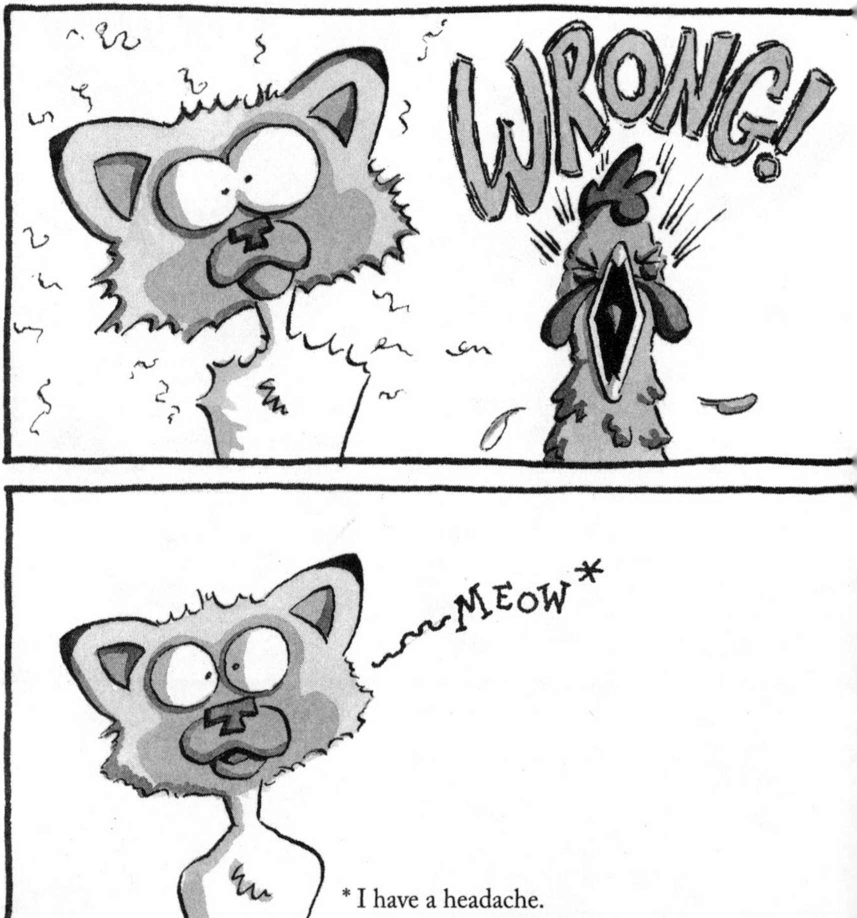
WRONG!
MEOW*
* I have a headache.

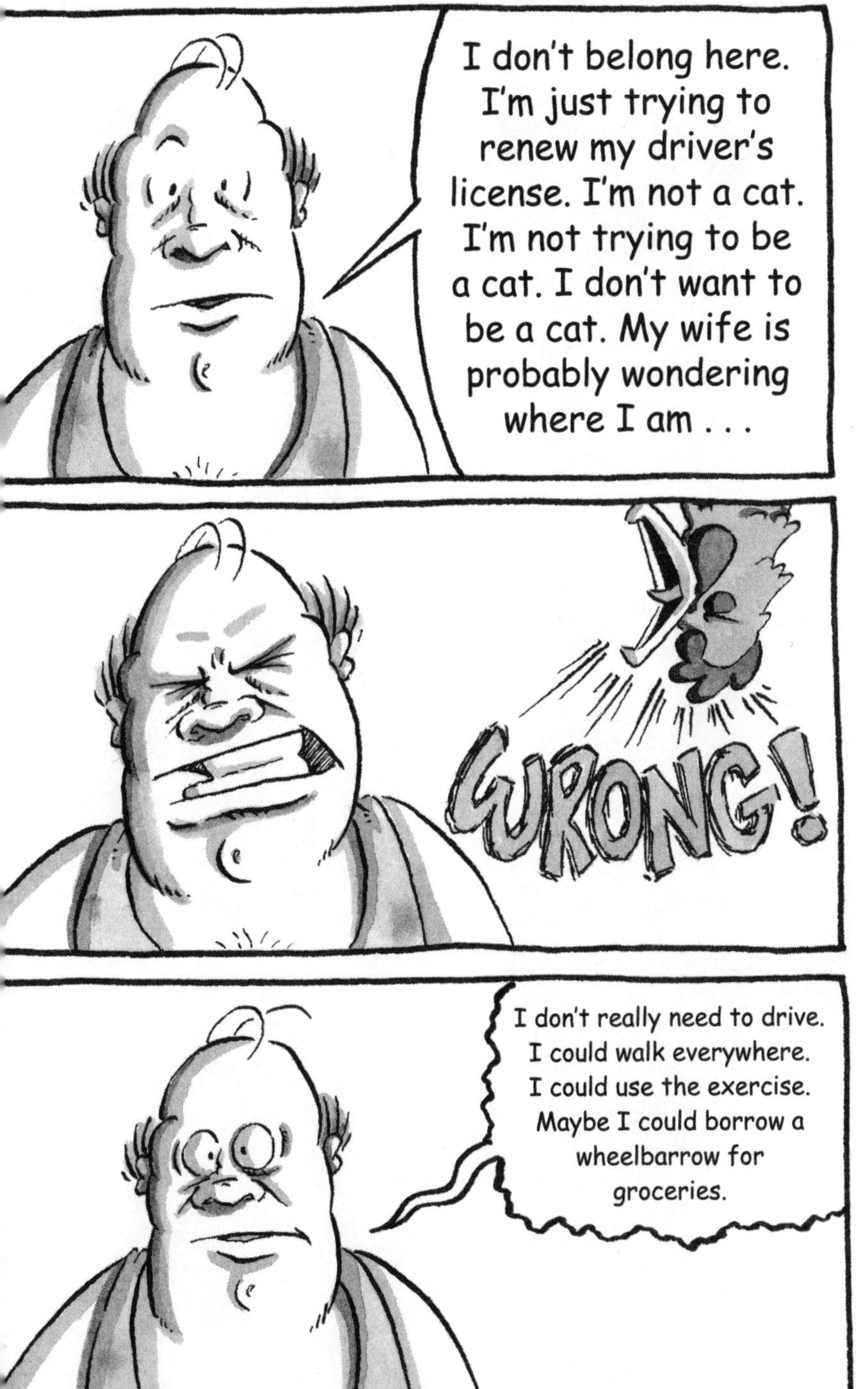
I don't belong here. I'm just trying to renew my driver's license. I'm not a cat. I'm not trying to be a cat. I don't want to be a cat. My wife is probably wondering where I am . . .
WRONG!
I don't really need to drive. I could walk everywhere. I could use the exercise. Maybe I could borrow a wheelbarrow for groceries.

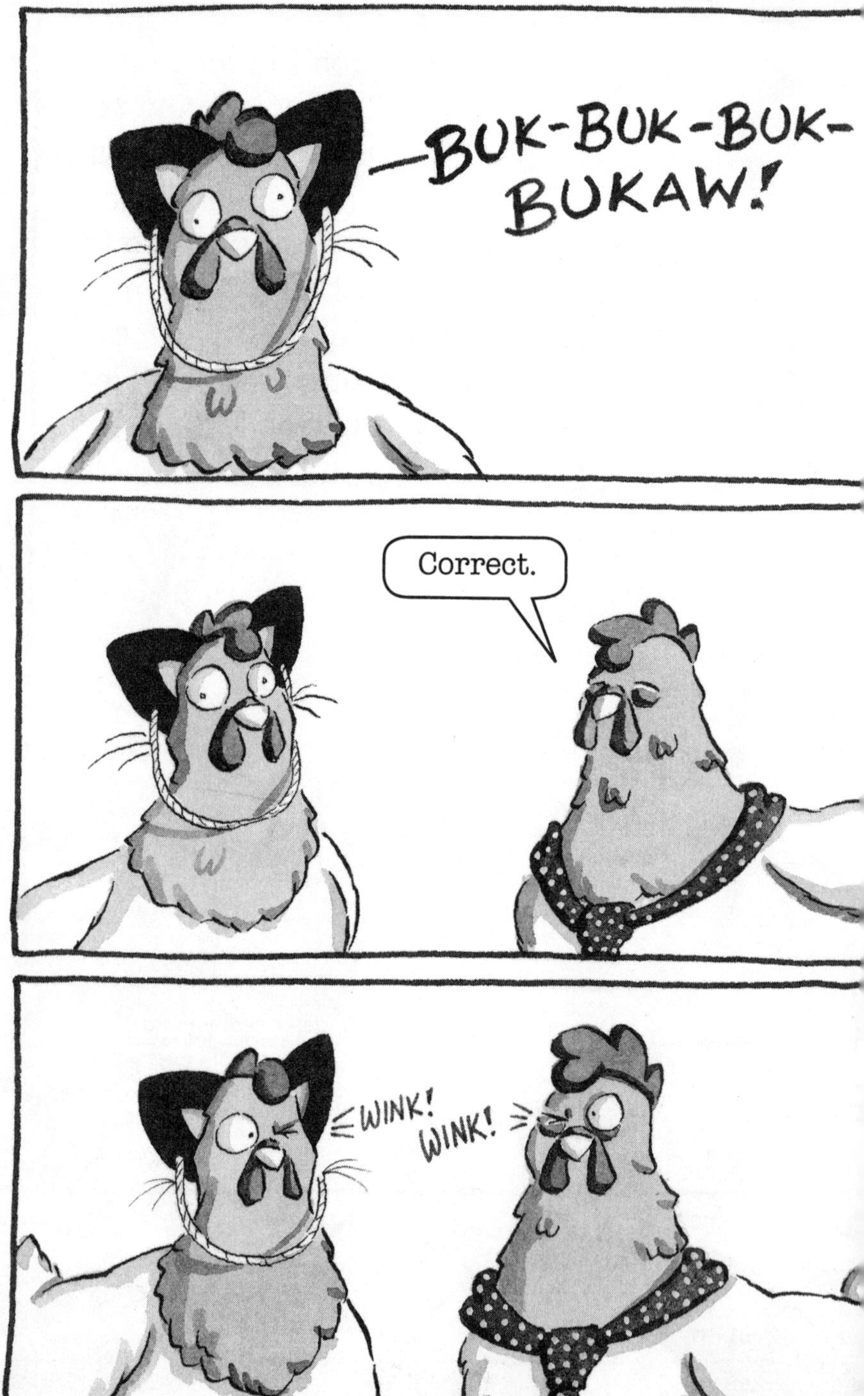
BUK-BUK-BUK-BUKAW!
Correct.
WINK!
WINK!

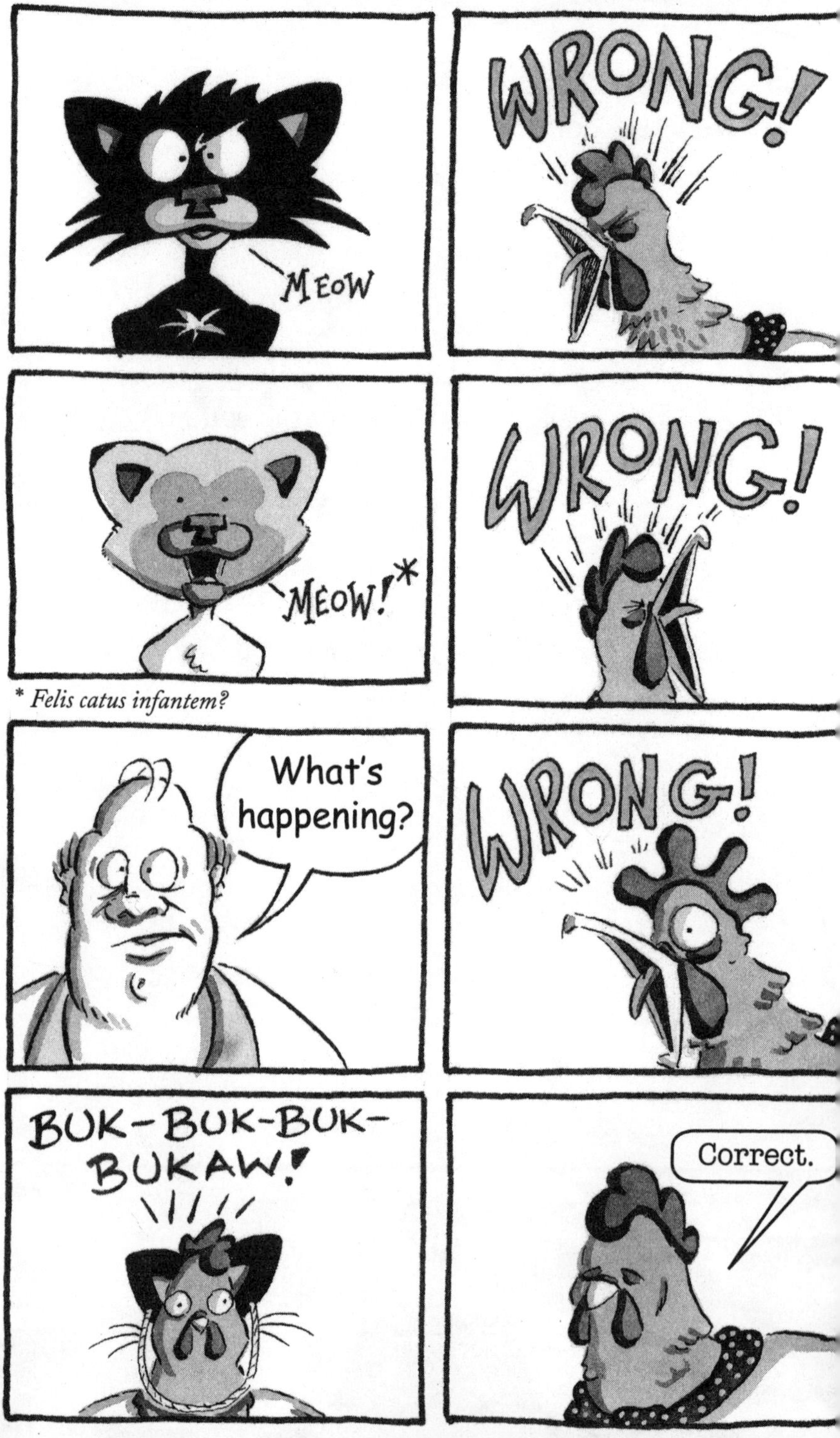
MEOW
WRONG!
MEOW!*
WRONG!
What's happening?
WRONG!
BUK-BUK-BUK-BUKAW!
Correct.

* *Felis catus infantem?*

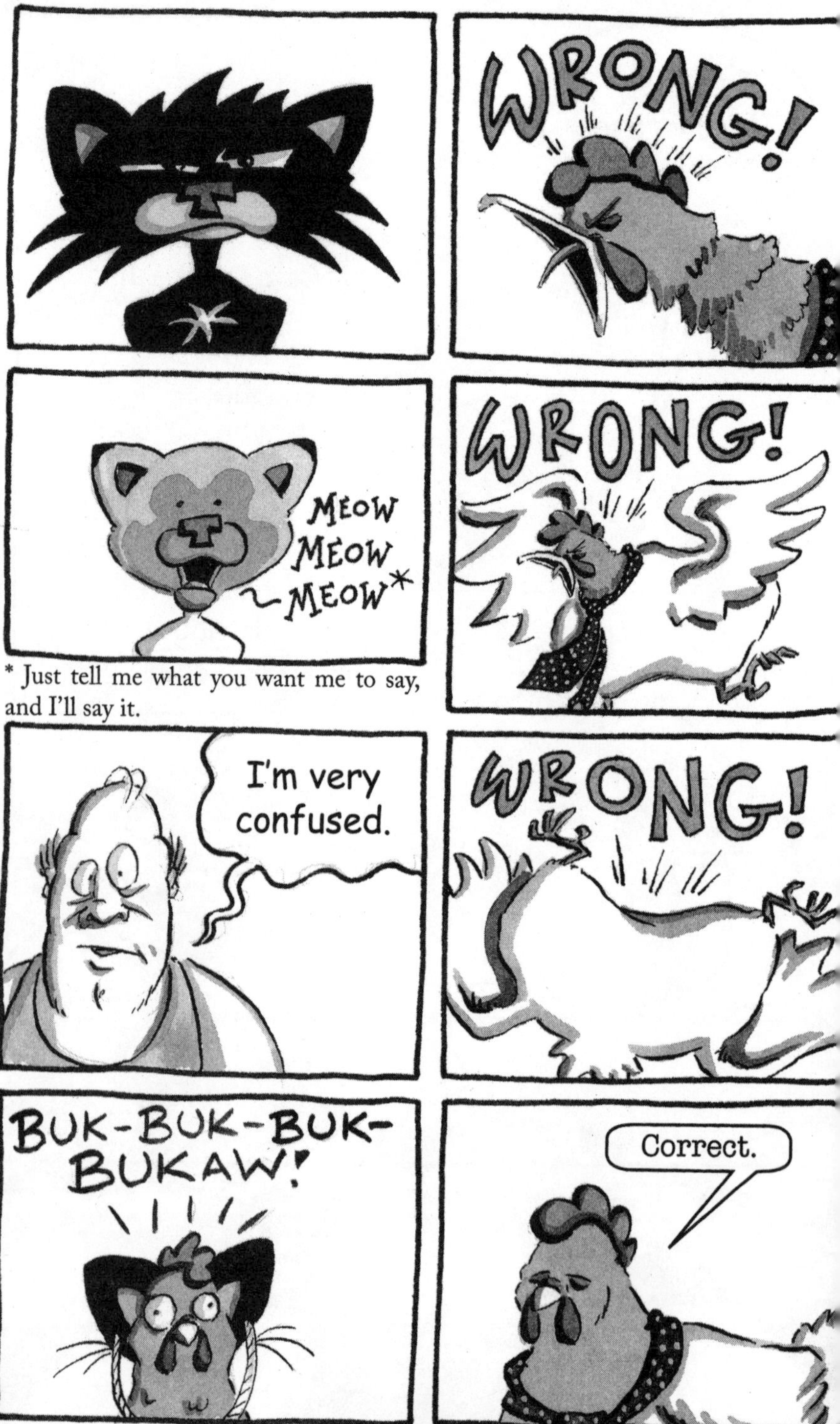
WRONG!
MEOW
MEOW
MEOW*
WRONG!
I'm very confused.
WRONG!
BUK-BUK-BUK-BUKAW!
Correct.

* Just tell me what you want me to say, and I'll say it.

If your students are failing, then ____________.

A) it's your fault, not mine
B) clearly you're not doing your job
C) maybe you should look into another line of work because obviously teaching is not for you
D) All of the above.

Answer: D

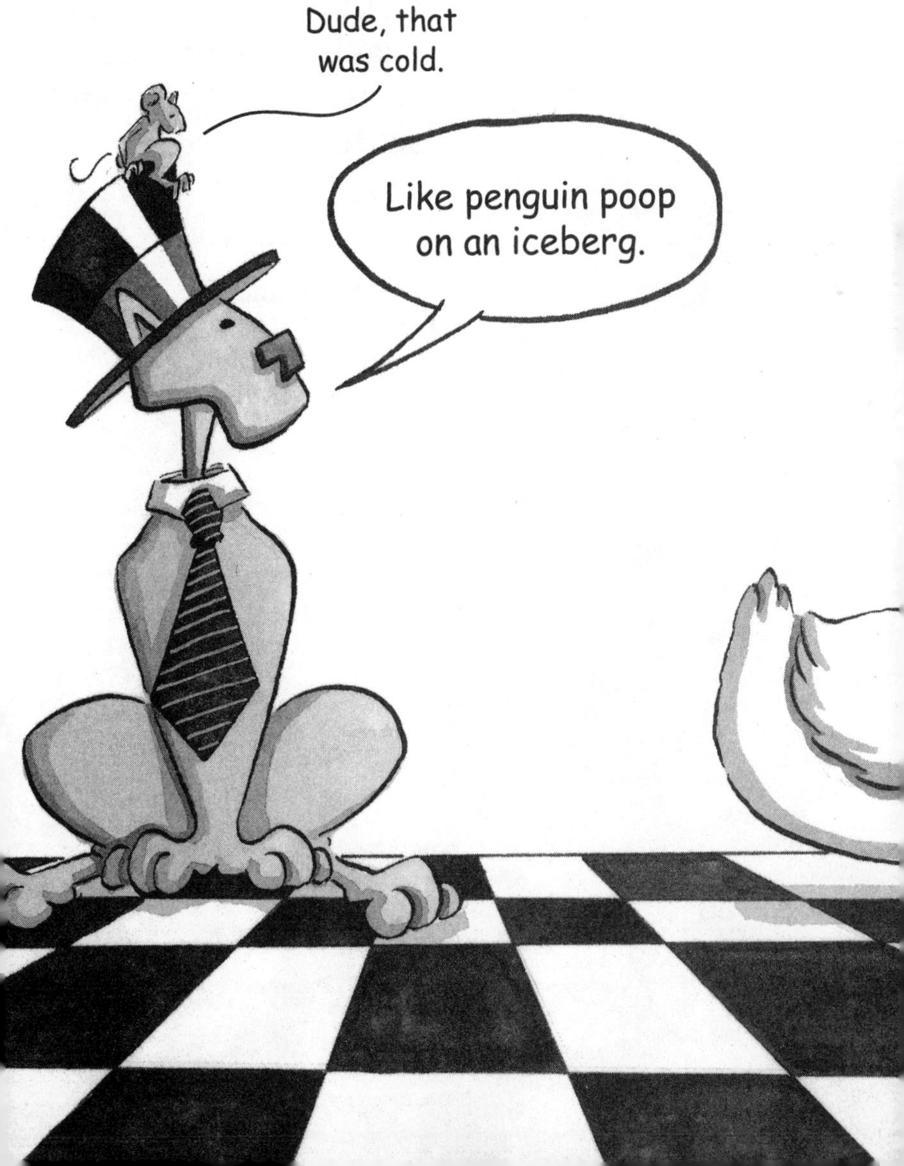
Dude, that was cold.
Like penguin poop on an iceberg.

•CHAPTER SIX•

THE FINAL CHALLENGE

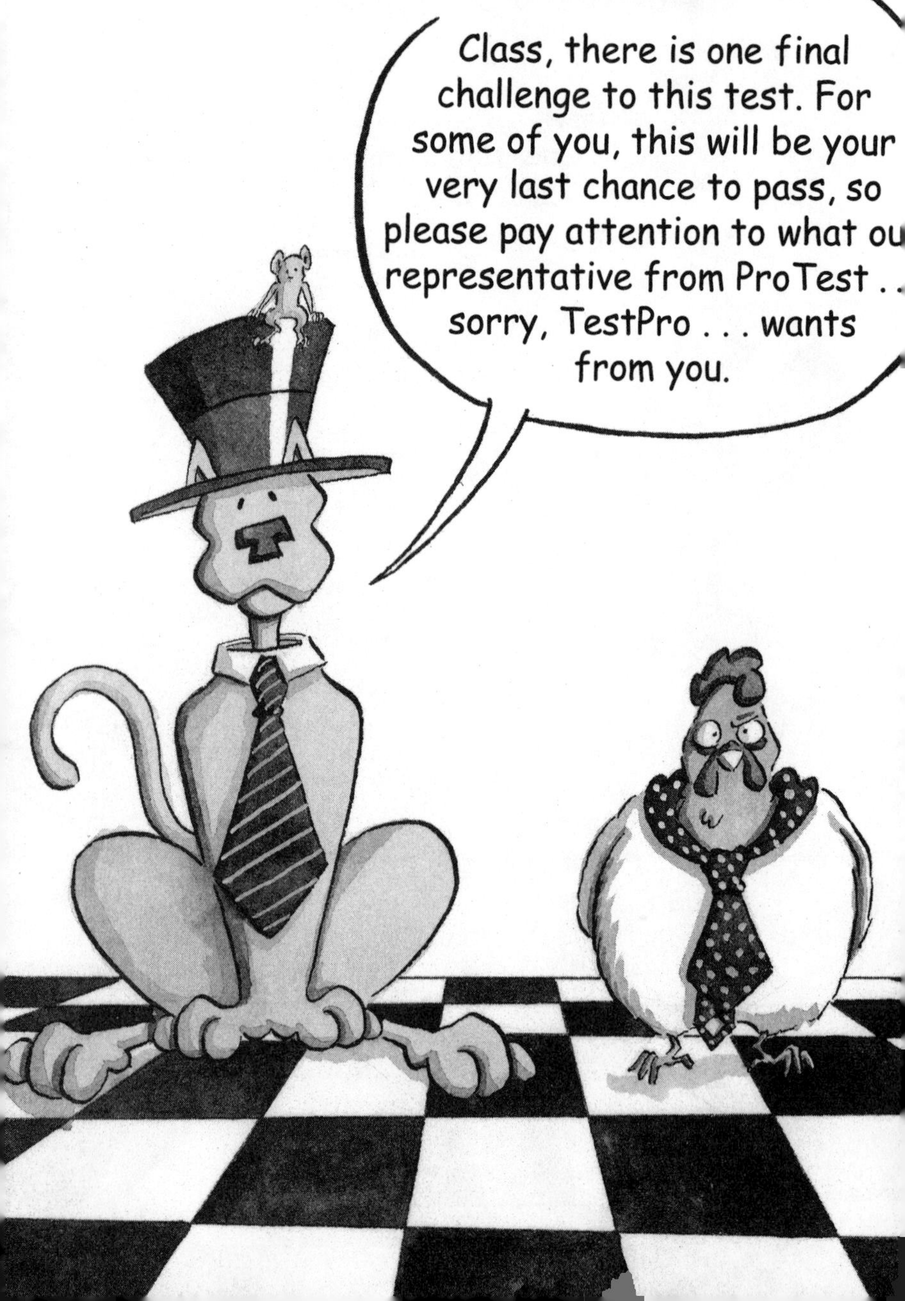

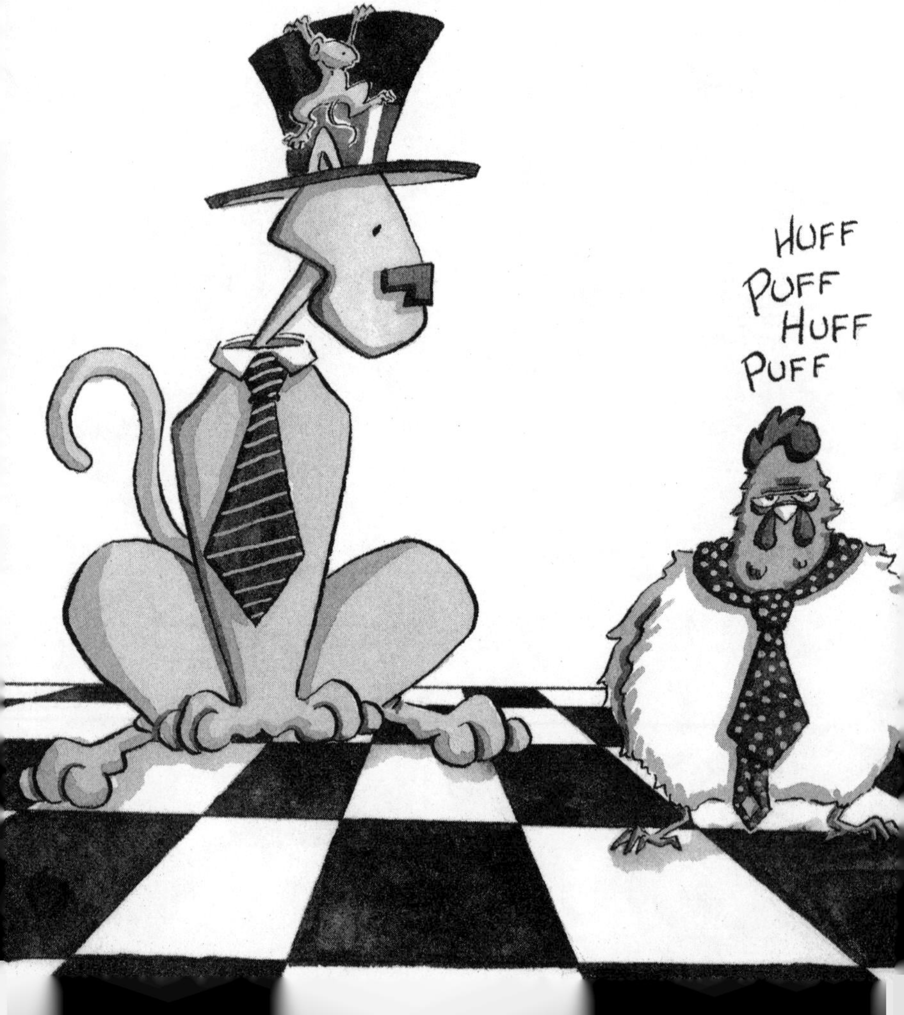
HUFF
PUFF
HUFF
PUFF

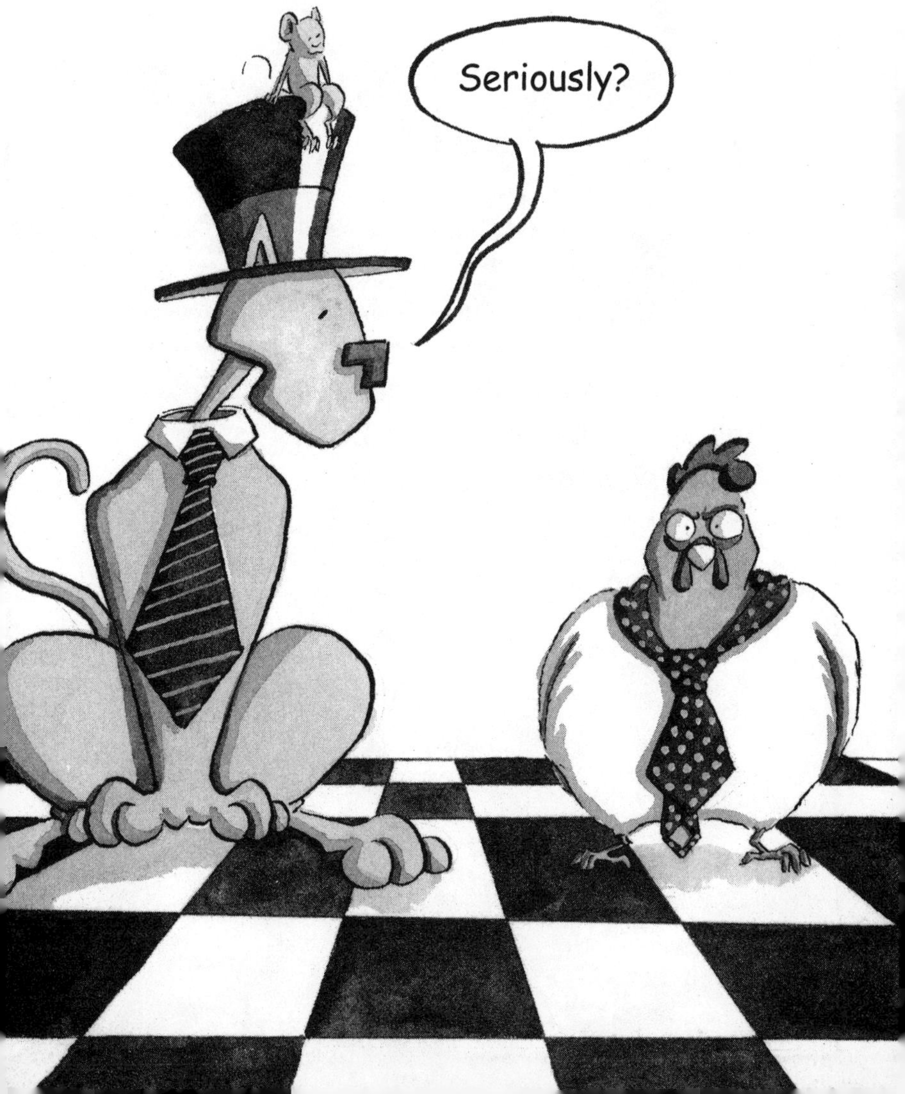
Seriously?

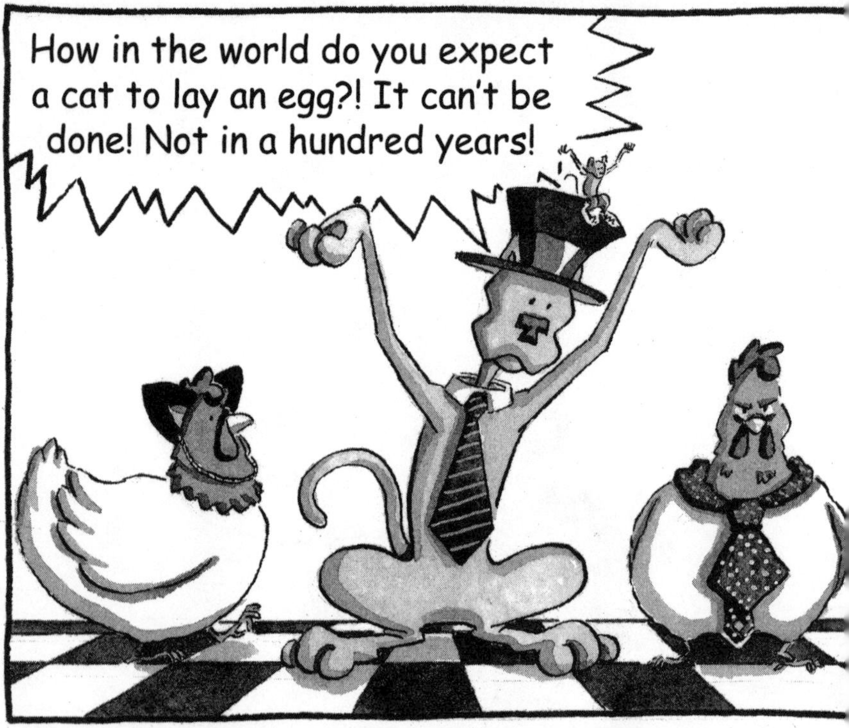
How in the world do you expect a cat to lay an egg?! It can't be done! Not in a hundred years!

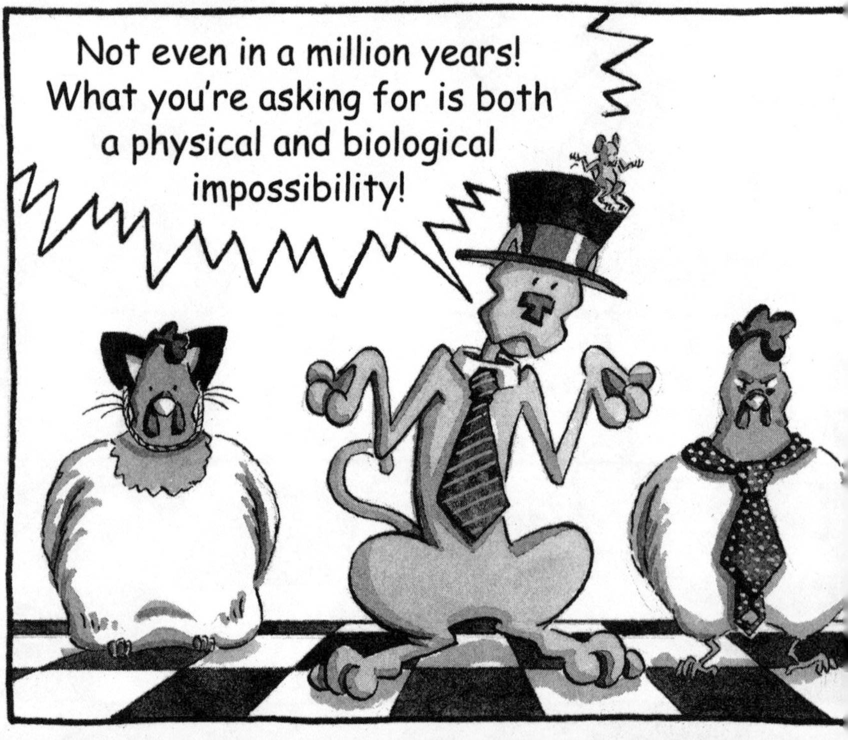
Not even in a million years! What you're asking for is both a physical and biological impossibility!

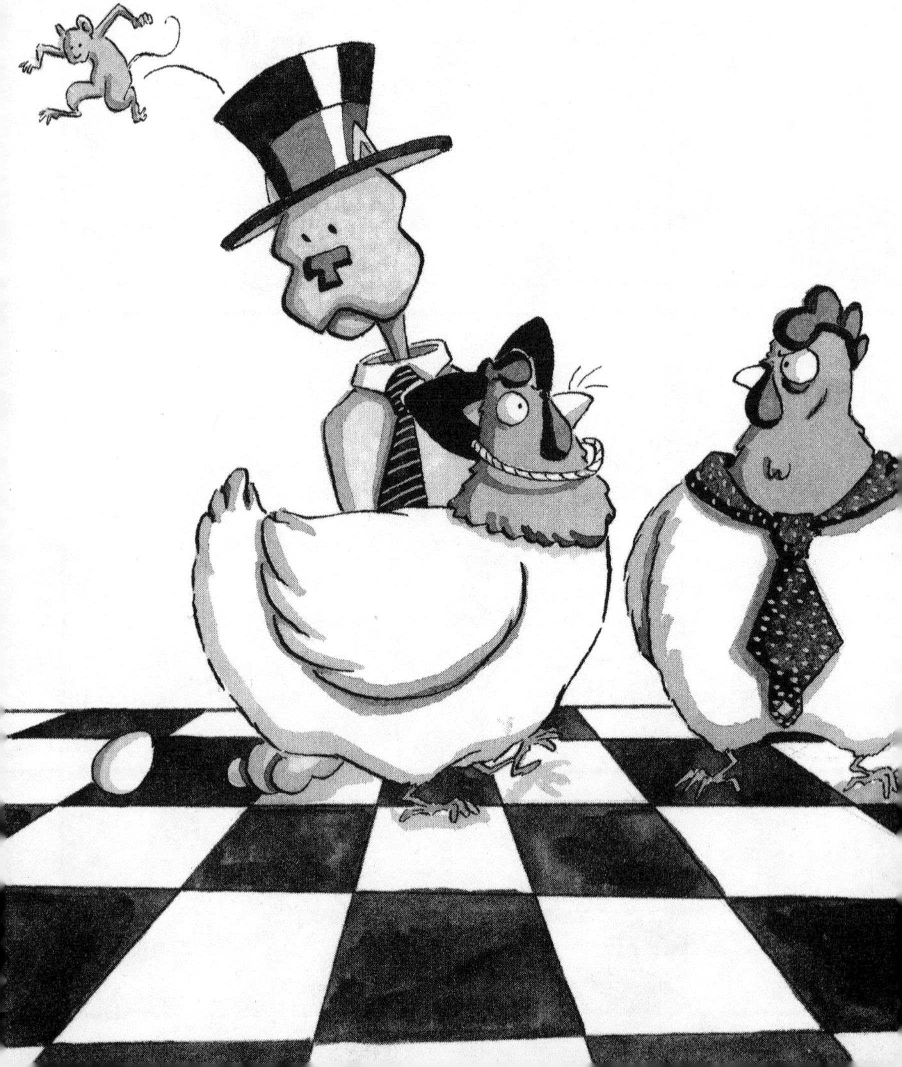

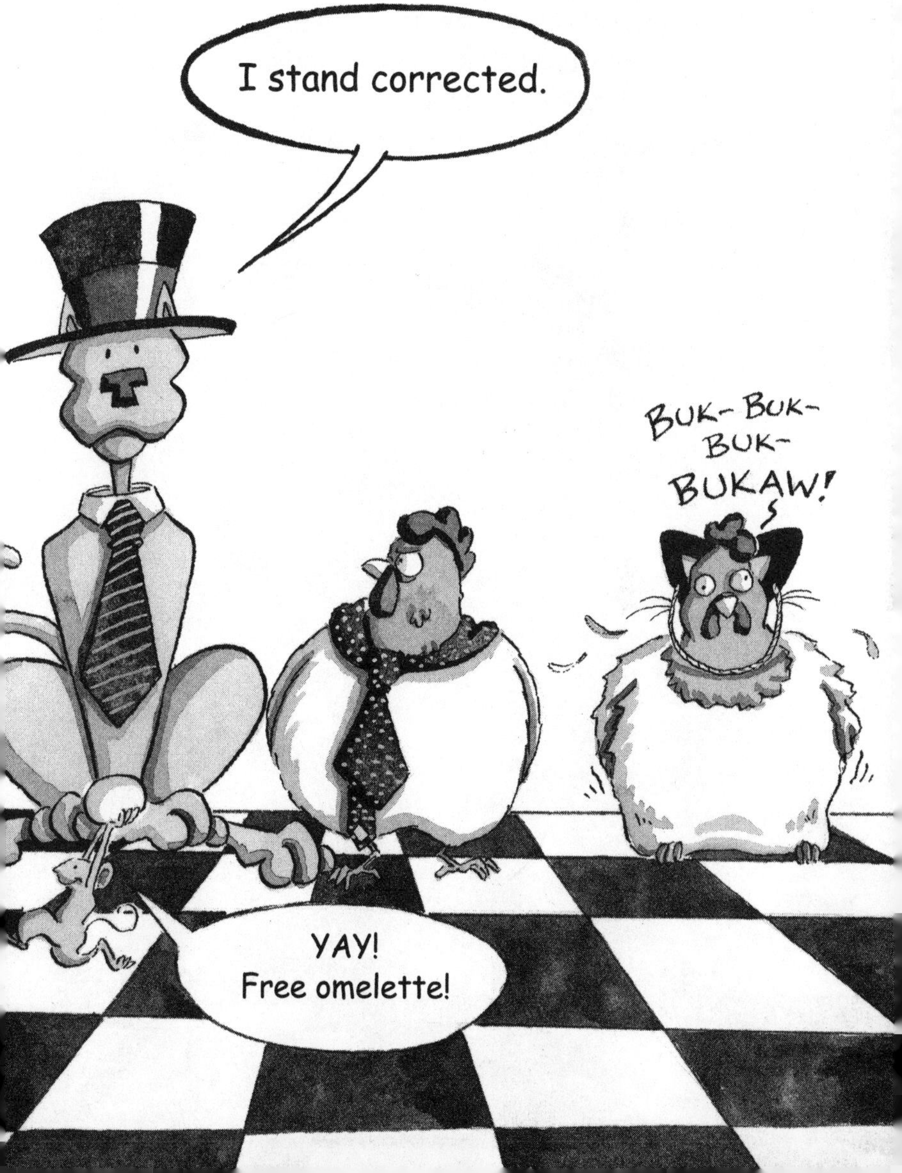
I stand corrected.
BUK-BUK-BUK-BUKAW!
YAY! Free omelette!

This proves that _____.

A) the test is fair
B) chickens are smarter than cats
C) this is definitely, DEFINITELY not, not, NOT part of an overall scheme to prove to the world that chickens are smarter than cats and always have been so that chickens will eventually be kept as pets inside nice, warm houses while cats will be served at dinnertime on a bed of rice next to potatoes and green beans
D) someday chickens will rule the world

Answer: A

Extra credit.

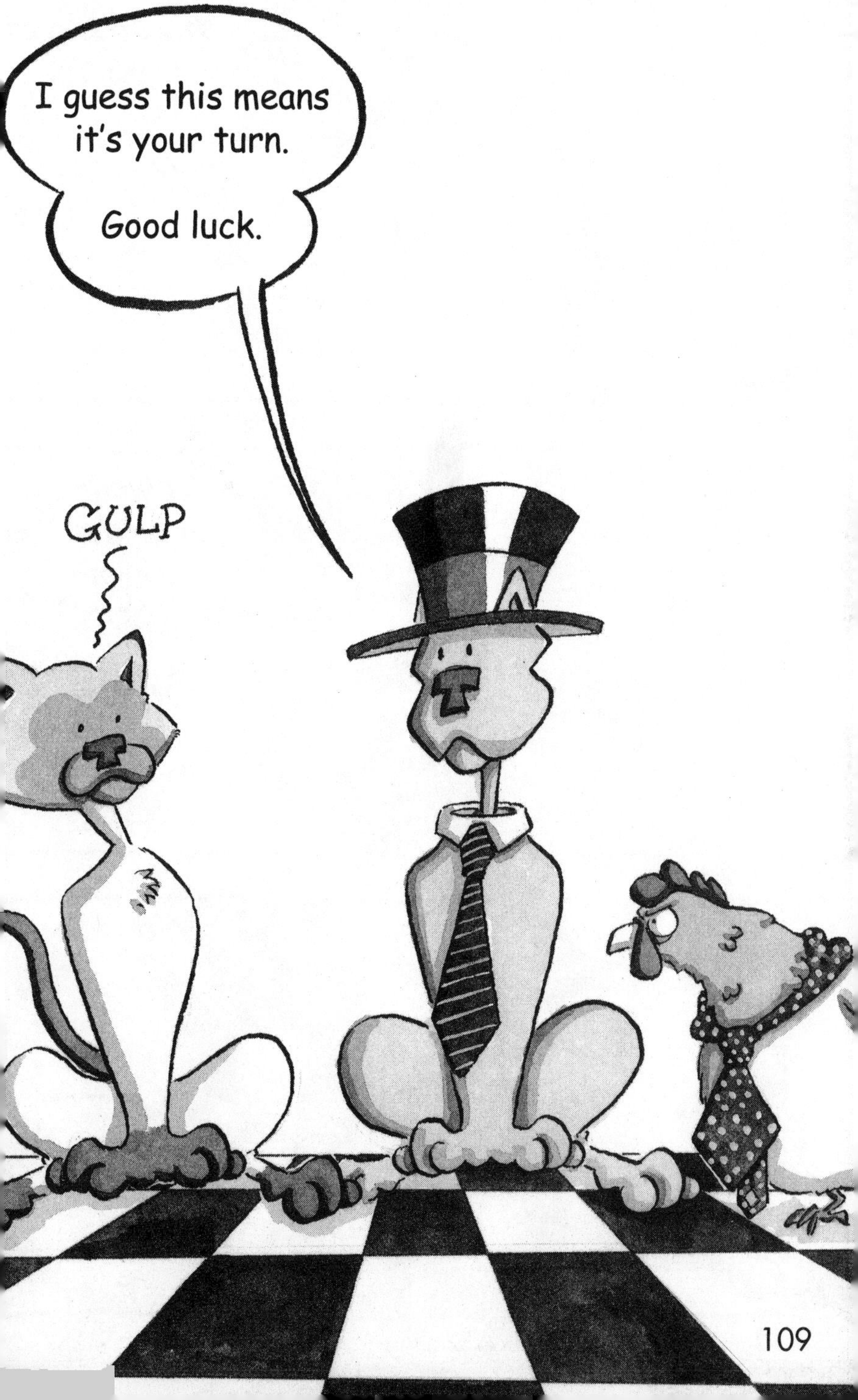

I guess this means it's your turn.
Good luck.
GULP

* I can't do it!

* What if I fail?!

* But everyone will think I'm a dummy.

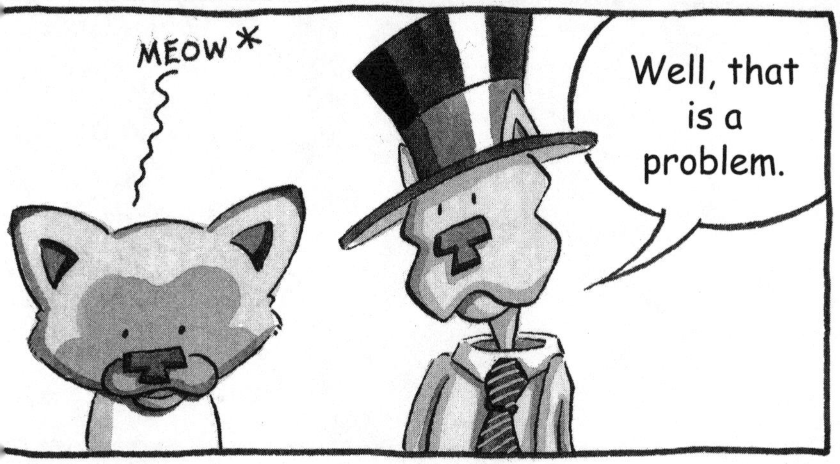
MEOW*
Well, that is a problem.

will. I'll feel like a dummy.

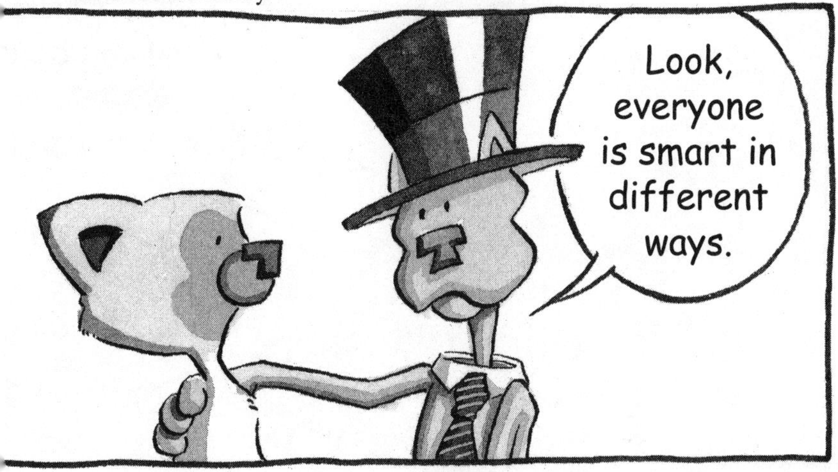
Look, everyone is smart in different ways.

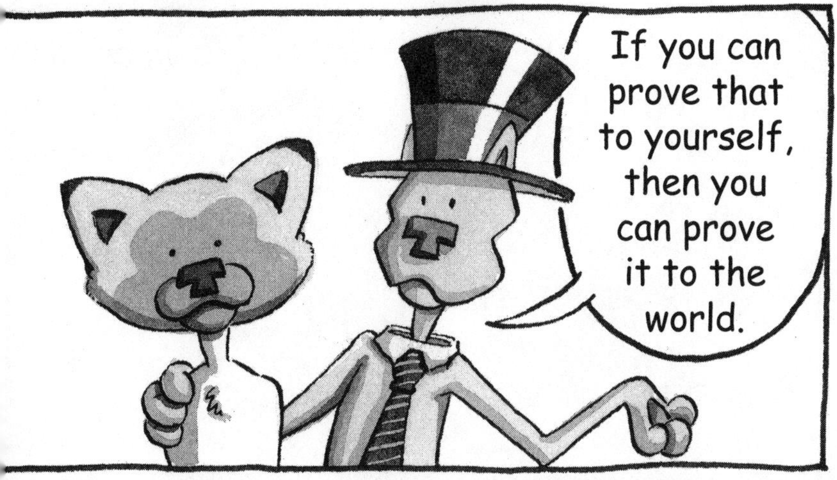
If you can prove that to yourself, then you can prove it to the world.

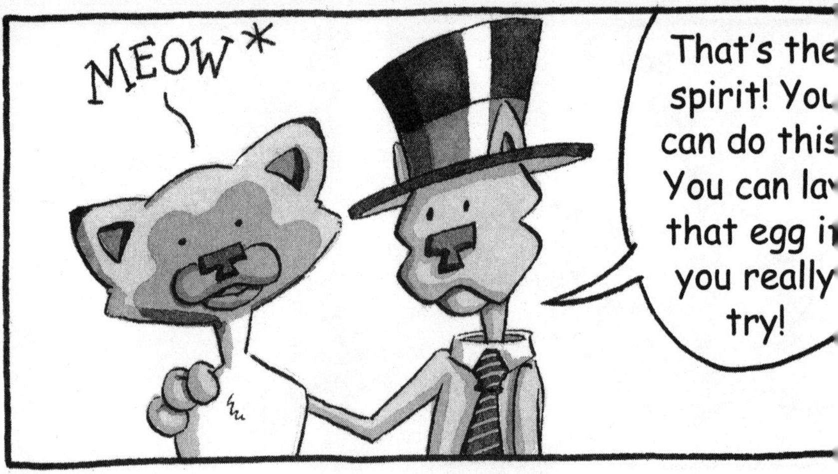
MEOW*
That's the spirit! You can do this You can la that egg i you really try!

* I'll try.

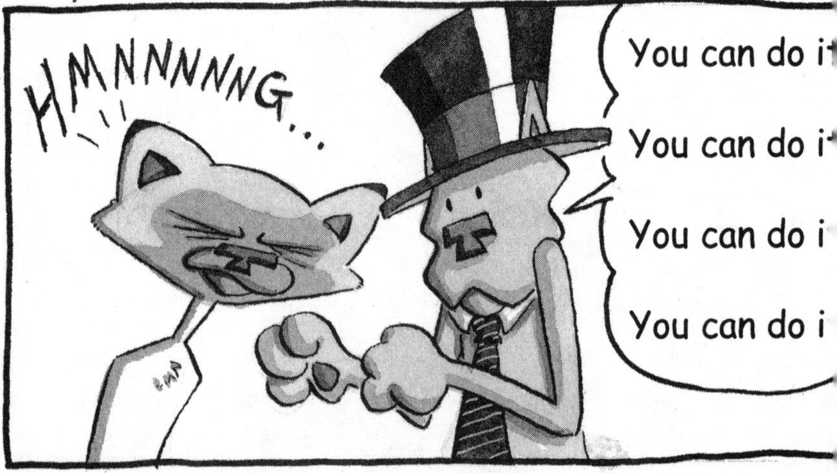
HMNNNNNG...
You can do i
You can do i
You can do i
You can do i

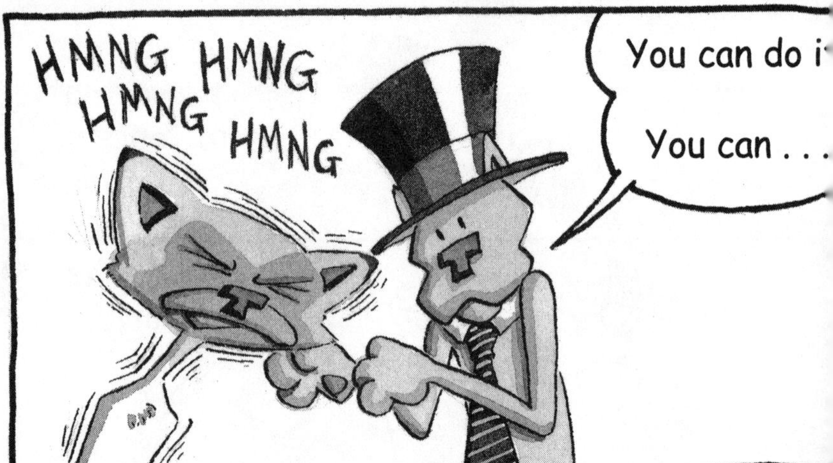
HMNG HMNG HMNG HMNG
You can do i
You can . . .

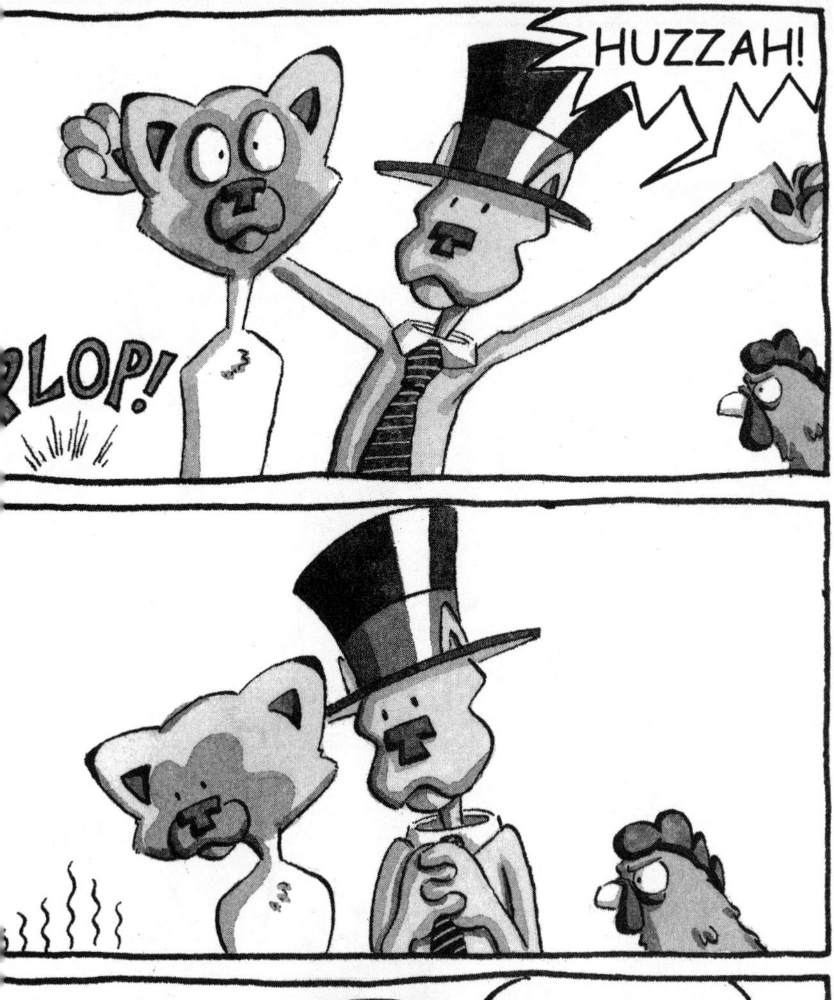
HUZZAH!
LOP!
MEOW! *
No, it isn't.
FAIL!

at's not an egg, is it?

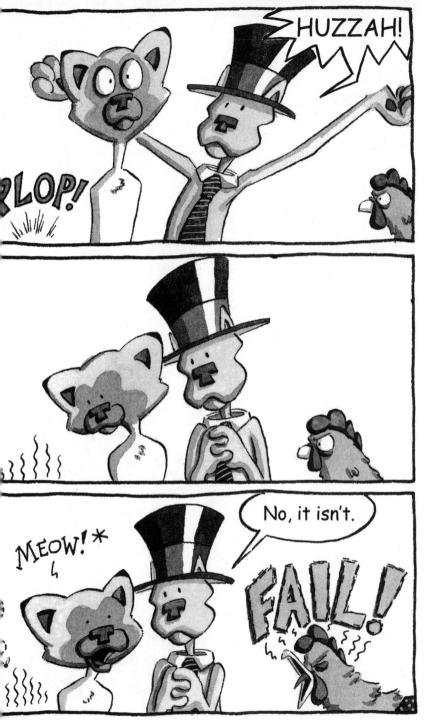

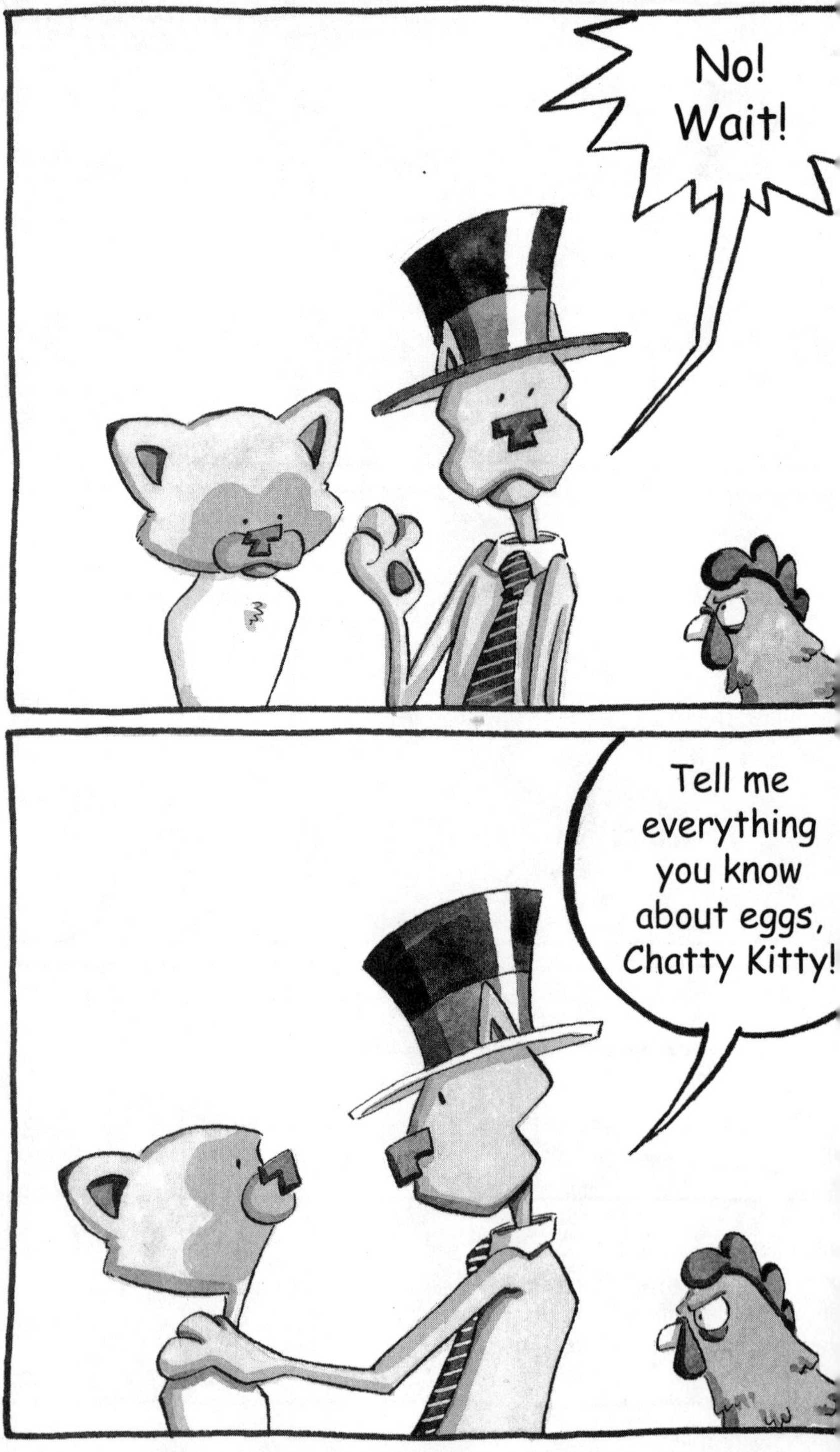
No! Wait!
Tell me everything you know about eggs, Chatty Kitty!

MEOW MEOW MEOW MEOW MEOW MEOW MEOW MEOW MEOW MEOW MEOW MEOW MEOW MEOW MEOW MEOW MEOW MEOW MEOW MEOW MEOW MEOW MEOW MEOW MEOW MEOW*

Approximately 1.1 trillion eggs are consumed worldwide each year, China being the largest producer. Roughly half of all eggs produced are white, and the other half are brown. The color of the egg depends largely on the color of the earlobe of the chicken that laid it: white earlobe, white egg—red earlobe, brown egg. Egg shells are composed primarily of calcium carbonate, which is also the main ingredient in some antacids, but I don't recommend chewing on egg shells if you have an upset stomach. The membrane inside the shell is semipermeable, meaning that it allows water and oxygen inside the egg while keeping dust and other debris out. The white of an egg is also called the albumin after the primary protein that inhabits it. If an egg white looks cloudy, that actually means that the egg is very fresh. The color of the egg yolk depends greatly on the diet of the chicken that laid it: the more yellow or orange pigments in the food, the more brightly colored the yolk. A monotreme is a mammal that lays an egg, and there are only five known species in the world, the platypus and four species of echidna. The largest eggs come from ostriches, which can weigh as much as 5 pounds, and the smallest eggs come from vervain hummingbirds, which weigh only a fraction of an ounce. And lastly, a person who is considered to be intellectually gifted is often referred to as an egghead. I've been called an egghead. I wasn't insulted.

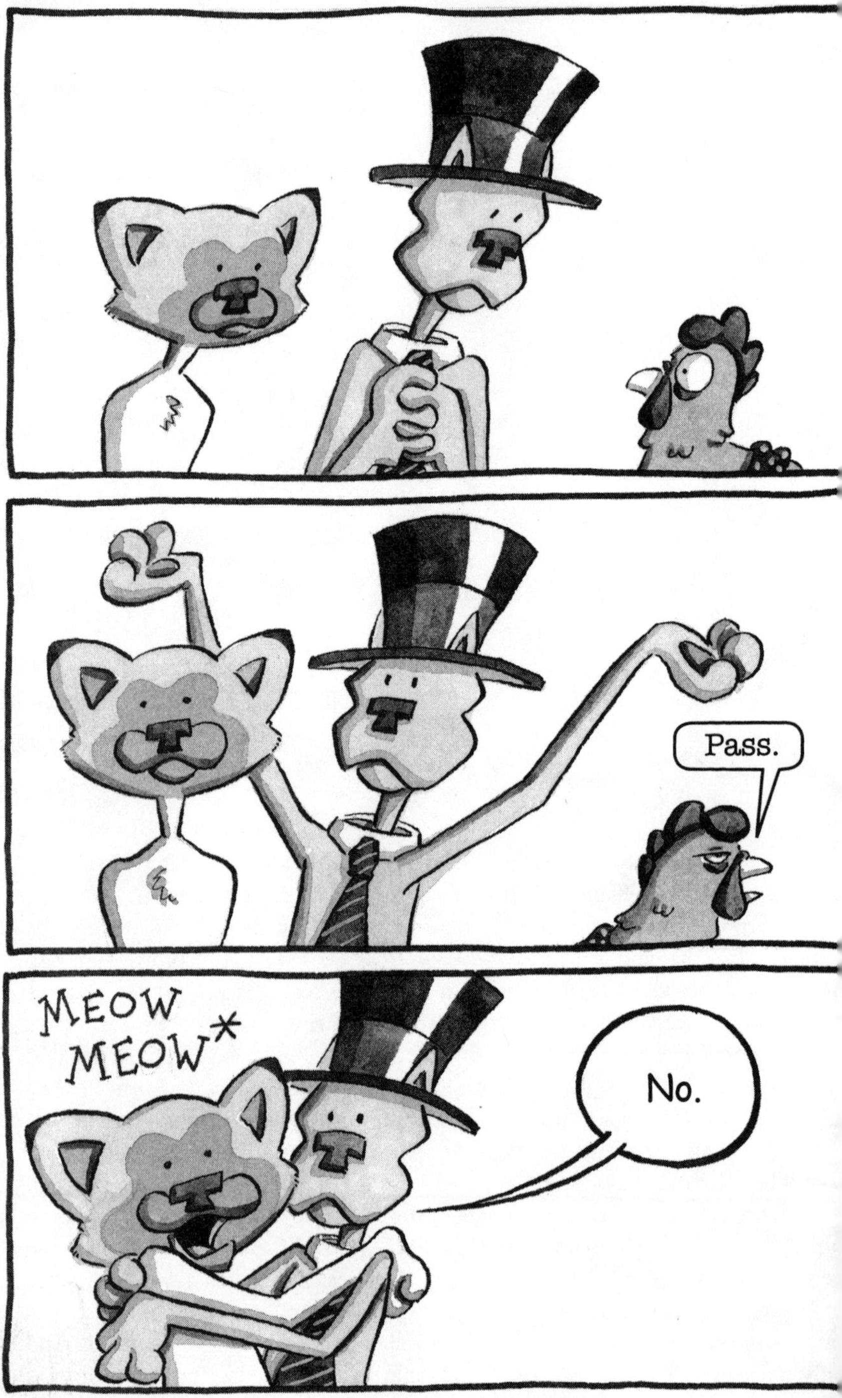
Pass.
MEOW
MEOW*
No.

* Shall I tell you everything I know about dishwashers?

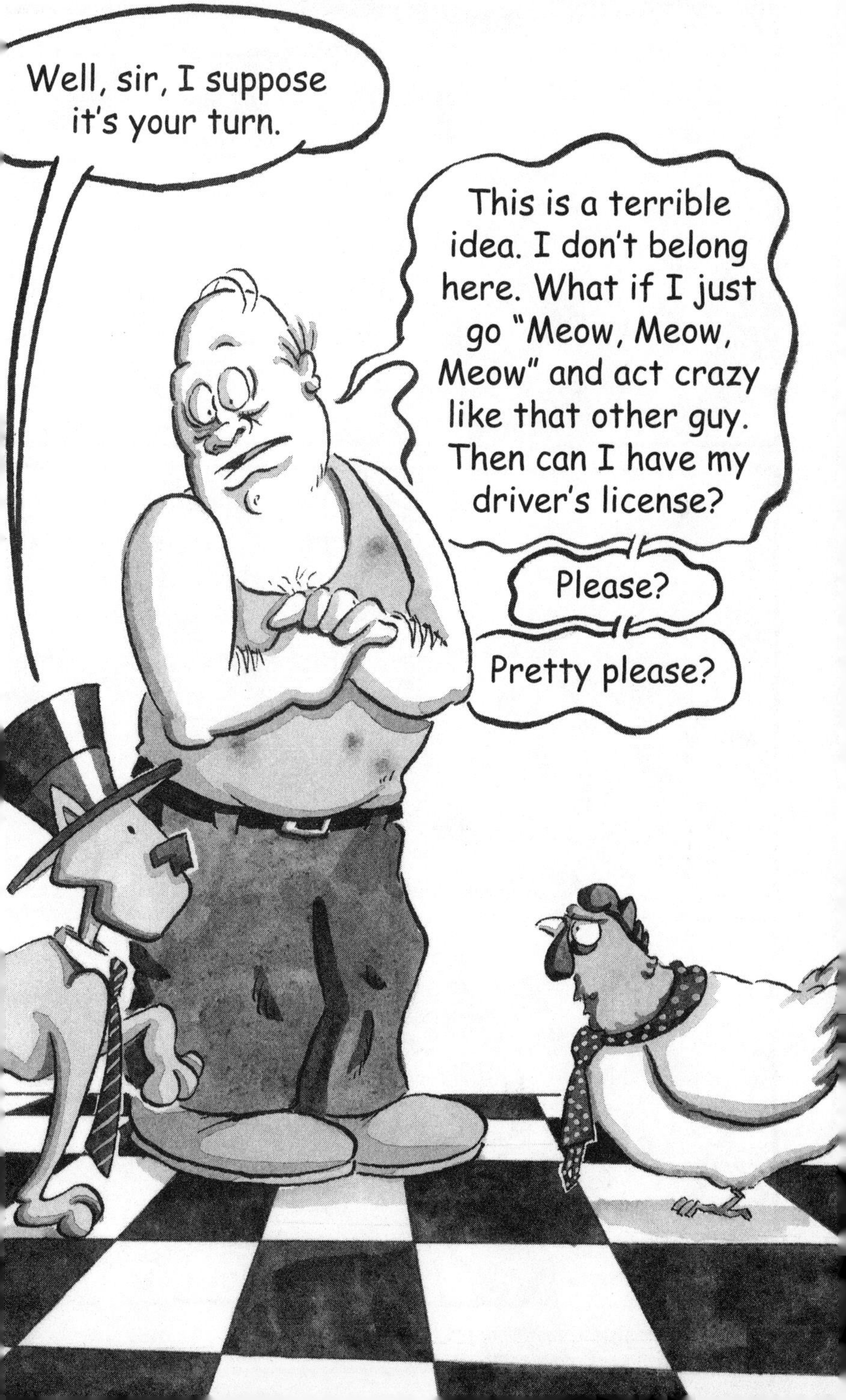
Well, sir, I suppose it's your turn.
This is a terrible idea. I don't belong here. What if I just go "Meow, Meow, Meow" and act crazy like that other guy. Then can I have my driver's license?
Please?
Pretty please?

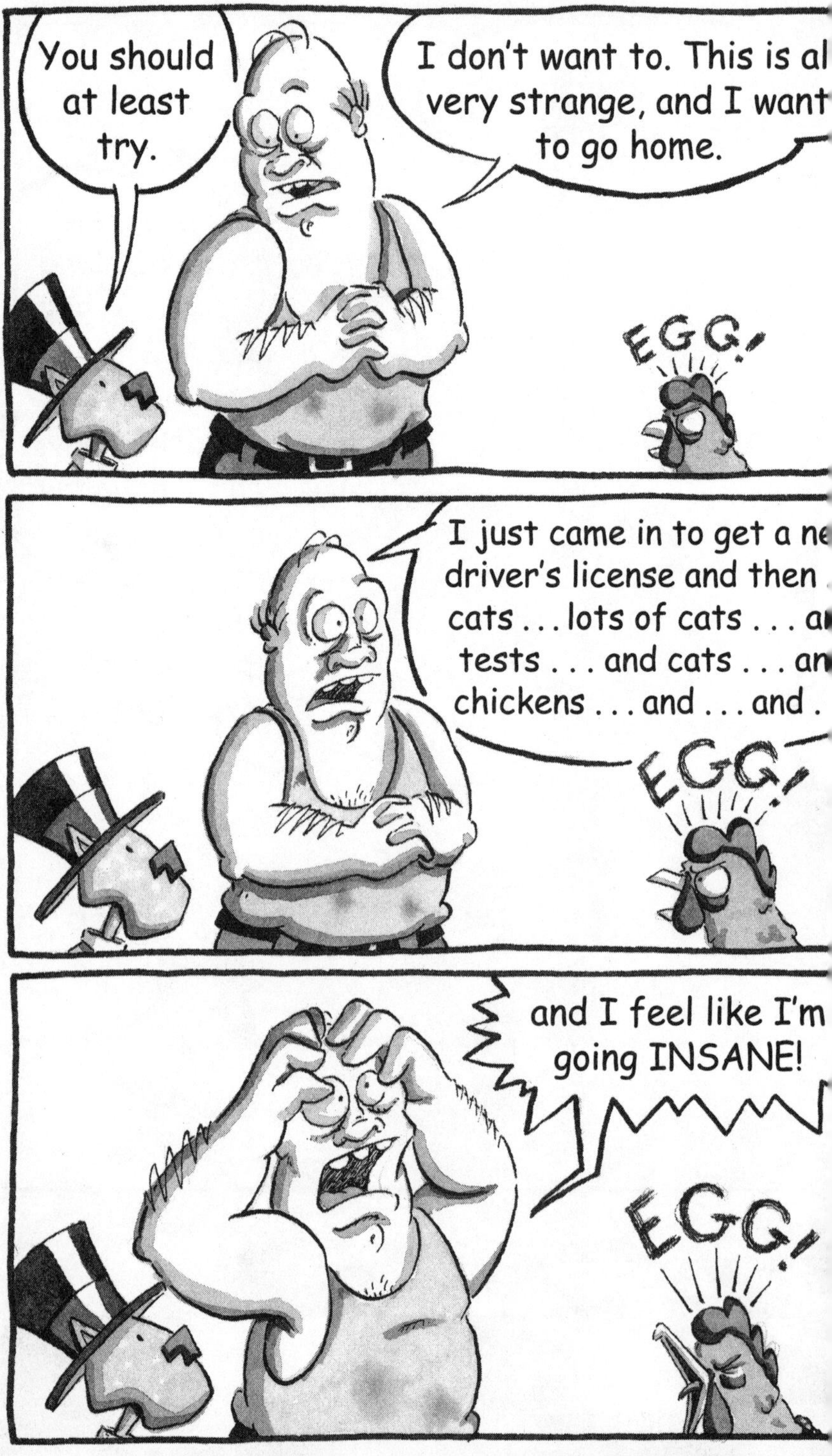
You should at least try.
I don't want to. This is al
very strange, and I want
to go home.
EGG!
I just came in to get a ne
driver's license and then
cats . . . lots of cats . . . a
tests . . . and cats . . . an
chickens . . . and . . . and .
EGG!
and I feel like I'm
going INSANE!
EGG!

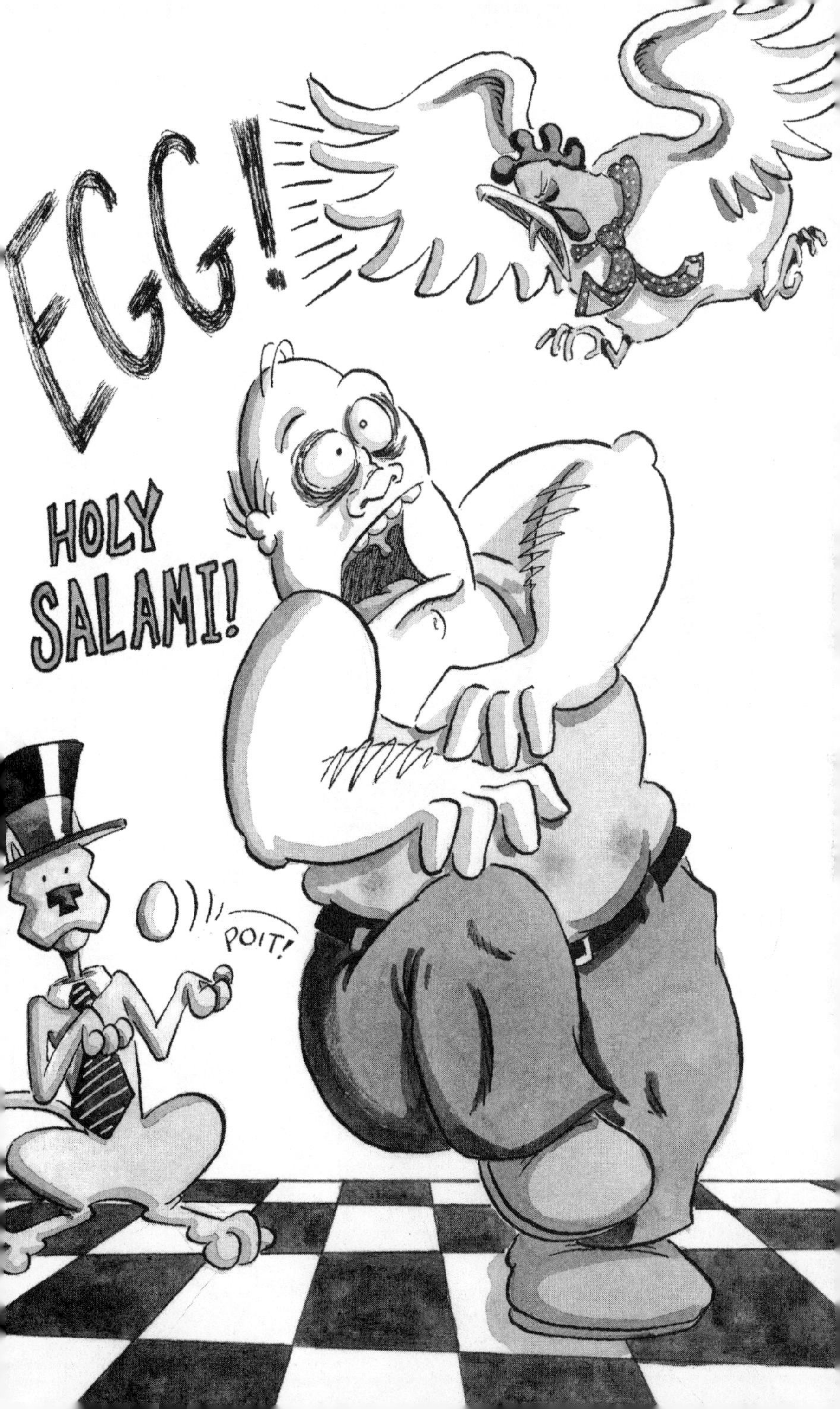
EGG!
HOLY SALAMI!
POIT!

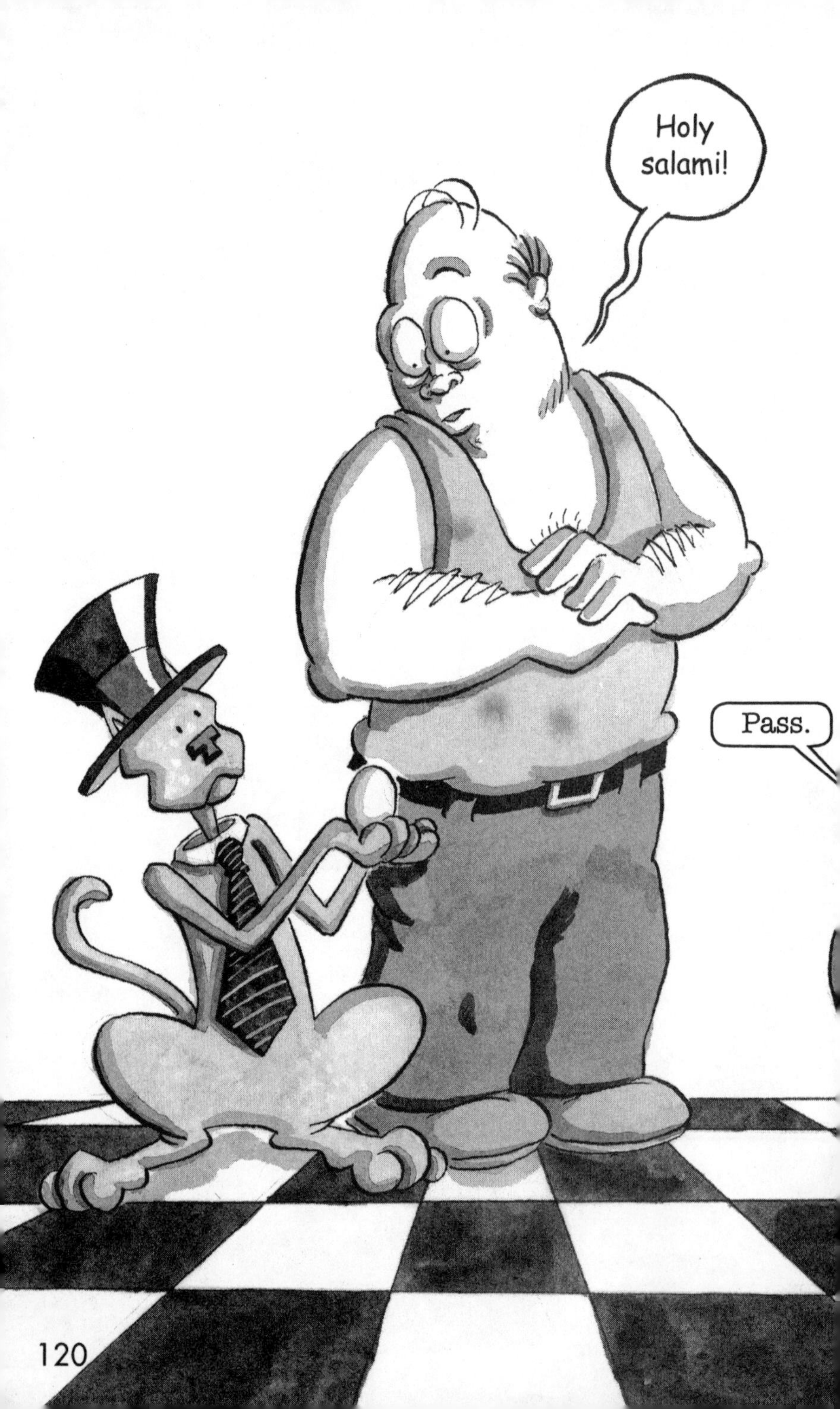
Holy
salami!
Pass.

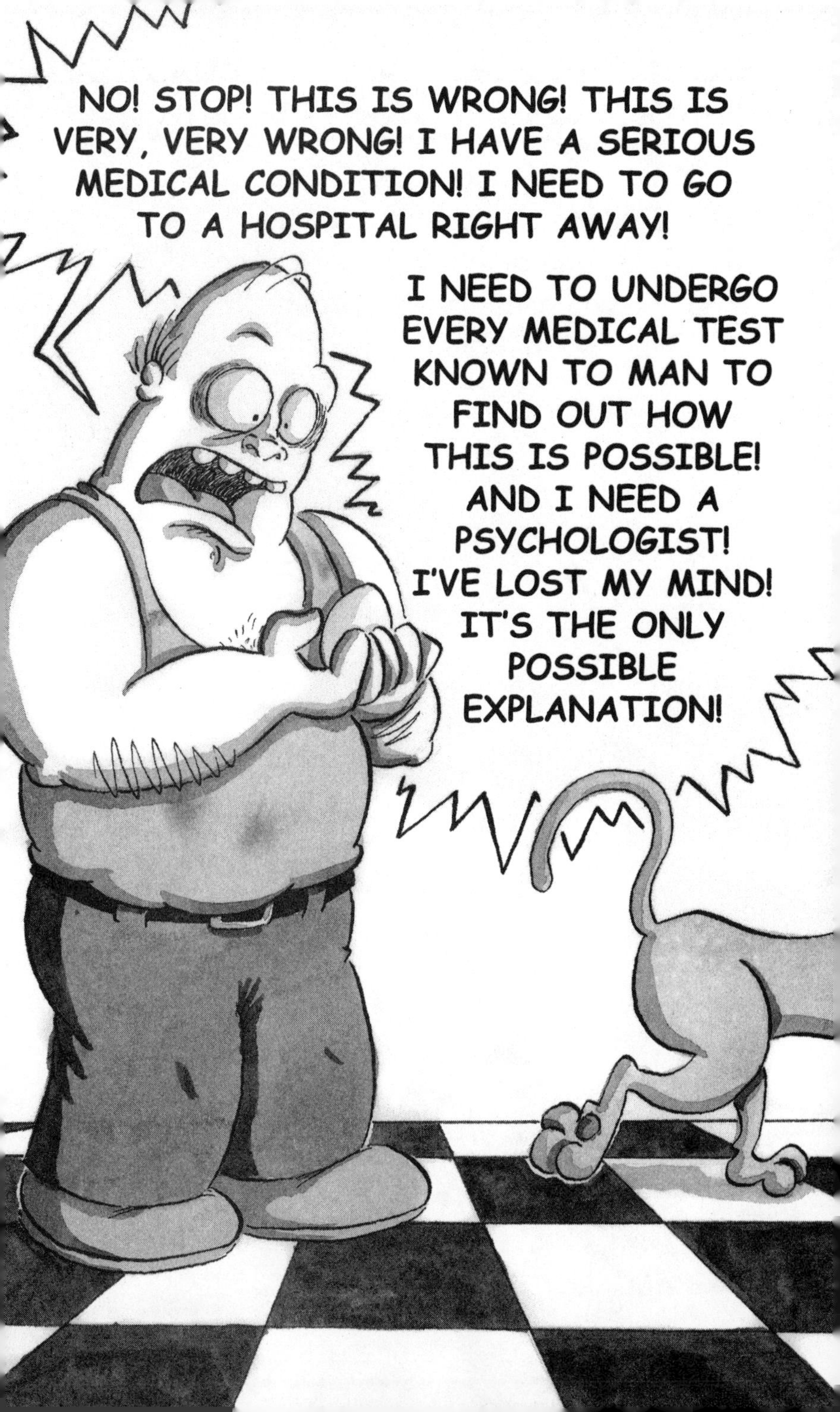
NO! STOP! THIS IS WRONG! THIS IS VERY, VERY WRONG! I HAVE A SERIOUS MEDICAL CONDITION! I NEED TO GO TO A HOSPITAL RIGHT AWAY!
I NEED TO UNDERGO EVERY MEDICAL TEST KNOWN TO MAN TO FIND OUT HOW THIS IS POSSIBLE! AND I NEED A PSYCHOLOGIST! I'VE LOST MY MIND! IT'S THE ONLY POSSIBLE EXPLANATION!

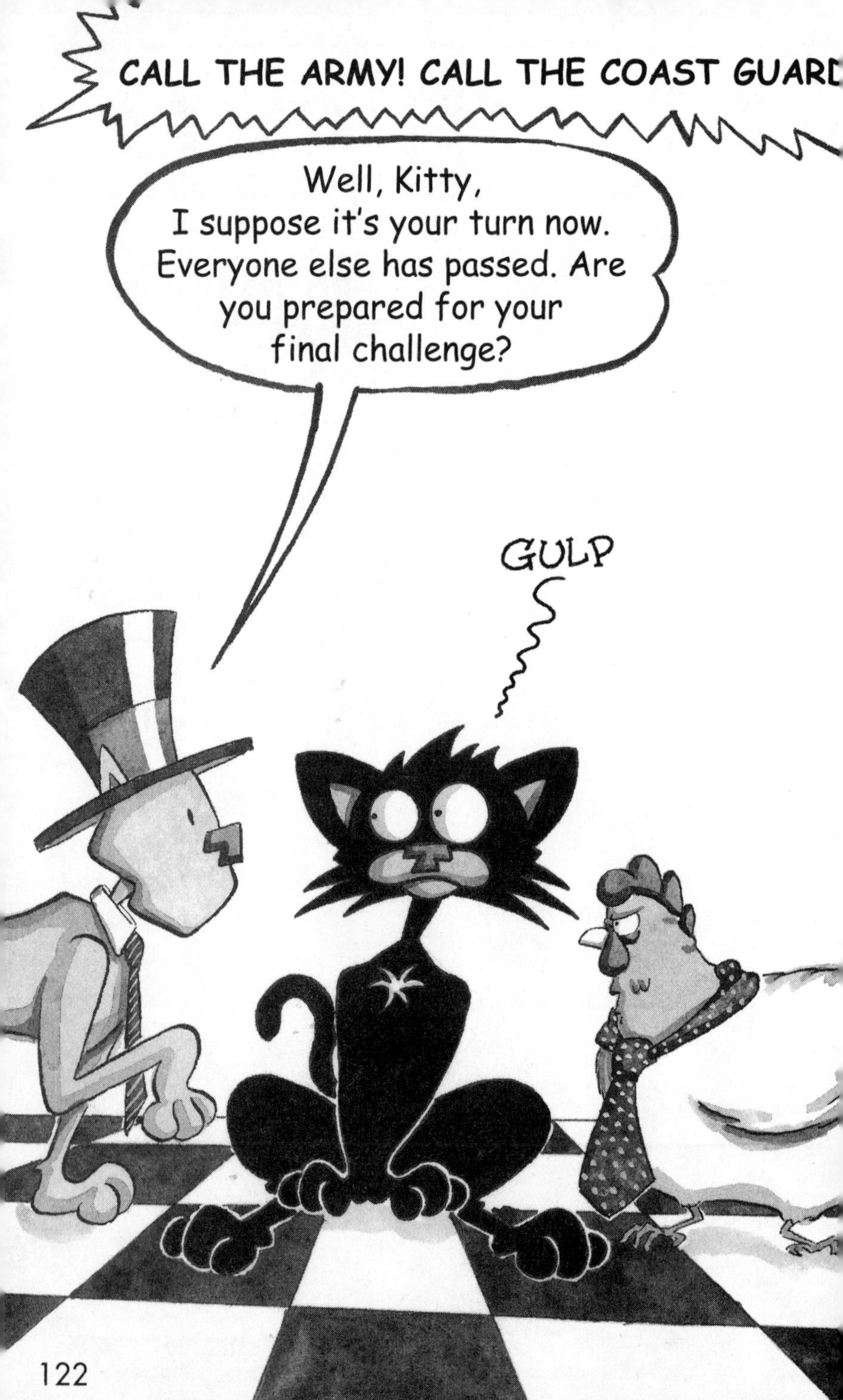

CALL THE ARMY! CALL THE COAST GUARD
Well, Kitty, I suppose it's your turn now. Everyone else has passed. Are you prepared for your final challenge?
GULP

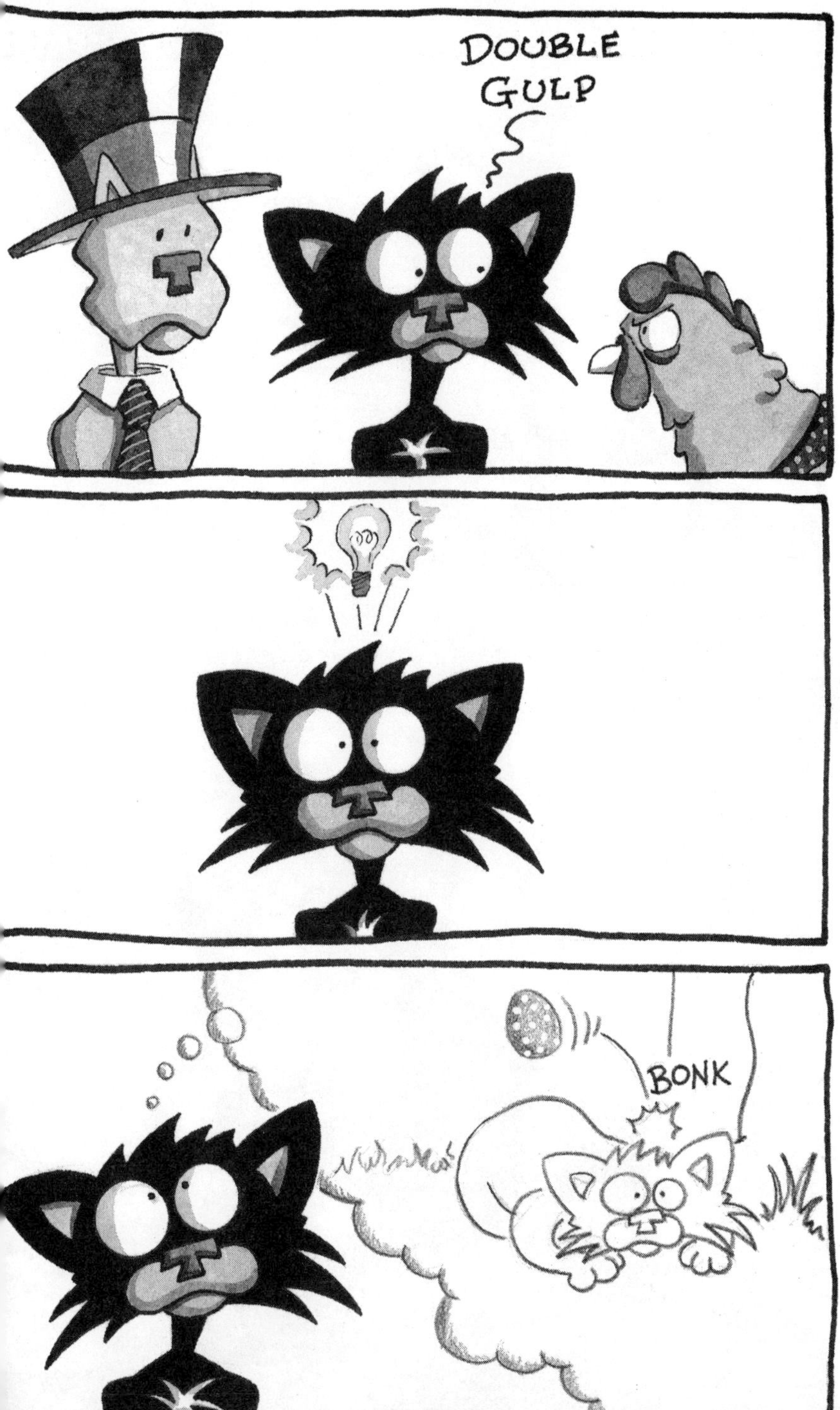
DOUBLE GULP
BONK

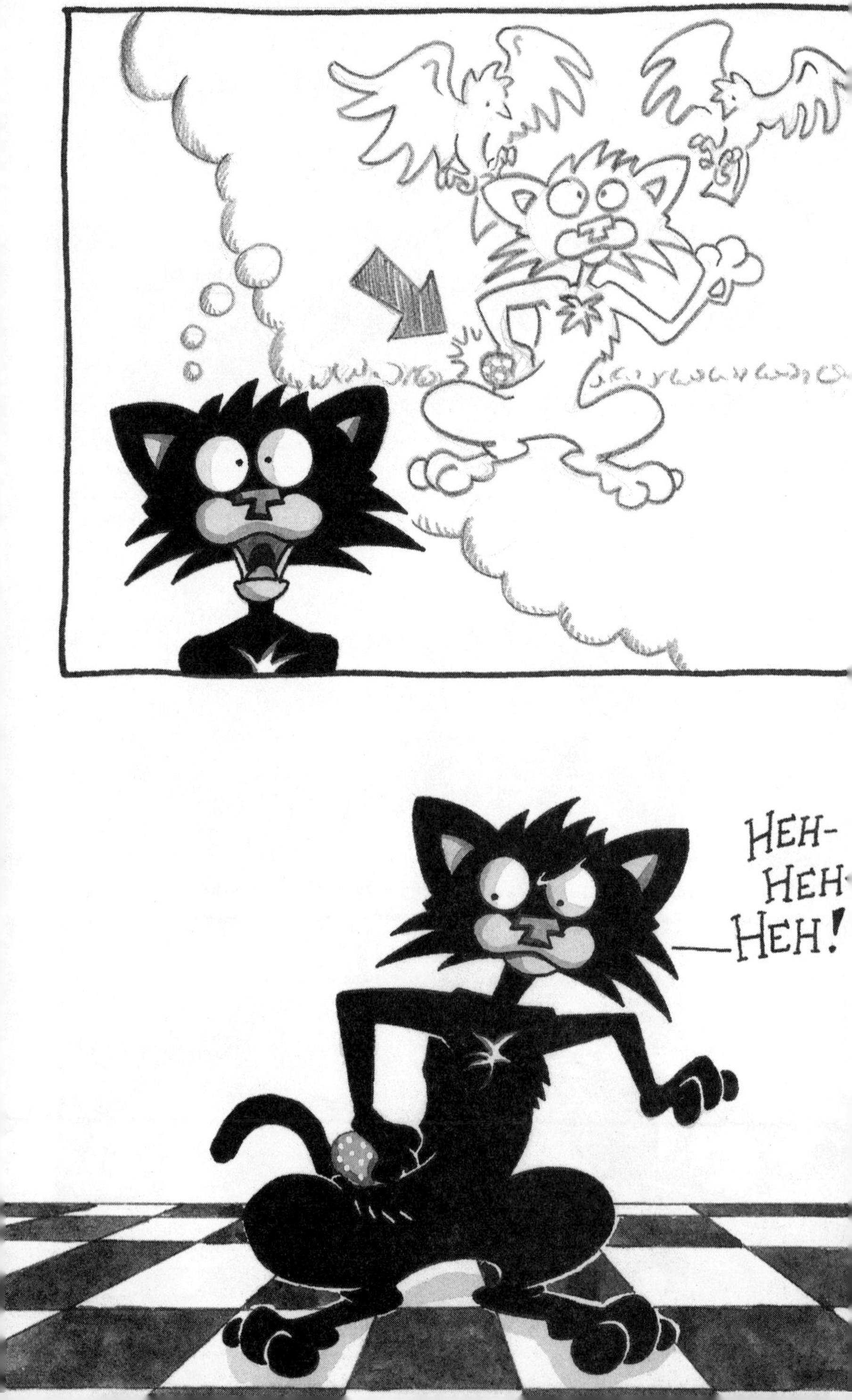
HEH-
HEH-
HEH!

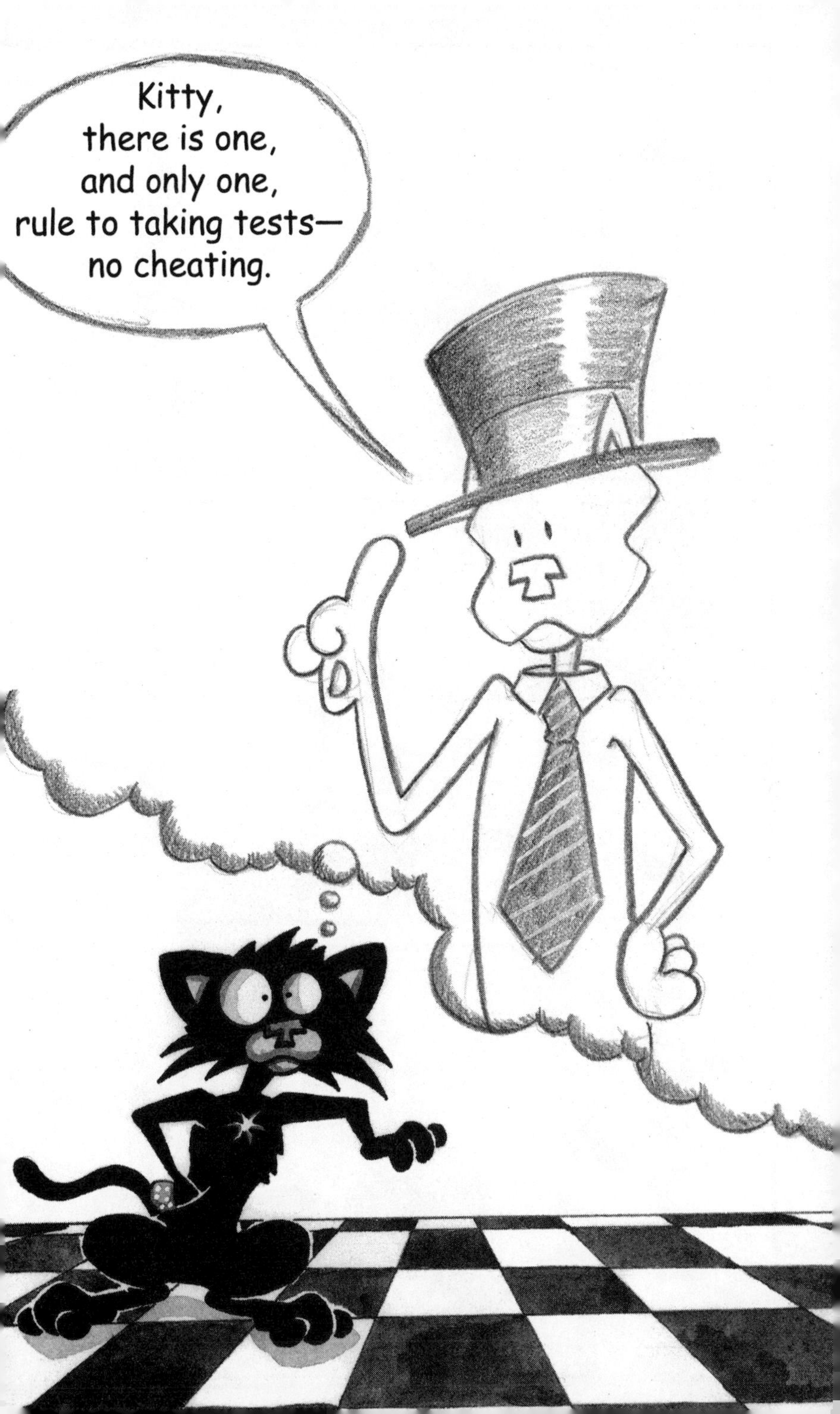
Kitty, there is one, and only one, rule to taking tests— no cheating.

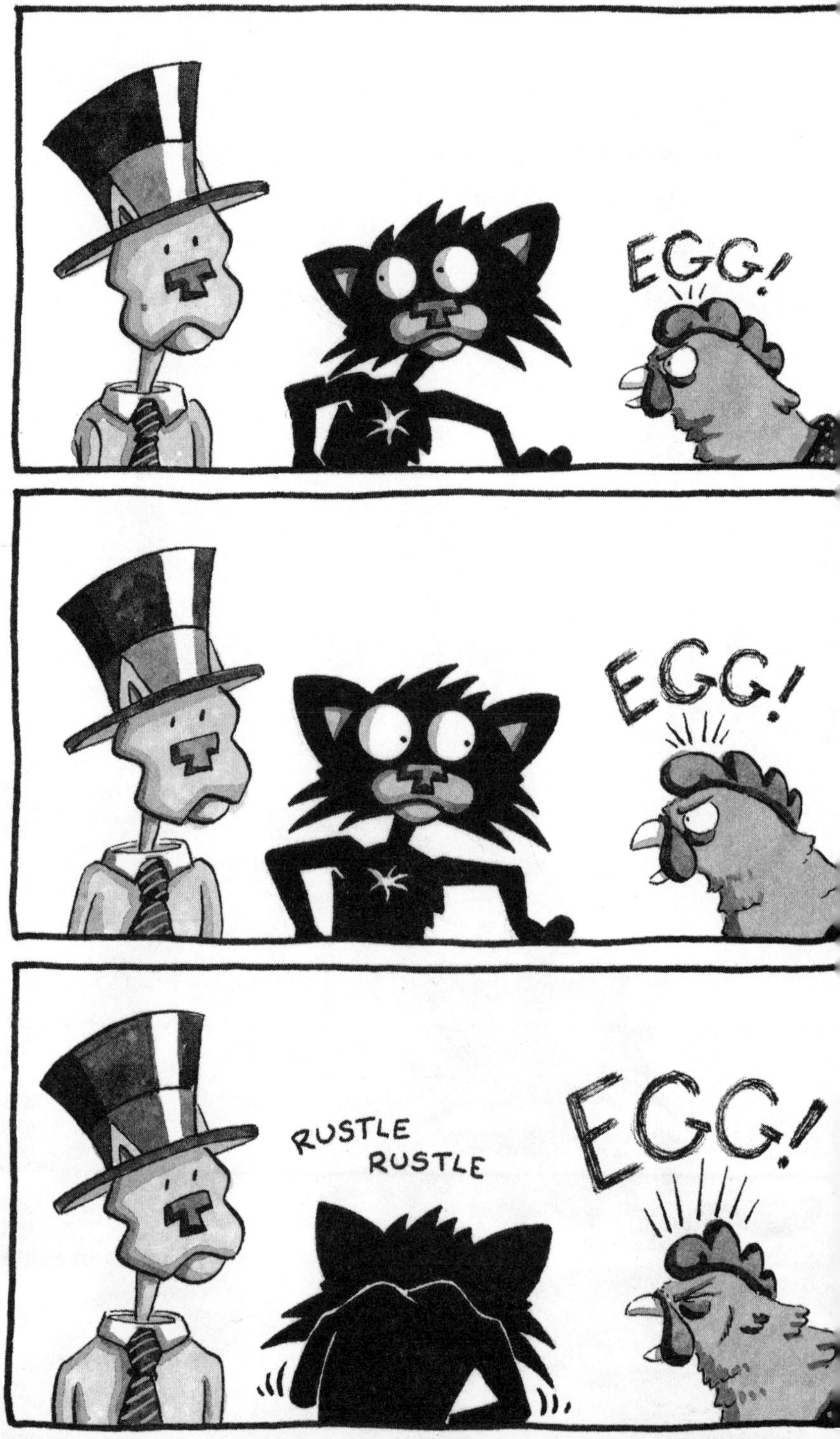
EGG!
EGG!
RUSTLE
RUSTLE
EGG!

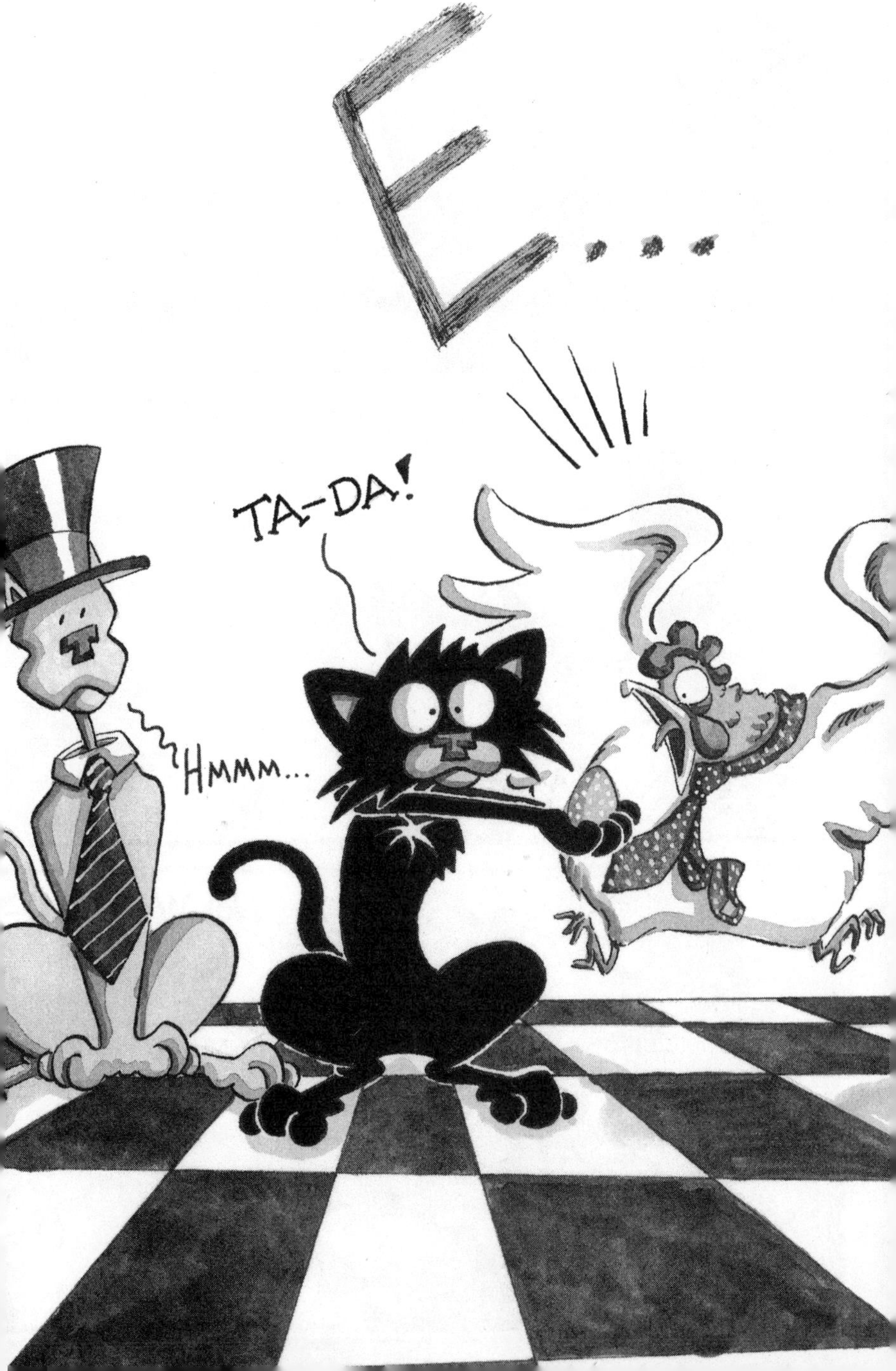
E...
TA-DA!
HMMM...

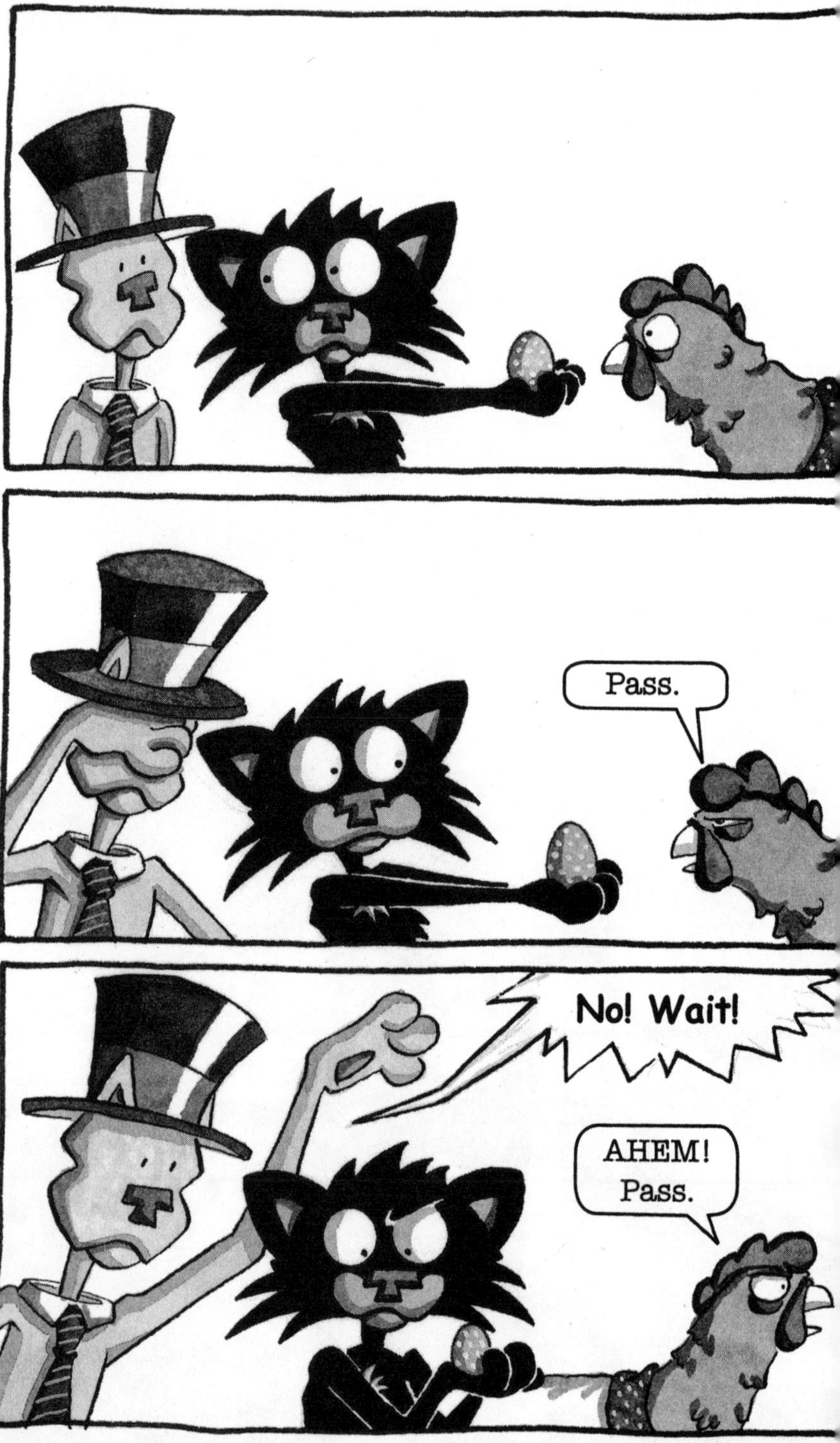
Pass.
No! Wait!
AHEM! Pass.

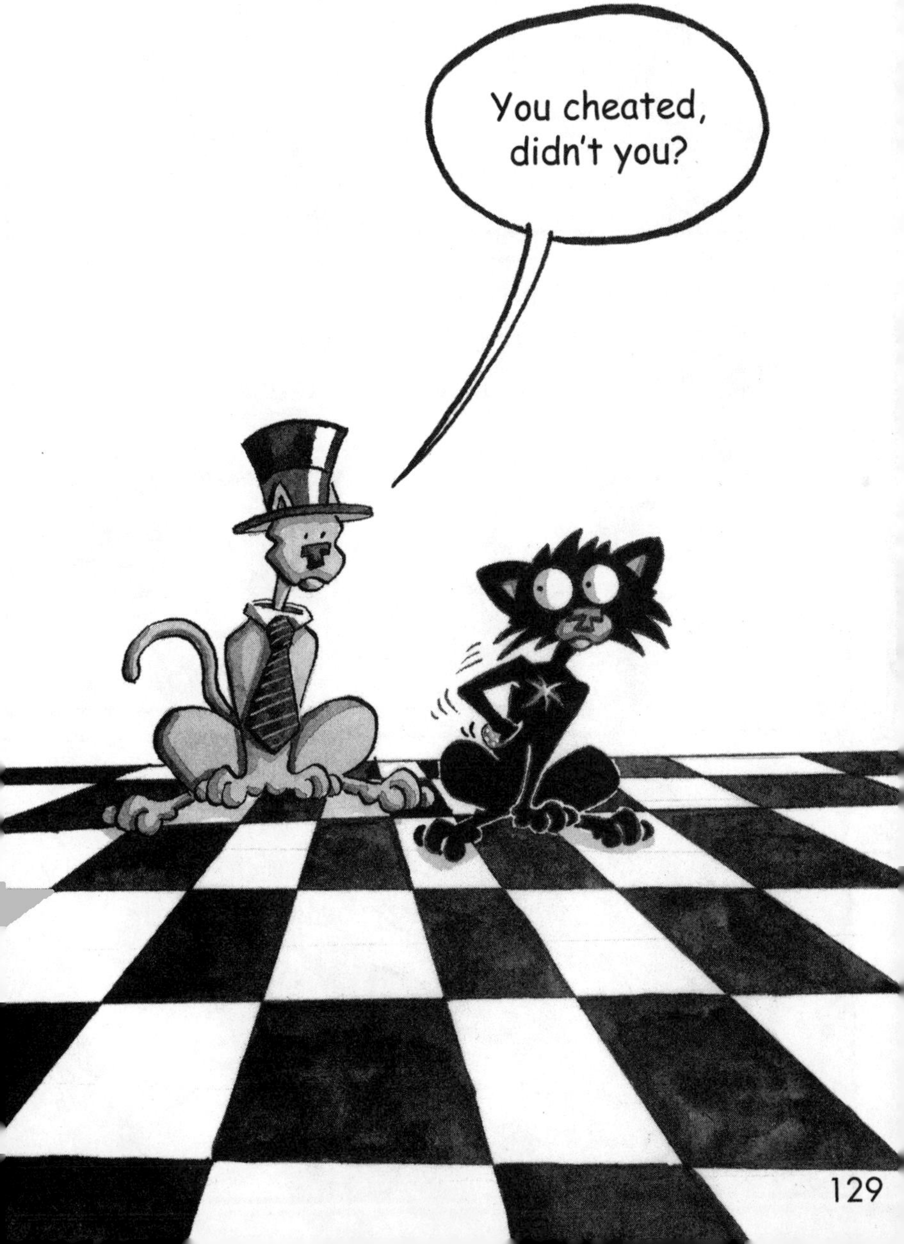
You cheated, didn't you?

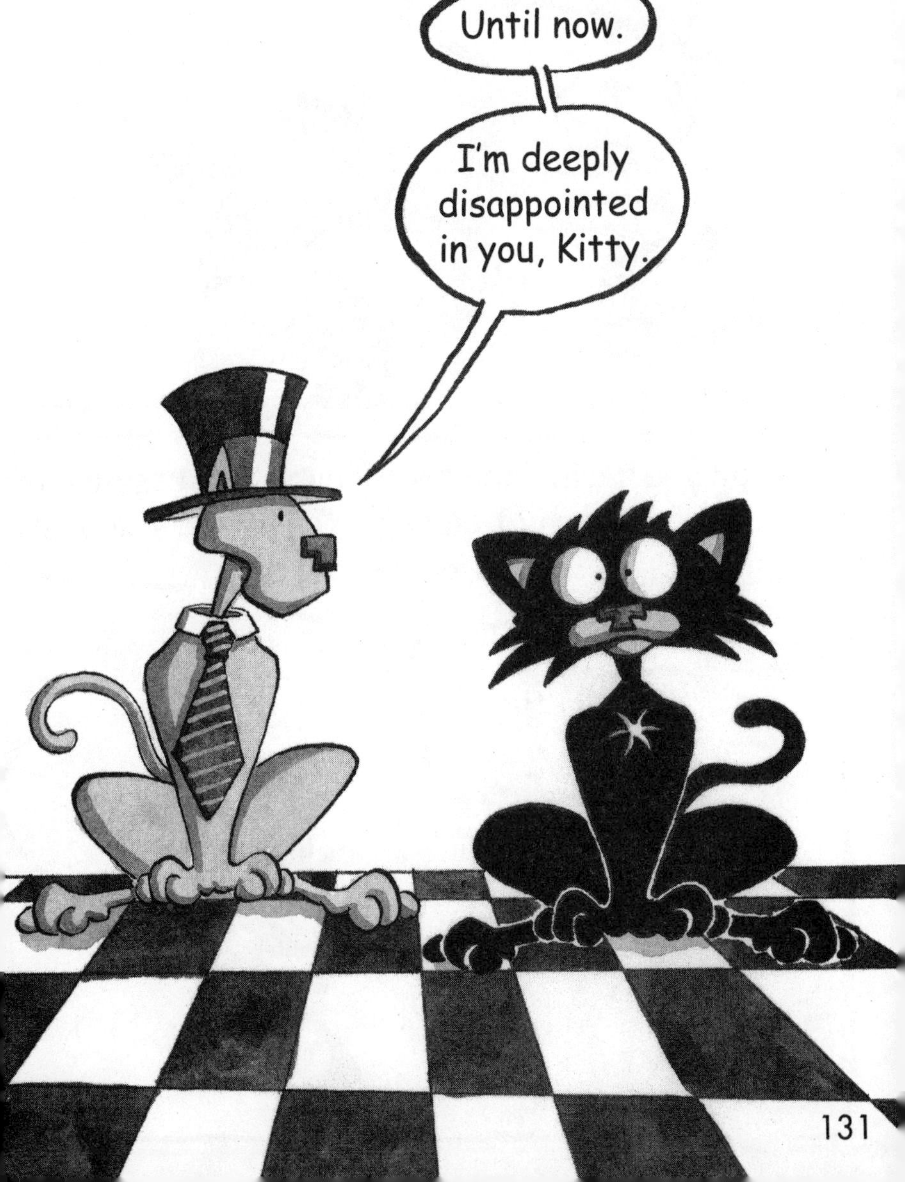
Until now.
I'm deeply disappointed in you, Kitty.

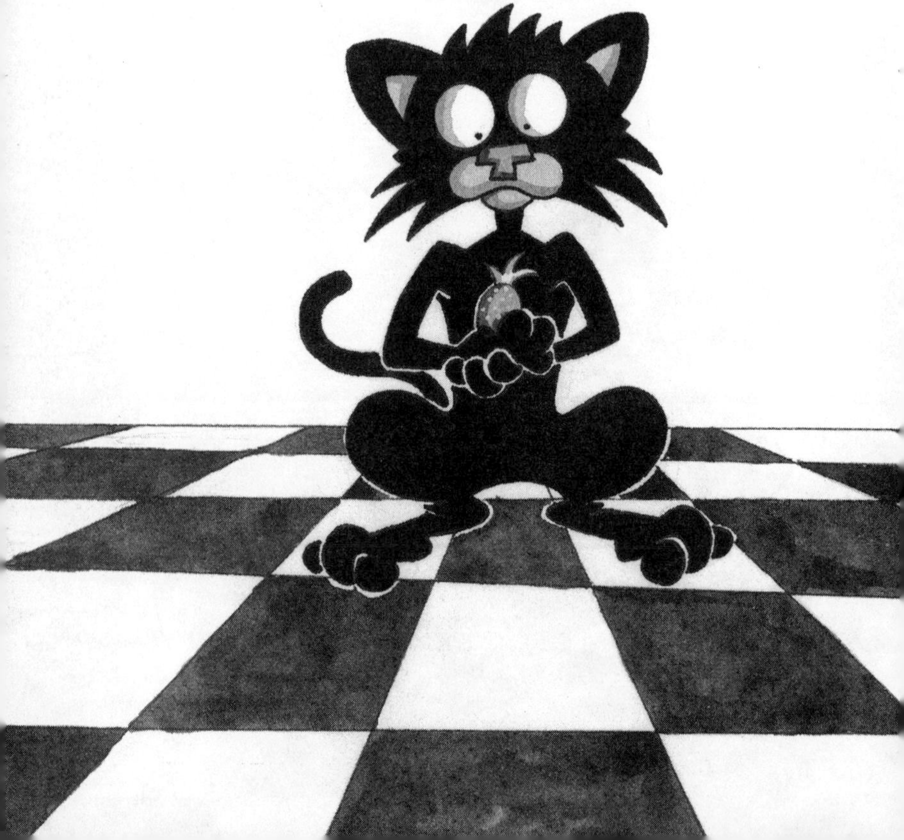

•CHAPTER SEVEN•

THE NEXT, NEXT, NEXT DAY

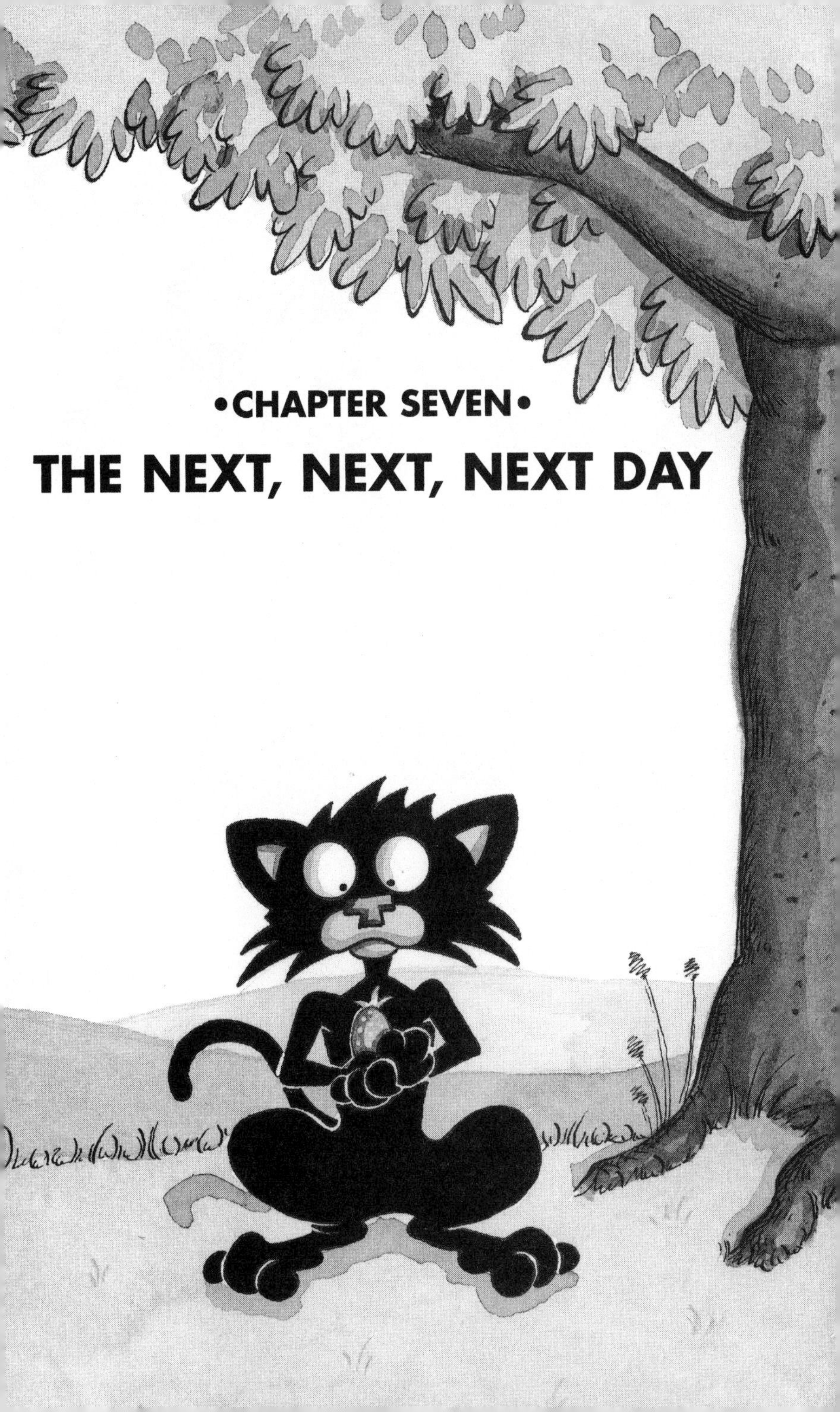

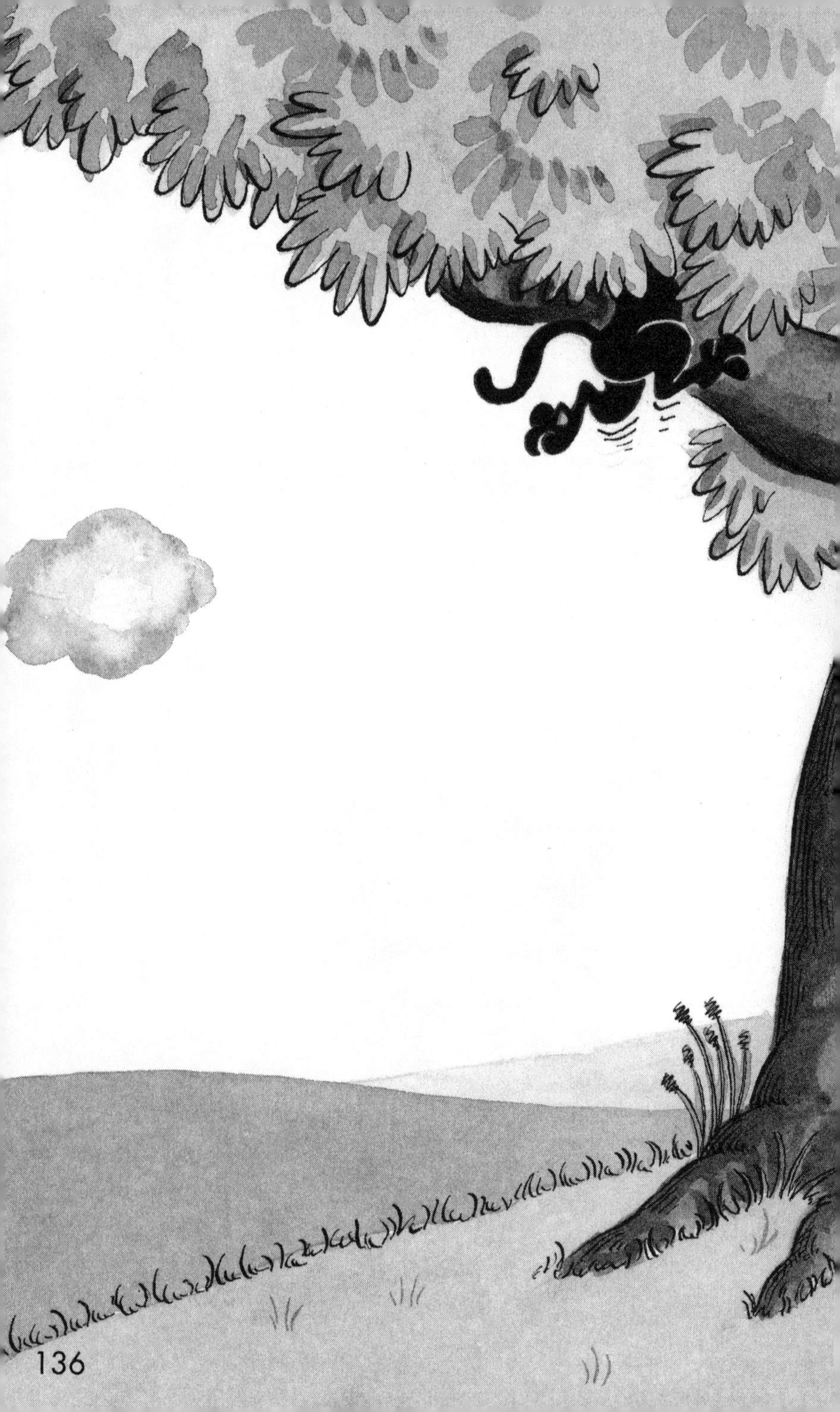

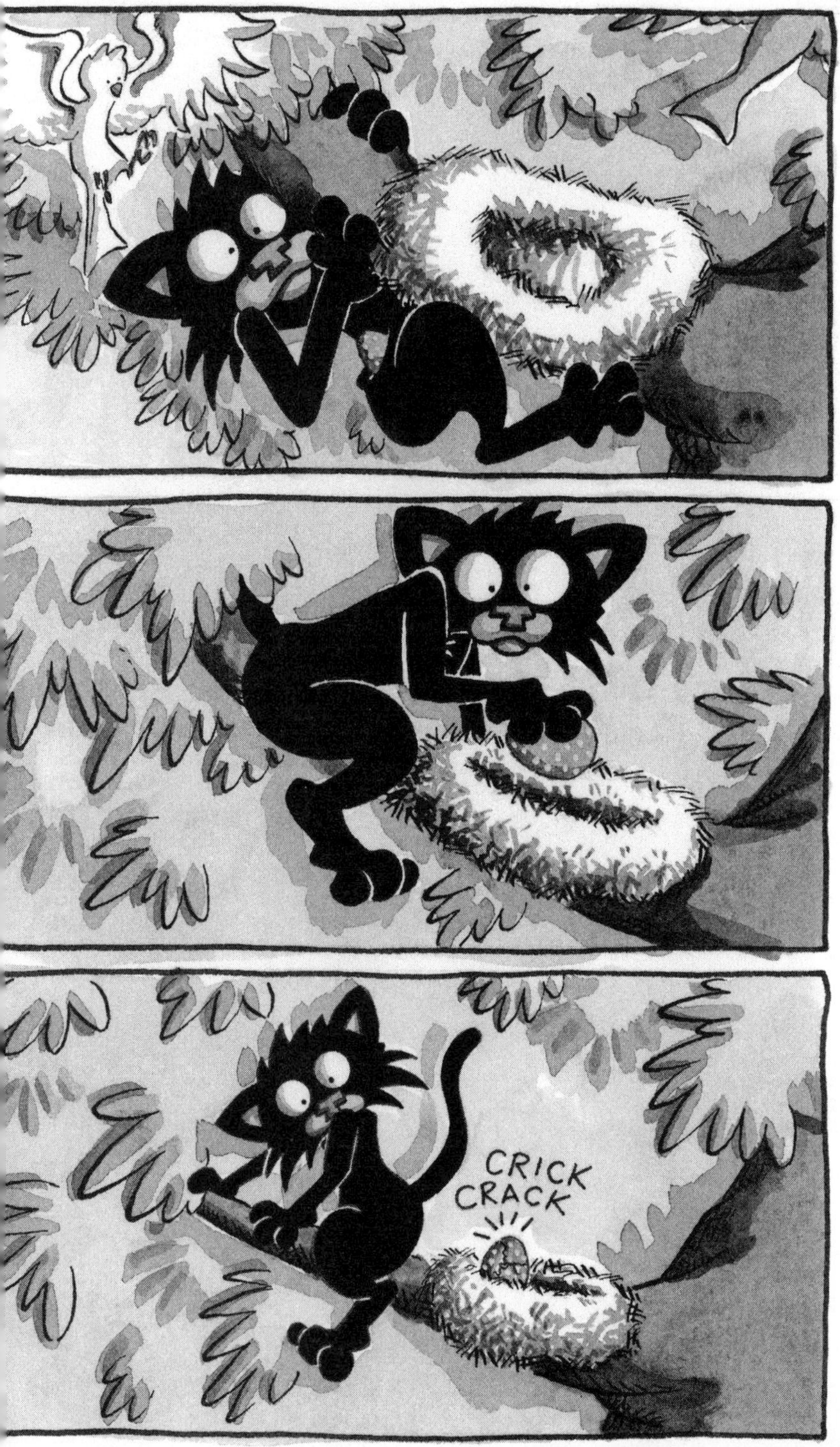
CRICK
CRACK

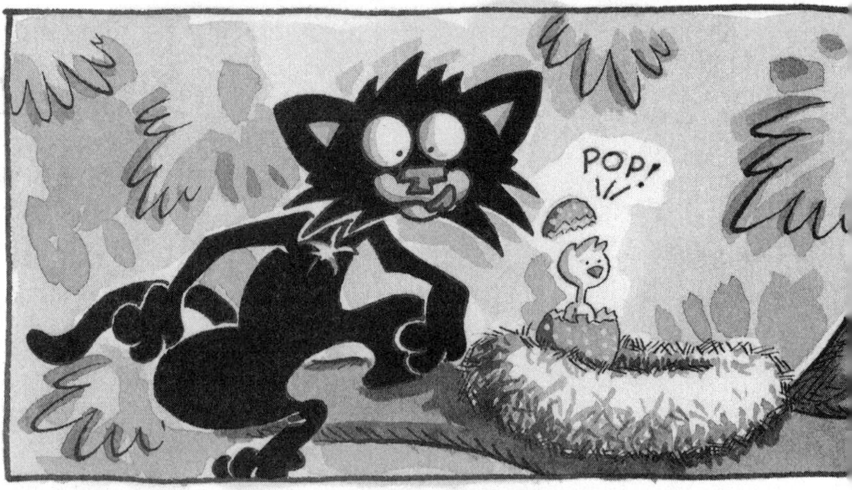
POP!

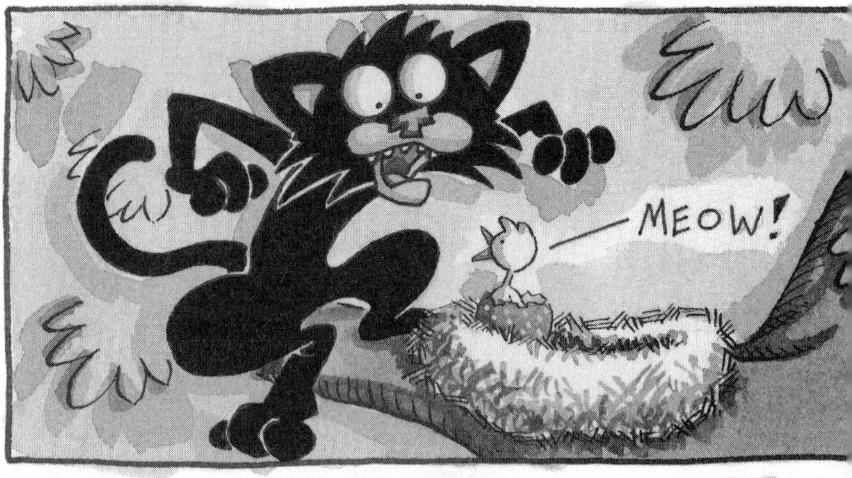
MEOW!

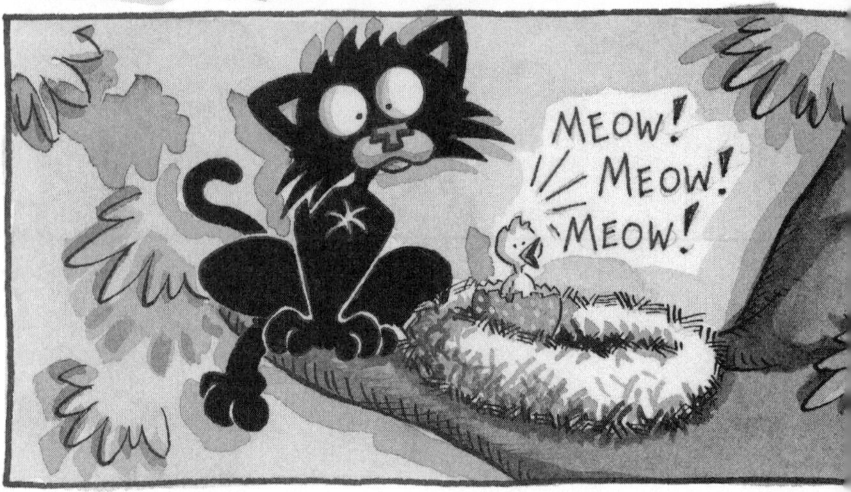
MEOW!
MEOW!
MEOW!

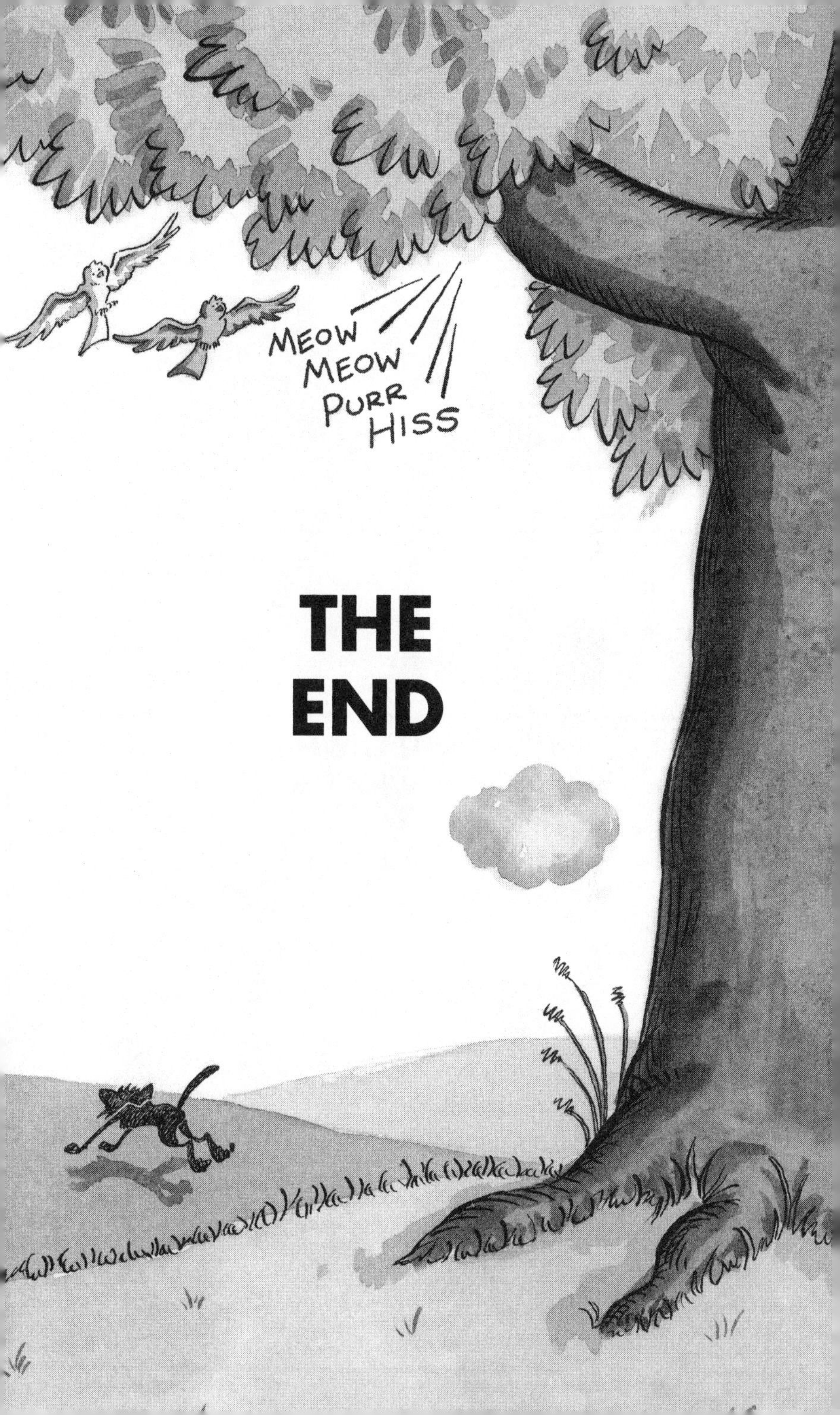
MEOW
MEOW
PURR
HISS

THE END

•EPILOGUE ONE•

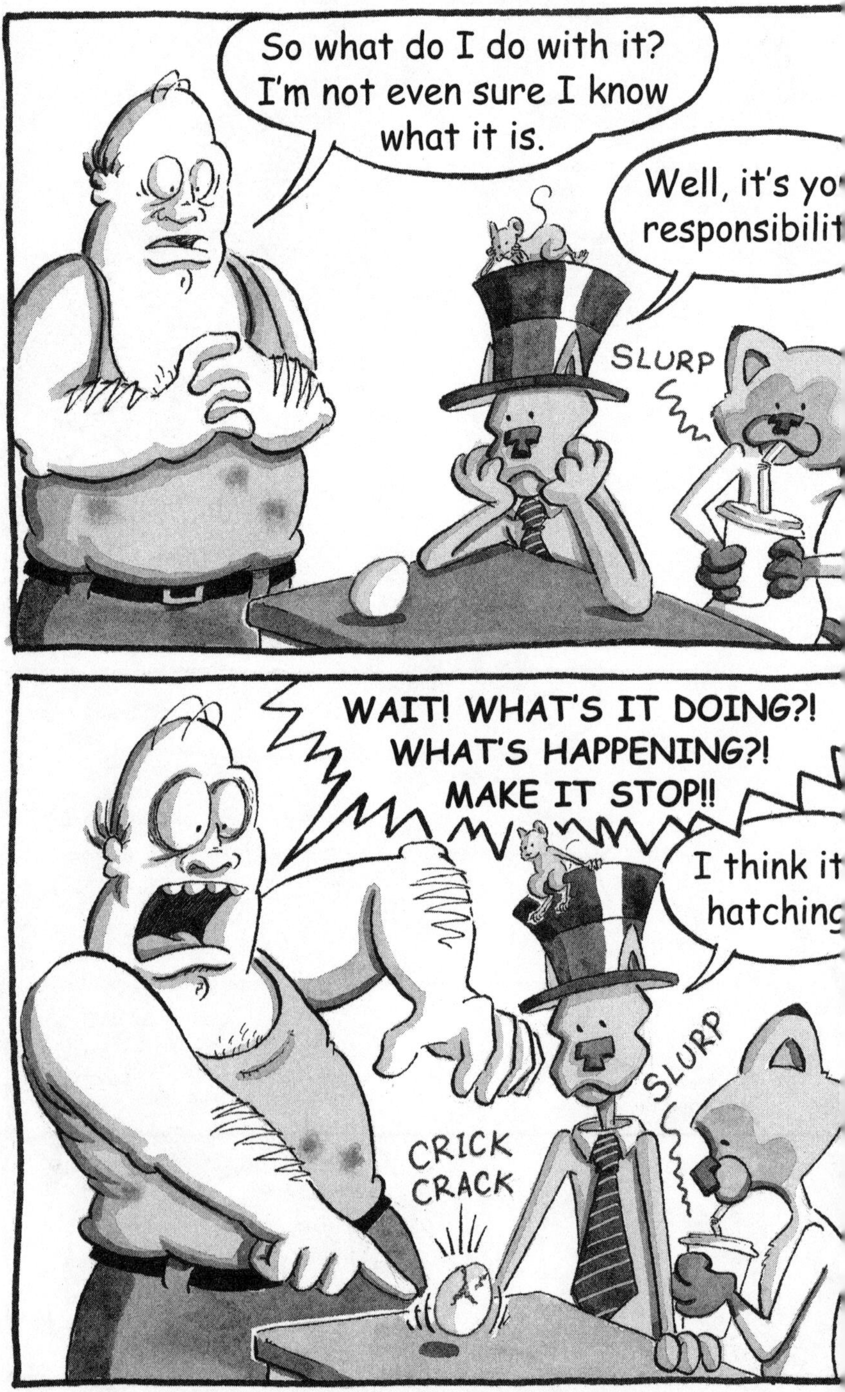

So what do I do with it? I'm not even sure I know what it is.
Well, it's yo responsibilit
SLURP
WAIT! WHAT'S IT DOING?! WHAT'S HAPPENING?! MAKE IT STOP!!
I think it hatching
SLURP
CRICK CRACK

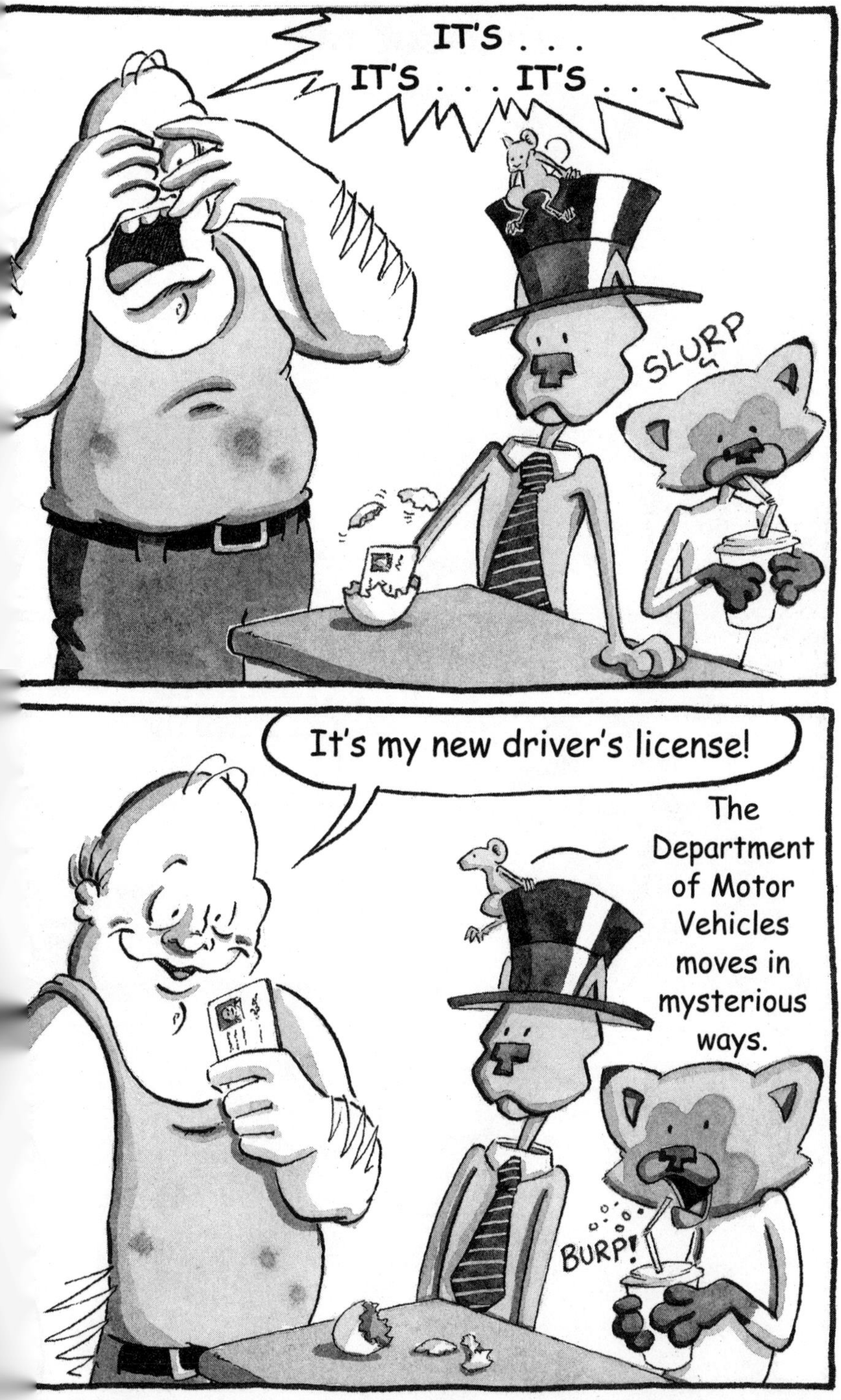
IT'S . . .
IT'S . . . IT'S . . .
SLURP
It's my new driver's license!
The Department of Motor Vehicles moves in mysterious ways.
BURP!

•EPILOGUE TWO•

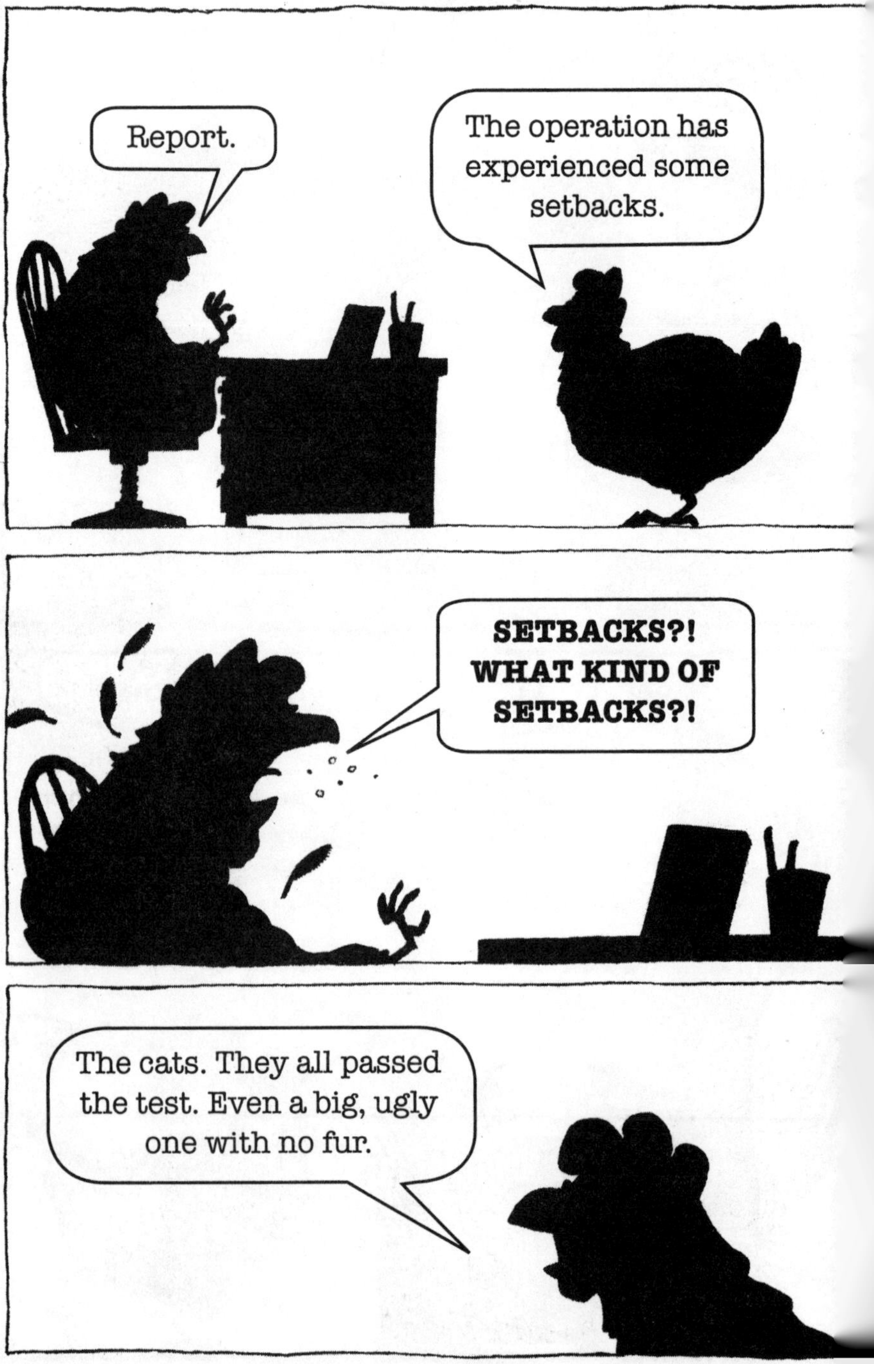
Report.
The operation has experienced some setbacks.
SETBACKS?! WHAT KIND OF SETBACKS?!
The cats. They all passed the test. Even a big, ugly one with no fur.

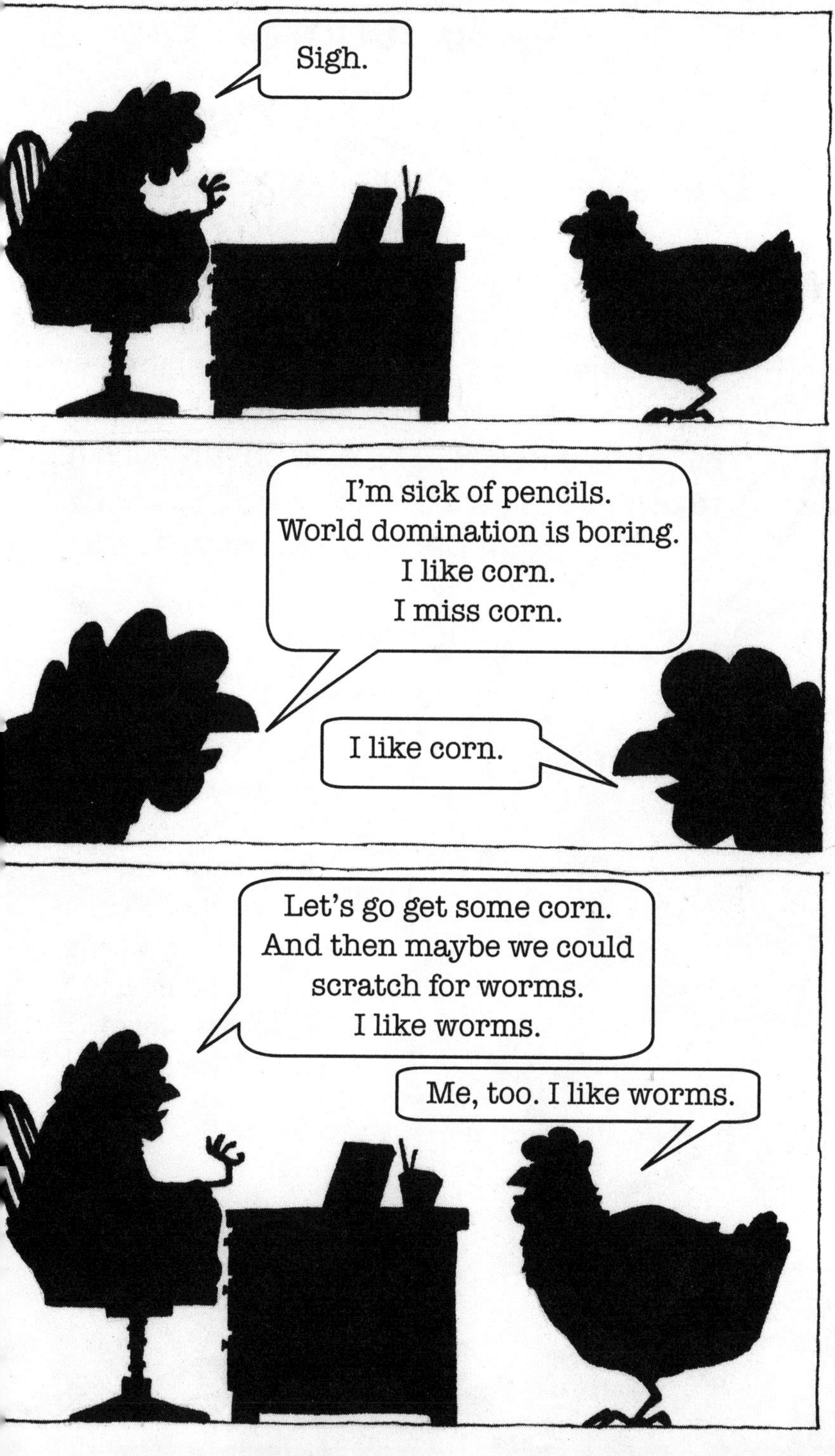
Sigh.
I'm sick of pencils. World domination is boring. I like corn. I miss corn.
I like corn.
Let's go get some corn. And then maybe we could scratch for worms. I like worms.
Me, too. I like worms.